The Poyson Garden

•AN ELIZABETHAN MYSTERY•

The *Poyson Garden*

KAREN HARPER

DELACORTE PRESS

Published by
Delacorte Press
Random House, Inc.
1540 Broadway
New York, New York 10036

The trademark Delacorte Press® is registered in
the U.S. Patent and Trademark Office.

Library of Congress Cataloging in Publication Data

Harper, Karen (Karen S.)
The poyson garden / by Karen Harper.
p.   cm.
ISBN 0-385-33283-1
1. Elizabeth I, Queen of England, 1533–1603—
Fiction.   2. Great Britain—History—Mary I,
1553–1558—Fiction.   I. Title.
PS3558.A624792P69   1999
813'.54—dc21   98-36420
CIP

Manufactured in the United States of America
Published simultaneously in Canada

February 1999

10 9 8 7 6 5 4 3 2 1

For those who helped to make
the Elizabethan Festivals
at Whetstone High School
so real and so rewarding:
Don Harper
Linda Thompson
Anne Barry
and our Brit Lit students

The Poyson Garden

The Prologue

"T HE QUEEN WISHES TO SEE YOU ALONE IN HER privy chamber, my lady."

So kindly, simply spoken, the twenty-year-old Princess Elizabeth thought, but not so kind or simple in fact. They always called her lady, not princess or even Your Grace, these swarming courtiers of the new queen, her half sister Mary Tudor.

Yet Elizabeth kept a set smile on her face as she sat across a small inlaid table for an afternoon repast with Her Majesty. The sweetmeats and tarts looked delicious, but under her stiff stomacher, Elizabeth's belly cramped with foreboding. She had always danced on sword points at court, but only in her sister's newborn reign did she fear she could stumble and impale herself.

"A beautiful day," the pale thirty-seven-year-old monarch said with a sigh and a sideways glance out the window. Set slightly ajar, the casement caught crisp October air blowing up from the Thames across the gardens and greens to Whitehall Palace. "And here I've done naught but read

---

1

and sign bills, grants, and warrants today—when I was not hearing holy Mass, of course."

"Your Grace works far too hard," Elizabeth assured her, gripping her hands together in the pale blue silk folds of her gown. "Would you not have time for a walk in the knot garden or a ride in St. James's Park?"

"*Dios sabe,* duty calls," Mary intoned in her masculine voice that always surprised people when they first met her. She reached for her goblet of claret and cradled it in her beringed hands a moment before putting it back down with a thump. "I'll not have them say behind my back that a woman cannot rule."

"Remember our father king said once, Your Majesty, that like lunatics, we women are so governed by the phases of the moon we could never command his realm?"

"*We?*" Mary challenged with an audible gulp. "*You,* sister, will never bear these royal burdens, for *I* shall have a son and heir—as *our* father also said!"

"God grant it, Your Grace, and I am ever grateful for your continued kindnesses to me."

Despite the queen's slow nod, Elizabeth's heart began to thud like horses' hooves. She fought down panic at her latest faux pas. Even an imagined affront could set the queen off. At least she was used to Mary's nearsighted squint always making one think she was frowning. Now those pewter eyes skewered her to her chair as the queen waited for her younger sister's next move.

But Elizabeth's one true—if necessarily covert—adviser at court, the young secretary Master William Cecil, had always said, *When in doubt, do or say nothing.* So with a pleasant countenance she sat stock still. In the aching silence Mary leaned forward to select a berry tart. With her other small, blunt hand, so different from Elizabeth's tapered, elegant ones, the queen clutched the heavy gold crucifix that swayed from an ornate neck chain. To stall further, Elizabeth took a tart that appeared to match Mary's. It oozed rich, red juice.

"So," Mary murmured with a heavy sigh, "these weeks since I was crowned you publicly declare you support me but will not even hear the Mass with me in private."

Elizabeth stayed the tart halfway to her lips. There they loomed again, those upturned sword points to tread upon as if she were some spike-walker from distant Araby.

"Your Majesty, you yourself said one must hearken to one's own conscience, so I only follow your lead to—"

"But my conscience is obedient to the true faith." She dropped her uneaten tart back on the table and seized her goblet again. "Eat, eat, sister," she ordered with a dismissive gesture. "Do not look as if I would devour you. We shall be more than family; we shall be allies forever in the holy church and in our daily—"

The tart tasted bitter in Elizabeth's mouth. And she bit on a cherry pit. She tried to chew and swallow but gagged and spit out the mouthful into her lavender-scented handkerchief. The smell of that made her explode in a messy sneeze.

"Bitter," she muttered, sniffling. "And within, a hard stone I cannot—"

She jumped as Mary's arm swept across the table to clatter goblets and dishes together. Tarts rolled and broke; the ewer tipped, spewing crimson wine, splattering Elizabeth's gown.

"Diversion and disobedience masked with pretty smiles, that has always been your game," the queen thundered, "for it is in your blood!"

"I—forgive me, Your Majesty, but the tart just tasted—"

"Poison? Is that what you would dare to say?" she shrilled, rising. Elizabeth leapt to her feet too. "Despite my good graces to you," the queen went on, "is that what you will accuse me of next?" She paced to the window so the afternoon light slanted in to gild her stocky form but obscure her features.

"No, of course, not, and—"

"In her own privy chamber the Catholic queen tries to poison her Protestant half sister, Elizabeth of England, beloved of the people. Is that what you and your tricky supporters will say next?"

"I have no supporters of my own, but all yours in loyalty."

"I'll hear no more lies. It would be justice indeed if someone did poison you, but not I—never I." As she paced, her skirts swished and her crucifix scraped her jewel-encrusted bodice. "I want only the best for you and your eternal soul, sister."

"But I spoke not of poison," Elizabeth whispered, yet her mind raced. She had swallowed nothing, but she still felt she choked down the sour taste of the tart. Surely it was

more than that some pastry cook had simply left out the
sweetening. With the back of her hand, she wiped her lips.
"I never intended—"

"You do know *that woman* poisoned my sainted mother,"
the queen said. She came closer. With both hands Elizabeth
held hard to the tall back of a carved oak chair. "At
Kimbolton Castle, where she died. It's true: poison."

Elizabeth knew *that woman* always referred to her own
mother, Anne Boleyn, who had supplanted Mary's in the
king's affections years ago. "No," Elizabeth protested quietly, "that cannot be true, since your mother was ill then, so
she simply—"

"I tell you it is God's truth, and you'll not gainsay me on
it. Queen Catherine wrote of it to me, and years later I had
it straight from her loyal Lady de Salinas, who was with her
to the end. That woman bewitched our father to send his
Catherine into exile, and your mother—the whore Boleyn—had her poisoned there. The queen wrote me she was
sore afraid. Her few ladies were reduced to cooking their
meat over the fire in her bedchamber to guard against poison, but still that witch—"

"That is a lie!" Elizabeth screamed, then, wide-eyed,
clapped her hands over her mouth. Despite knowing she
should hold her tongue or just withdraw, her fists shot to
her waist. She shook her red head so hard her headdress
rattled its pearls. "No, Your Grace, it cannot be," she said in
more measured tones. "I cannot warrant that—"

"Get out—out! I cannot bear to have you here. I thought
we could be sisters, allies, friends. But there is too much bad

blood between us, and not of my making." She had come so close, Elizabeth could now see her own reflection in the haunted eyes.

Elizabeth's survival instincts rose to the fore. She bridled her temper, dipped a curtsy, and bent her head. "Whatever passed between our long-departed mothers, my queen, I love and honor Your Gracious Majesty. I am your loyal subject, and this talk of poison is painful to me, for God knows, I am innocent of any—"

"No one, especially you, is innocent," Mary said, hissing the last word. "Like your dam, you are poisoned by bitterness and bound by iniquity. Go back to your country house and keep clear of plottings against your God-given queen!"

When Elizabeth left the chamber, she was so distraught she ignored the veiled woman who stepped swiftly back into the shadows.

Chapter The First

HE TWO RIDERS URGED THEIR MOUNTS FASTER through the deepening gold and scarlet forest on the road to rural Wivenhoe. In the brisk autumn wind their black capes flapped about them like raven's wings.

"So long gone, but I see you've not forgotten the way, milord," Will Benton, Henry Carey's man, called to him over the steady tattoo of their horses' hooves. In the chill afternoon air both men's breaths made small clouds that darted quickly behind them.

"These five years Bloody Mary's held the throne seemed eternity, Will, and we're not well out of it yet. But I'd never forget the way home to my lady mother. I just pray we are not too late, since she's sore ailing. It takes letters damnably long to find me and Catherine hidden away like scared rabbits in Switzerland."

"Not scared, not you, milord. Just careful and waiting for a better turn of the times. If'n your cousin the Princess

Elizabeth mounts the throne, then we'll see English sunlight again, all of us, eh?"

Henry did not answer. It was no doubt unhealthy to shout her name even out here where no one could hear. He tried to summon up her form and face, but his younger cousin seemed a red-gold-haired, haloed vision to him. He recalled her toddling about in leading strings—three years old she was when her mother, Anne, his aunt, was beheaded—but he had seldom seen the woman grown. As children they had spent fleeting moments together when their common cousin Catherine Howard was queen. Later, Boleyn kin as they were, he was forced to stand afar off while Elizabeth passed in the London coronation procession of her half brother, the boy king, Edward.

Henry shook his head and shifted farther forward in his saddle. Now Bloody Mary had declared herself pregnant. Finally, thank God, the royal physicians had declared her full only of a festering belly tumor.

"And vile venom," Henry muttered.

"What's 'at, milord?"

"Let's just ride, my man. Food and a fire await us just beyond this last stretch of forest."

THE FOUR MEN HUNKERED DOWN behind massive oaks and sycamores that lined the road to Wivenhoe. Thickets as well as tree trunks would hide them until their prey rode into the snare. The bend in the way here should slow even fast-ridden horses.

The leader pointed to move one of them farther back and put his finger to his lips. That kept the two across the road from stomping their feet to keep warm in the ankle-deep pile of dry leaves at their feet. Saints be praised, he thought, for at least the woods still held most of its bounty to shield them from the man she had promised would come ahorse this afternoon.

When he heard distant hoofbeats—not more than one or two men were in the party—he gave the first signal. His men fitted their arrows into their strung bows and, aligning their sights, lifted and steadied them. The arrows were perfectly fletched, the tips sharp and well-anointed with the thick paste she had made from hellebore and something else she said could kill wolves and foxes. *Be careful if you have a cut,* she had warned, *not to so much as touch the paste to your skin.*

To kill wolves and foxes: Her other words echoed in his mind as only two riders came into view, slowing their mounts for the turn, just as he had hoped. *Wolves and foxes.*

"Now!" he yelled.

Four bows spewed arrows. One rider shouted, then screeched. As the other noisily drew his sword, his horse panicked, reared, and whinnied, throwing him. Both were dressed alike and on first glance, looked alive. But it didn't matter: They had to kill them both.

When he strung his next arrow and ran out slightly into the road, one horse had fled. One man lay writhing on the ground, three arrows in him. Hellebore worked quick all right, and that was certain. Still, he stood astride this one and, slinging his bow briefly over his shoulder, seized the arrow protruding from his stomach. The man squinted up at him, perhaps hopeful of help. With both hands he thrust the arrow deeper with all his weight. Pinned to the road, the wretch grunted, groaned, then lay stone still.

"Is that one Lord Carey then?" his man at his elbow asked.

"Hell and be damned if I know," he said with a shrug, stepping back to look around.

His other two men came out of the woods. He saw the second horse standing not far down the road. "The other one," he cried. "Where is he?"

"Don't see 'im," someone behind him said. "Thought we 'it 'im too."

"Beat the bushes. A knife or sword blade will do, but these poison arrows be better."

SHAKING WITH SHOCK AND AGONY, Henry Carey huddled behind a fallen tree in a bramble thicket just off the road. He was certain he had broken his sword arm when his horse threw him. And there was blood on his hand when he touched his chest. Had one of the brigands' arrows nicked him, or had he gotten cut by his own blade when he fell and rolled?

"A pox on you. Canna you jackanapes find him?"

That voice didn't have the local burr, or had he been away too long? It was the first thing they had said that he could discern. He heard them come closer, thrashing through the brush and dry leaves. But with his arm useless and this cut, with his pistols in his saddlebag, he would die. His mother was dying too, but he'd never see her now this side of heaven.

"Someone's coming on the road."

That voice came so close he knew they'd find him. He squinted his eyes shut tight in pain, in childish hope they would not see him. He tried to picture his wife, still in Switzerland with his sister, Catherine. And in his last moment he cursed himself that, once again, he dared not— could not—just stand up and fight for what was good and right.

"We canna be leaving this half done."

But Henry heard his chance at deliverance now: more than one man's voice in some rollicking song. Or had he died and was being welcomed at the sacred gates to leave behind this regret, this fear and pain?

"Let's fly then, and we'll be settling later with them all."

The next cry clanged in Henry's ears like doomsday bells.

"Down wi' the bloody Boleyns—e'en the royal one!"

EDWARD THOMPSON, ALIAS NED TOPSIDE, stopped singing when he thought he heard some sort of shout just up ahead on the road. He couldn't discern the words, but it was definitely not someone joining in his romping chorus of "Between your thighs your beauty lies."

"You hear that, Uncle Wat?" he asked, turning his head

to survey the new leader of their troupe. Wat Thompson had taken over when Ned's father had died of the sweat this summer. Wat rode their only horse at a plodding pace that kept up with the cart the mule pulled. When they emerged from this dense woods, Wat would ride ahead to a tavern or manor house to inquire if they wished a revel, masque, or play from The Queen's Country Players.

Meanwhile, Randall Greene, a pompous popinjay Ned secretly called Grand Rand, rode the cart because he felt peckish today, the sot. The two boys, Rob and Lucas, who did the women's parts, walked as Ned did, their high voices echoing his deep tones.

"Don't think that man's shout was a hurrah we're coming, sounding clear out from Colchester, not out here," his uncle said, seeming to rouse himself a bit. "Best fetch our pikes and stage swords in case we meet up with some rural louts ahead, eh, lads?"

But Ned had already reached for one of the ax-headed pikes that protruded from the bundles of costumes and makeshift bits of scenery. He was not a tall man, but wiry and strong. Despite his shock of curly black hair and boyish-if-rugged face, he'd long yearned for the meaty roles—the Italian dukes, English kings, even villains—the ones Wat usually took himself or gave to Grand Rand. Ned wearied of his uncle making him play the fond lover or young captain just because the ladies liked the turn of his leg and the mere hint of his smile.

But worse, he hated playing the fool, the clown, the country rustic whenever a comedy came along, however good his ear for it. And right now he was sure that voice up ahead had not been some rural lout at all. Though he could not discern the words, it had been a defiant if lilting shout.

Gesturing for them to slow, Ned strode ahead on the bend of road and came first upon a nervous horse, well-fed and curried, lathered yet from a run. He smacked its flank to send it along the road to his companions.

"Stay back," he warned when young Rob came first around the bend. Wide-eyed, the boy nodded and seized the horse's dangling reins. "And tell them to halt the cart till I call the all-clear."

Warily, Ned advanced, then stopped and stared. A body studded with arrows lay ahead in the middle of the road, not moving. Eyes darting both ways, Ned shuffled carefully forward. A corpse dressed well enough, with his jerkin all bloodied and his warm wool cloak splayed out under him black as night. His first instinct was to hurry everyone past, for some folks didn't trust the likes of traveling troupes and might blame them. But that would be unworthy of him and of what he promised his sire just afore he died.

And then he heard a rustle in the bushes. Instinctively, he shouted and charged with his pike, just as he did in act the third of *Victory at Agincourt.*

But in a sudden bramble brush he banged his shins and took a tumble over a tree trunk—and a second body. Gasping, Ned knelt over him. The man's pale face clenched in pain. He was bloodied, but at least for now he was among the living.

"I AM BORED TO DEATH with all this waiting," the tall, red-haired woman muttered to herself as she dismounted. *"To death."*

The sudden cloudburst wet Elizabeth Tudor clear through to her skin, but she turned her face up, reveling in the strength and sweep of it. No dangerous lightning or thunder with this, but it still suited her mood. And it pleased her that she managed to be out here nearly alone when the Popes had gone back with her Barbary falcon, the servants, and the remnants of the food.

She dismounted and leaned against the strength of the great oak for what cover it could give. Gazing into the distance toward her small rural realm, she sighed. The old palace of Hatfield House where she lived in exile—watched closely by the queen's man Sir Thomas Pope and his wife Beatrice—would have to do since she could not be at court. She could yet be rotting in the Tower of London if her royal brother-in-law, Spanish King Philip, hadn't taken a fancy to her and asked Queen Mary to be kind while he was away.

"But that is as kind as it gets, Griffin," she told her favorite horse and stroked the black stallion's muzzle to quiet him. "Some of my people at least have been returned to me, and you, of course, my dear boy."

The horse whinnied as if he understood and cherished every word. " 'S blood," she whispered and patted him again. "Sweet talk to horses, that's what has become of the most marriageable virgin in the kingdom."

"You say this place has you talking to horses now, Your Grace?" her faithful lady Blanche Parry teased as she pulled up under the tree and dismounted. Unlike her princess, Blanche huddled in her hooded wool cloak to avoid the wet.

"At least," Elizabeth said with a smile, "I know they are to be trusted."

They shared a little laugh that faded, drowned not by the downpour but by quick horse's hoofs. As with hearing someone running in a house, Elizabeth had learned to fear fast feet of any kind, for they had seldom boded well for her.

But it was her groom, Stephen Jenks, whom she jestingly called her Master of the Horse in Exile. He usually stuck to her skirts like a burr, her unofficial bodyguard and one she relied on, but she thought she'd lost him in the storm somewhere.

"Your Grace, beggin' your pardon, but you want to go back in now? You'll catch the ague out here," the young man blurted as he dismounted.

Jenks's wit was for horses. Elizabeth was quite sure that when he talked to them they truly listened. As for people, he was good at taking orders but not usually at giving them. Still, strangely, he looked as if he'd like to command she go inside right now.

"I'd only get wetter going back to the house," she told him and patted his slick shoulder. "And I'm in no hurry to return to the watchful eyes of Her Majesty's second-most favorite Pope."

But she startled when Jenks pulled one side of his leather jerkin open to flash a folded letter at her, then patted it to his body again as if to preserve it from the rain and prying eyes.

She studied his eager face. His blue eyes were alight with a message she, for once, could not read. His chestnut eyebrows lifted to touch his straight, sodden hair, cut low across his forehead. Though Blanche was one of her two trusted ladies, he had cleverly blocked even her from seeing what he had.

A secret letter for her. Pray God this did not mean a new attempt to snare her in another plot like the one that had cost her her reputation and Tom Seymour his head, or the aborted Wyatt Rebellion, which had put her in the Tower.

"You know, Blanche, I think Jenks has a point. The rain looks to be letting up. Let's ride back."

With his linked hands under her foot, Jenks gave her a quick boost up, then helped Blanche remount. Because of slippery grass and the warren of rabbit holes in this meadow, they went slowly toward the russet-brick Tudor palace, now gone shiny in the rain.

Eighteen miles north of London, Hatfield House had become her refuge, though the queen had seen to it that it was invaded by far too many spies. Yet Elizabeth loved its quadrangle overlooking the central courtyard. She admired the modest great hall, not that she ever dined or entertained there, but her parents had in their brief happy years together before the Boleyn downfall. On sunny days the solar was her favorite haunt, even for her studies, for it overlooked the fish pond and flower gardens. But today that letter loomed.

When they dismounted in the courtyard, Jenks thrust the letter quickly into her hand. She folded it once and shoved it up her sleeve just before Thomas Pope and his lady, Beatrice, called Bea, came out to greet her. Elizabeth saw that they had both dried off though not yet changed their riding garb.

"You mustn't go off by yourself like that when we are all out riding, my lady," Sir Thomas scolded by way of greeting. "It is our duty and honor to protect you."

"The storm and skittish horses separated us, my lord, not I," Elizabeth told him, brushing quickly past. "I'll change these sodden garments and see you a bit later for supper."

She could feel it now against her skin, the letter. She would read it once and burn it if it were anything to incriminate her. Didn't they realize—those most loyal to her who wanted to raise a rebellion—that only in this solitary waiting game in exile could she hope to survive?

"Oh, no, I knew it," Kat Ashley, her childhood governess and the closest thing Elizabeth had to a mother, cried when she met her at the door to her chambers. Kat's plump face framed by graying hair was its own raincloud. She threw her hands up, then smacked them on her skirts. "Oh, lovey. Look at you, soaked to the skin. Drenched hair despite the cloak and quite bedraggled."

"Yes, Kat, I know."

"I'll not have you catching your death of cold or anything else."

"Do not fret, my Kat. Just build up the fire, and I'll undress before it. And lock the door," she whispered as she swept in and went directly to the hearth. "Blanche is no doubt changing, but she'll be in here fussing over what I'm to wear soon enough."

"Just so she doesn't bring the Buzzard with her," Kat muttered. She closed and locked the door and hurried over to throw a new log on the others in the broad, open hearth, but she kept her eyes sharp on Elizabeth.

"The Buzzard" was Kat's name for Beatrice Pope, who she said was always hovering, watching, just waiting for bones to pick. Despite the fact Elizabeth knew Bea was sent with her husband to keep an eye on her, she appreciated Bea's quick wit and even temper—and her beautiful handwork. She'd had far worse jailers, and she'd even overheard Bea sticking up for her privileges in private when the Pope had ranted on about keeping her more closely confined. Still, Kat at times seemed so put out by Bea that she looked as if she'd like to stab her with her own sewing needle.

While Kat hurried to the clothes press for a dry linen smock, Elizabeth put a foot up on the iron fender and pulled the now-damp letter from her sleeve. Though both Kat and Jenks would know she had a missive, unless she chose to tell them, they'd know nothing else of it.

But now she saw something caught in its tiny loop of red ribbon the sealing wax held. She recognized it instantly and sucked in a silent breath.

A three-tiered pearl eardrop, the mate to the other the Duchess of Norfolk had given her years ago during the

Twelve Days of Christmas—Catherine Howard was queen then, briefly.

This was your mother's once, one she wore the day she was arrested, the duchess had whispered, *so do not wear it openly. I meant to get the other of the pair for you, but I hear someone in your mother's family has it for a keepsake. Hide it, and do not speak of it,* she had insisted as she thrust the dainty thing into Elizabeth's palm and fled back into the crowd of masked, laughing courtiers.

Now, as new flames at her feet caught and leapt, Elizabeth's eyes widened and her lower lip dropped in shock. She skimmed the letter in the delicate but shaky scrawl.

It could not be. This eardrop with a letter from a woman long dead. The forbidden past resurrected from its tomb. And a summons she was desperate to keep but one that could mean the utter end of her.

Chapter The Second

LIZABETH CLASPED THE PEARL EARDROP IN her fist as she read the letter:

To My Dearest Niece Elizabeth,

I know we have had no dealings these long years since the fall of the Boleyns, and that has grieved me sore. But it was, indeed, the best for you and the only way for me to survive. How many times I have longed to write you from my voluntary exile or, since I lost my beloved husband last year, to steal to you. But I know, especially now with Mary queen, that would be impossible, and I vowed once to your father I would remain silent to my grave if he would but let me live my own life away "from the heat of the sun," as he said.

But, my beloved Elizabeth, I must break that promise now. I believe you were informed that I died here at Wivenhoe several years after your mother's death. That was a falsehood I willingly upheld to protect you and my children from my first marriage, Henry and Catherine Carey. Even now they must live abroad in

*exile from Bloody Mary's England. I assure you they are your
loyal future subjects and friends who pray daily for your rightful
succession, as I do.*

"What is that letter?" Kat's voice interrupted Elizabeth's
concentration. Kat tried to peer over her shoulder, but she
shrugged her off and turned slightly away. "Lovey, what?
You look as if you've seen a ghost."

"I have," she whispered, not looking up. "Now, let me
read."

"Not if that is from another dangerous rogue or whoreson traitor like Wyatt."

"Leave me be, I said."

*People have claimed cruel and wretched things of your
mother, my poor sister, but she loved you. She fought and
died for your rightful place, so never forget that. And I, as a
mother, dying now, must fight for the safety and future of my
children.*

*Therefore, I long to see you to explain further certain
things in person. God be pleased, at my manor house at
Wivenhoe, west of Colchester, Henry is healing from an attack on his person. We are not so distant from you at
Hatfield, dearest niece, but so far these long years apart.
Henry insists there is something he must tell you. Beware for
your own safety, for he believes, even after all these times and
trials, that the Boleyns of your generation, your royal self
included—perhaps especially—are in grave danger.*

If you will, come not by the Marks Tey forest road, but

cross the River Colne near the village. Say you are Lady Penelope Cornish of Ightham Mote in Kent come to visit. She and I have corresponded for years, but my people do not know her face.

Loyally, with respect and love,

Mary Boleyn, Lady Stafford

The coffer lid banged down; Elizabeth jumped. "What is it, then," Kat demanded from across the room, "if not some silly or solemn plot?"

"In a way, my own plot a-hatching," she declared, pressing the letter to her breasts. She lay it slowly upon the carved oak mantelpiece as if on an altar. Frowning, she freed her long hair from her flat velvet cap and snood. She let Kat drape her tresses over the front of her shoulders to begin unlacing her bodice in back. She felt frozen with fear—*when in doubt, do nothing,* Cecil had said—but she thought only of sweeping to action. She would have to make ready as fast as possible.

"Not a tryst then, is it?" Kat asked, her voice even sharper. "Not after that disaster with Tom Seymour, I warrant."

"I told you not to speak of that again." Elizabeth gripped the mantel, then slowly loosed it to turn toward Kat. "This hardly bodes a tryst for love—romantic love. But I must get away, and I know I can trust you to help me with this ruse."

"Get away? Ruse?" Kat sputtered. Hands on ample hips,

she gasped for air like a beached fish. "What talk is that?" she whispered. "I would go back to that purgatory of the Tower with you, die for you, but I'll not let you go off God knows where. And how would you escape from this velvet prison the queen's got you in?"

Elizabeth spun her back to Kat for her to finish the unlacing. Reluctantly, the skilled hands crept back to their task. "In answer to your query, I'm afraid, my Kat, I feel one of my wretched head pains coming on." She hurriedly untied her own petticoats, wriggled out of them, then jerked her damp shift over her head.

Naked but flushed, she waved away the linen towel Kat had to dry her. She wrapped herself in her favorite old green velvet robe and thrust her feet in woolen mules. She retrieved the letter, kissed it, and pressed it to her forehead as if she could emblazon the words in her brain.

How dare the Tudors keep her from her mother's people? It was the worst sort of treason, fragmenting a royal family. Trembling, she unfolded and read the letter again, then thrust it into the flames, where it flared to silver ash and floated up the chimney.

"You're not acting one whit like a sick head pain coming on," Kat groused, grunting as she bent over to gather the garments. "But at least, once I tell everyone, you will have to stay here. The last time you lay abed two nights and the day between with no one allowed in footfall but me. And with the drapes all pulled tight and the bed-curtains closed and no noise or visitors, not even wanting food . . ."

"Exactly," Elizabeth declared and watched Kat slowly catch her intent. "And after my getting caught in the storm, even the Pope and Bea will take our bait whole."

"*Our* bait?" Kat echoed, dropping the garments by the door for the laundress to fetch. "You'll tell me where you're off to or I'll not lift one finger," she insisted, coming back toward the hearth, wagging that finger at Elizabeth as if she were her girlhood tutor again.

With the hand not holding the eardrop, Elizabeth seized Kat's finger in her fist and bent close to her round, florid face. "Go find Jenks, because he'll have to get us the horses. Tell him four sturdy ones so we can spell the beasts, and not from the stables here, for they'd be missed. For him and me—not you. And take some coins to give him."

Kat pulled her finger back, then grasped Elizabeth by her slender shoulders. "Your Kat Ashley will do naught of the sort, on my mother's soul, Your Grace, till—"

"No, on *my mother's soul,* I will do this, and you will help me. And *now,*" she added, shrugging off Kat's hands and lifting her chin to stare down her nose at the shorter woman.

Kat collapsed to a long, low curtsy. It always shocked them when the gulf of privilege and power gaped between them.

"Kat, rise," she said, helping her up. "Heed me and never speak of this to a living soul but me. This letter came from my aunt, Mary Boleyn, from what sounds like her deathbed."

"But she's already dead. Has been these long years so—"

"Shh! That is what they told me, my lord father and my sister, years ago. But they both hated the Boleyns then—and no doubt me, for my bad Boleyn blood, as Mary once put it. I must see my aunt, and they'd never let me, not even if I begged."

Her usually bell-clear voice snagged. "Now, listen to me, Kat. Jenks and I will leave tonight and have but one swift day there before coming back. And tell him I need some boy's garb—and if there are fleas or mites in it, I'll have his head."

At her choice of words they both stared wide-eyed at each other. Kat's lip pushed out in a trembling pout; the sting of unshed tears made Elizabeth blink.

"You're sure 'tis safe," Kat whispered, "and cannot be a trap?"

"I have had enough of both to smell them out. Besides, see, she sent the other of the pair of my mother's earrings, the ones they said she wore when the king had her arrested, before everything . . . went so wrong."

"Aye, went so wrong," Kat echoed as she stared down into Elizabeth's trembling palm.

"REIN IN HERE and hold the horses," Elizabeth called to Jenks. She looked only slightly less a lad than he. They stopped abreast of an apple orchard, with the distant village of Wivenhoe barely in sight through predawn mist. "I'm going to don my gown."

"Here?" he gasped, frowning and craning his neck to

scan the area. "Thought you packed that gown for when we got there, Your Gra—I mean, milady. How you going to do it without at least a tiring-girl out here?"

Jenks looked entirely rattled, as if battle drums or bagpipes had beat in his ears all night instead of horse's hooves. Before he could dismount to help her down, Elizabeth swung her leg over her mount's broad haunch and slid to the ground. She dug the rumpled gown out of her saddle pack, grateful that the mud puddles, which had splattered them the first twenty miles, had not dirtied it too.

"I can't carry off being a lad once we get there," she told him, "even if the folk at Wivenhoe don't know me. I'll put the gown on here, and you can lace it."

Ignoring the fact that he looked as if she'd ordered him to dance barefoot on hot coals, she stepped behind a cluster of trees and yanked off her jerkin, shirt, and breeks. The gown was not a good one, though she'd have loved to go in fine fettle to see her aunt and cousin after all these years. And she'd brought no petticoats, so it was going to hang as if she were some rustic milkmaid.

" 'S blood!" she cursed in the voluminous folds as her cap came off and a hairpin snagged something. She yanked harder and could breathe again. She shook the gown's warmth about her legs. The weight of the cloth would have to smooth the wrinkles, that and the patches of fog out here. She pulled the pins from her snarled hair and flung it back loose over her shoulders. Since she'd forgotten a proper hat, the hood on her cloak would have to do.

"Here, lace me," she told the now dismounted Jenks as

she held up her skirts and strode to him. She shoved the boy's garb in her saddle pack, then spun away and lifted her hair so he could get at the back laces. "Pretend you're cinching saddle straps or some such," she prodded when he didn't move.

She could tell her bold lad's hands were shaking at the task, when little scared him. Still, her mind raced ahead, then back to Hatfield, where she had sneaked out at night like some love-struck swain gone courting. But so much more than a lovers' assignation was at stake. She offered up a swift prayer that her Kat could hold off the Popes and that all would go well here.

"Done, but don't know if it's right, your—milady, I mean."

"Lady Penelope Cornish of Ightham Mote in Kent, and don't forget it. Come on now, boost me up and don't be chatting overmuch with Lady Stafford's stableboys or scullery maids."

"I know," he said as they urged their tired horses to a trot again. "But Mistress Ashley made me swear I'd go in first to see if'n it's a trap."

Her first sight of the modest manor house awed Elizabeth more than the vast grandeur of a castle or opulent palace ever had. She stared, wondering if it had been enough for Mary Boleyn to live here with a commoner she loved, one she had chosen herself though it angered her king and family. As if in answer to her unspoken question, pale dawn gilded the gables in pure gold. Autumn frost pearled the gray thatched roof. Silver smoke curled from brick chimneys, and the mullioned windows blinked like brilliant gems. Yes, this place and life had been their riches, and she ached with deep envy for something she would never know.

Her stomach began to knot itself like a noose. She settled deeper into her dirty brown traveling cloak and hood and stayed back as Jenks rode into the center courtyard, pulling the two extra horses behind him. She heard him call out, "What, ho!" then other voices. Squinting up at the diamond-shaped windowpanes for a welcoming face, she shifted in her saddle. She knew she would be sore from riding astride, but it was worth the pain, the risk—at least she prayed so.

Jenks appeared on foot and windmilled his arm. "The Lady Stafford left orders for the Lady Cornish to go direct in to see her," he called as she rode forward. A man and woman, stout and simply dressed, stared up at her in the cobbled central courtyard, curiosity easy to read on their open faces, so different from those at court or even Hatfield.

Jenks helped her down. "Welcome, my Lady Cornish," the man said, as the woman managed a half curtsy so awkward Elizabeth instantly knew how it had been for her aunt these years of willing exile. Queen Anne Boleyn's sister Mary had never brought ceremony here and had been much the better for it.

The two servants introduced themselves as Piers and Glenda, the household steward and his wife. As she entered, Elizabeth saw that the great hall lay dim and silent but for the low crackle of fire on the hearth. Jenks walked a step behind her, rotating his flat cap in one hand, his other still resting warily on the hilt of his sword.

Along the upstairs gallery that overlooked this large room, a chamber door banged open. From above a flicker of firelight threw a long shadow of a figure on the high-beamed ceiling. A woman clothed in a white shift or night rail with long silver hair ran forward to clutch the banister and lean toward them, wavering like a specter who would take flight.

"Is it you?" the woman cried. "Bless God, is it you?"

Glenda started up the stairs. "My lady, you're not to be up. I'll skin that girl Meg for leaving you alone and ailing. This here's the Lady Cornish, come like you hoped she would—"

But Elizabeth was quicker than Glenda up the stairs, around the turn of the landing. Her skirts dragged, but she lifted them and almost sprinted. Unladylike, unroyal to run, but she had never dared to dream of this reunion.

Mary Boleyn's face was gaunt and haunted, white skin stretched over fine bones, eyes once deep blue, now washed almost colorless by tears and pain. Mary pressed one hand to her belly and breathed through her mouth. How could it be that this once blond beauty could look so faded and frail—and old? Elizabeth had always pictured her young, laughing like those muted memories of her own mother, but Mary Boleyn must be in her middle fifties now.

Yet Elizabeth saw in a closer glance that her inner spirit flamed. Mary held up a trembling hand to halt her woman's approach and said, "My friend, Lady Cornish, will help me

back to my bed. Please fetch her a hearty breakfast—now."
She looked as if she would be ill, but she only dry-heaved
once, pressing her palm to her mouth. She leaned for
strength with one hand on the banister. Glenda turned and
plodded back down the stairs, mumbling.

"Dear aunt," Elizabeth whispered, "let me help you."
She put one arm around the woman and her other under
her elbow. How skeletal she was under the linen night rail.

"I will be fine now," she insisted through lips thinned
with pain. "Everything will be fine now." They shuffled
into the bedchamber, and Elizabeth closed the door behind
them. Though she leaned her aunt against the bed, the
moment she let go to reach for the mounting stool, Mary
Boleyn slid back to her knees on the woolen rug.

"Not the strength to curtsy anymore, can't manage it,"
she murmured as Elizabeth knelt beside her, then lifted her
again. "Besides, there has been no one else for years, no one
who truly deserved my curtsy after he killed my—our—
family."

"Don't talk now," Elizabeth insisted. "No one here must
curtsy to anyone. Save your strength so we may talk."

Suddenly, huge tears began to pour down the woman's
wan face. Elizabeth, trained by duty not to cry but when
alone, held her aunt to her, blinking back tears.

"Oh, my dearest," Mary Boleyn said in a rush, as if Elizabeth would disappear if she were silent, "you have your
mother's slimness, her dark, snapping eyes, and long, elegant hands too. His red-gold coloring, of course, but not his

ruddy face. A porcelain complexion, just like hers," she went on, leaning back to study Elizabeth. "You are Boleyn as much as Tudor, and you must never forget it, no matter what threatens."

As she spoke, the door swept open. A russet-haired man with broad shoulders filled it, stepped in, then closed it quickly. "Mother, Glenda says you got up and almost fell, so I'm glad Meg's finally back out of her own sickbed to help—" he began before his eyes focused on Elizabeth.

He squinted at her before his frown relaxed in surprise, as if he hadn't known Mary had sent for her or had not fathomed she would come. Because he wore a white shirt, it was only when he stepped slowly closer that she realized his right arm and upper chest were bound in bandages and he wore a sling.

"Princess Elizabeth," Mary said, her weak voice gaining power in obvious pride, "may I present your cousin and devoted subject, Henry Carey." She leaned against the bed, clinging to the heavy carved post so that Elizabeth did not have to hold her up. "His sister, my Catherine, is still in Switzerland with Henry's wife and their children. But Henry came home to see me before . . . before—"

"Before I could miss her more than I already did," he finished gallantly. He was broad-faced, with wide-set eyes and a prominent nose much like her own, Elizabeth thought, a handsome man with a trimmed auburn beard, though he looked older than his thirty-some years. She could not place him as the lad she had met fleetingly years before. He was of middling stature, but his manly bearing made him seem tall. Indeed, she did resemble him, even more than she had her half brother. She liked him instantly.

"Cousin Henry," she said, extending her hand, "it gives me great joy and comfort to meet you, even—and especially—in these tenuous circumstances and times."

"Your servant and liege man always, Your Grace," he whispered. He went down on one knee before her. Inclining his head, he lifted the hem of her soiled cloak and kissed it, then the backs of her fingers before, still kneeling, he raised his face. She clasped his shoulders lightly to raise him, and they exchanged proper kisses on each cheek. She saw the outer corners of his eyes crinkled and his hopeful expression turned up a bit on one side of his broad mouth. Tremulously, she smiled into his eyes, brown ones shadowed by lurking sadness or grief.

Together, they helped Mary Boleyn back into her big bed, for she seemed to have instantly fallen asleep right where she leaned. Henry indicated they should walk out. They huddled in the hall by the bedchamber door, he now suddenly silent, she looking to him for further explanation.

"My eyes," he said, when she stared a bit overlong, "are glad of your sweet face. When I see you here so strong and sure, I know we can face and solve this murder plot together."

"Murder plot?" she gasped. "Whose murder? You mean the attack your mother mentioned was attempted murder? Tell me."

"I will," he vowed, lifting a finger to his lips. "Let's go outside where none may overhear."

But it was her own inner voice now screaming the question in her ear that terrified her most: *This is my murdered mother's family, and now are they—we—in grave danger of murder once again?*

Chapter The Third

ELL ME EVERYTHING," ELIZABETH DEMANDED
as they walked downstairs.

"But you've obviously just arrived and
should rest and eat," Henry insisted.

"I can do naught until you tell me."

She wanted to show him how much she respected him
and didn't mean to take over. Still, she could not help but
blurt, "But we must fetch someone to sit with your mother.
Who is this Meg you and Glenda spoke of?"

"Meg Milligrew, her favorite girl, just the kitchen herbalist, really," he explained as he escorted her through the hall
toward the back of the house. "The chit is down with
greensickness and can't even seem to dose herself back to
health right now. The thing is, forgive me, Your Grace, but
she somewhat resembles you, and that's who I thought you
were at first glance."

"Resembles me?" Elizabeth asked, stopping so suddenly
he almost bumped into her. Her tone and glance were more
withering than curious.

"I mean in hair color, height, and form," he added quickly. "She hardly has your fine features, bearing, or presence. No grace like yours, cousin. She's a bumbling sort, but Mother quite favors her. I'll just stop in here." He indicated a door that had to be, by the smells and sounds emanating from it, the kitchen. "I'll have Glenda send someone up to Mother. When she exerts herself, she sleeps for hours. I've been sitting with her when I wasn't weak with blood loss myself."

Elizabeth followed him a little ways down the dim hall. She was surprised to realize she still wore her cloak, though her hood had long fallen down her back. "And tell Glenda," she added, "to give my breakfast to my man out with the horses. *Ask* her, I mean, will you?"

He inclined his head in a hint of bow as Glenda came out with a tray. While Henry explained, the woman's narrow eyes shifted back and forth between the two of them. She nodded with a sniff, muttered a curse against poor Meg, and bellowed for Piers to come take the "fine lady's tray" to the stables.

No, Elizabeth thought again, they didn't stand on ceremony here. Ordinarily it might have amused her, but she felt only foreboding as a male servant appeared to swirl Henry's cloak over his shoulders and give him his cap before they went outside.

A bench against a brick wall in a patch of sun overlooked the kitchen herb garden. It was laid out in neat rows surrounding a cleverly knotted central pattern that the early frost had not yet blighted in this wind-sheltered place. Beyond lay the kitchen door and a window with its view partially obscured by hanging, drying clumps of herbs.

"Please, sit, Your Grace, and I shall tell you all."

"Will you not call me Elizabeth when we are alone together?" They sat, of necessity, close on the narrow bench. "Or you know," she went on, her voice almost wistful, "here I almost feel I should be just plain Bess and be quite at home, except for what you have to tell me."

He nodded and flushed—unless it was the crisp breeze that curled around the corner that suddenly burnished his cheeks. "Of course. And you must call me Harry as my friends do. Elizabeth, I did not mean for Mother to summon you here, but I am heartened she did." She saw he was more distraught than he had let on at first. He kept shifting his position, and his deep voice faltered. "I was afraid to put this—this dangerous disorder—to you in writing. The attack on my man and me in the forest not far from here was no accident—when I thought I had come home covertly to see my mother before she—she . . ."

"But are you certain she is dying?" she asked, leaning slightly toward him. "Can we not bring in some skilled apothecary or physician?"

He hung his head, staring at his hands gripped on his knees. "She's had all the local ones. The thing is, she's given up the will to live since my stepfather died last winter. She's been wasting away with worsening signs like watering eyes, nausea, stomach pains, and general weakness. Though I am glad you came, I fear that now that she's seen me and you at long last . . ."

"That she will have naught else to live for?"

He looked up sharply. "You read my mind. But to this other dreadful business. My man and friend Will Benton was killed riding next to me not a quarter hour before we would have arrived here."

"Killed? Then, *that* is the murder. I am sorry, cousin, for him and you," she said, covering his hands with one of hers. "Thank the Lord you will mend, but I am sorely grieved for his loss."

"He was ever your loyal subject. He attached himself to my faded star, but it was you he longed to see in power." He slumped slightly. She held his hand tighter. "In a way it's my fault he's dead," he went on, his voice shaky. "He was hardly the target of such a quick and painful death, but I, his sponsor—his better—a Boleyn. Three arrows felled him, one driven clear into his gut. Pardon my rough tongue, Your Grace—Elizabeth."

"Never apologize for the truth," she insisted, standing and beginning to pace before turning back to him when he jumped to his feet. "You must tell me all of it, Harry. Are you certain you were the target? Can you describe your attackers?"

"It is such a black whirl in my brain now. I never saw but only heard them, at least three, I think. I fear they were watching and waiting for me. Somehow I had been spied on—they knew I would come to see my mother and when. And pox on it, but I might have fought back but their first volley missed when my horse reared, and I was thrown and fell on my own damned sword." He hung his head again like a whipped boy. "And was saved," he added quietly, "by a ragtag group of players to whom I owe my life."

"You are certain it was not they who assailed you? Some country troupes are bands of thieves. They could attack, then hope for reward by miming a bold rescue. Or could it not have been local rogues just lying in wait for any hapless traveler? Times are terribly hard for the common folk, too, under Mary's taxes for her Spanish husband's foreign wars."

He shook his head so hard his cap went askew. "No, I am certain the assassins were driven off by the player called Ned Topside. I believe him. He says he did not see them either, only heard their terrible shout from afar. He's yet my guest, staying at the Rose and Thorn in the village, and I've asked them to do some pretty speeches to cheer Mother tonight. But Elizabeth," he went on, stepping closer, "I know it is a plot because I, too, heard the blackguards—at least one of them—shout that threatening battle cry when they had to leave their murderous work undone."

His eyes, now wide as coins, looked beyond her as if he saw it all again.

"Their battle cry?" she prompted.

He flinched as if he'd been struck, then spit it out between trembling lips. "Down with all the bloody Boleyns," he whispered, "even the royal one."

ELIZABETH ATE AND WASHED but refused to lie down, though she had a real headache working on her, as if an unseen tormentor screwed a tourniquet tighter about her forehead. She supposed it served her right for lying to her people at Hatfield. At least this head pain wasn't *that* crippling. Her stomach and balance seemed sound enough for now.

She sat with her sleeping aunt awhile, then walked the walled gardens of the manor house with Harry again, trying to catch up on years apart and yet make some plans to counter this current danger.

"Where did you bury him, your man Will?" she asked when she saw the churchyard with its mounded humps of turf and a few tilted gravestones just through an iron-gated door at the back of the grounds. A charnel house where old bones were eventually stored stood against the far wall of the graveyard. Over all loomed a stalwart stone church, one Harry had said lacked a minister since King Henry rooted out Catholicism from the kingdom.

At first he only gestured in a general direction, but when she continued to peer through the bars, he took a big, rusted key from a chink in the wall and unlocked the gate. It creaked open. They walked through, just to the edge of the yard where several fresh graves lay bare of grass.

"Will lies in this one," he said, pointing to a rectangle at their feet with a crude wooden cross stuck in the somewhat sunken ground. He sighed. "Sadly far from his home in Sussex. I have written to his mother, though she can't read. I had him buried quickly. I couldn't bear the way he looked. The arrows made black spots around the wounds, sores the likes of which I've never seen."

"Spots? Small ones, like with the pox?"

"No, black blisters dreadful to see, yet nothing like buboes of the plague," he added hastily, as if to comfort her.

But a shudder racked her. She had risked everything to come here and found only dying, death, and danger. And yet she could and would not draw back like some craven coward.

"Do you still have the arrows that struck him?" she asked. "Mayhap there is something to identify the attackers or the maker, a particular fletching pattern or marking on the shaft or even the point. My father always used to make his fletchers set his feathers just so when he shot at the buttes or hunted."

"But for the one arrowhead I had to leave in him, I wrapped the bloody, sticky things and put them in a box with my own shorter arrows from boyhood visits here. My stepfather taught me to shoot," he said with a glance at the little church where, no doubt, the grave of Mary Boleyn's beloved lord lay out of the elements that battered these of lesser rank. "The box is in the gardener's shed we just passed," Harry added and escorted her back into the manor grounds. The gate scraped closed behind him; he relocked it and restowed the key.

But there were no wrapped arrows in the interior of the wooden box he peered in, then showed her. Not his boyhood ones or those that had been used to murder Will Benton. Cursing under his breath, Harry ransacked the shelves of the shed, knocking things off, then throwing them.

"Did anyone know you put them here?" she asked, raising her voice over the din he made.

"I told no one—didn't want to keep the dreadful things in my chamber, but I see I should have." He looked ready to tear the place apart. She realized and understood his devastated poise; no one had ever taught him to stand stiff and still no matter what befell. Besides, she'd seen the result of choleric humors all her life, especially in men. His face clenched in a frown, he hunched against the crooked doorway.

"We've two gardeners I'll question," he said, his voice tight. "And that herbalist Meg uses this place, as is evident enough with all this hanging rubbish."

A sweep of his good hand bounced bunches of thyme, marjoram, and rosemary hanging over their heads by tiny nooses from the crossbeam. On their way out he shoved a spade into a wooden rake until a row of tools toppled as he slammed the door of the ramshackle place.

Elizabeth let the incident go at first. She wouldn't blame a gardener or herb girl for burning or burying some horrid, bloodstained murder weapons kept in the garden shed he or she used. For one moment she almost wondered if Harry himself hadn't destroyed them in a fit of rage. Or perhaps he had been annoyed he hadn't kept them and didn't want to admit his hasty, ill-reasoned mistake to her. She had seen that inbred arrogance from men before too.

Though she had a good nerve to question the servants herself, she spent the waning afternoon with her aunt, treasuring Mary's memories of her mother from their girlhood days. Mary described their home of Hever Castle in Kent, their days being educated at the French court, their heady return to England when first Mary caught the king's eye and then Anne. Elizabeth asked about her Uncle George, who had died on the block with her mother, and asked Mary to describe her Boleyn grandparents. But she did not pry into how Mary became the king's mistress before he turned to the lively, clever Anne—and Anne held out for marriage and the crown.

"I was ever the fond, gentle one," Mary whispered, as a tear tracked down her wan cheek, "and she so clever and strong. You, of a certain, are like her."

The hours slipped away and Elizabeth became more exhausted, more weak with the pounding in her head. But she told no one and even let them talk her into attending the entertainment tonight. "My dearest," her aunt had said before she slipped off into one of her instant slumbers, "don't fret anyone will guess it is you at the play. We're having only the manor staff in, and if they don't think you're really Lady Cornish—I overheard Glenda has her doubts—they will think you are merely my Meg . . ."

That snagged Elizabeth's attention again. She wanted to see this girl who looked like her, who so held her aunt's affections when others seemed to dislike her. She decided to speak with her before she left, no matter what.

She ate an early supper with her aunt and Harry in Mary's bedchamber, dreading the coming entertainment, then her departure, and the long ride back to Hatfield. Though Mary drank a good deal of what she called mead, which Harry later said was hard cider sweetened with honey, she ate only a few small saffron cakes.

"No wonder you are thin, aunt," Elizabeth said, leaning toward her chair where she reclined against plumped cushions. "Cannot you take a bit of this meat pie to build your strength?"

"No appetite anymore, my dearest," she replied with a tiny shake of her head that was almost imperceptible from her constant trembling. "Not for food, not for much but my happy memorics."

Harry put his goblet down a bit too hard and wine slopped out. He reached to clasp one of their hands in each of his. "Three of Boleyn blood gathered together," he intoned as if in prayer. "That is a memory to cherish." He cleared his throat and frowned. "And that would make the queen choke on her own bile, eh? Pray, don't tell your sister I said so, Your Grace," he added, his serious face almost gone playful for a moment. He loosed her hand and lifted his goblet. "To the next queen of England!"

He saluted her and drank, but Elizabeth read despair in his voice and eyes. Mary tried to lift her tankard of mead, but again, Elizabeth had to help her get it to her trembling lips.

"FRESH-COME FROM THE STREETS of fashionable London," Ned Topside announced with a flourish of his short cape and a graceful sweep of his feathered hat after he had introduced himself, "our band of players oft does histories and tragedies. But tonight we shall play mostly trifles and tom-fooleries to lift hearts and light smiles, especially for the Lady Stafford."

By rushlight and sconce, the five men who dubbed them-selves The Queen's Country Players had swept into the cen-ter of the great hall to present themselves before their scenes and speeches. Mary Boleyn, Lady Stafford, had loved such pleasantries in her day and often, as the fairest lady at court, Harry told her, played the parts of Diana or even Venus. Tonight she segued between smiles and stupor, her head tipped back on her chair cushions. Elizabeth sat on her right and Harry on her left while manor folk, including Jenks, crowded two benches along the side.

Elizabeth scanned the women's faces for someone who could be Meg Milligrew, but there was nonesuch. Besides, Harry had said she was still puking and he hadn't talked to her yet. The gardeners had denied any knowledge of seeing or taking the arrows, and he said he believed them.

"We hope to amuse and amaze," the older man named Wat Thompson intoned with his deep bow as he introduced himself.

"And to sweep you away from this place to other sites in this world, though none so grand as our fair England," Randall Greene announced, with entirely too much ges-turing and posturing for such a simple sentence, Elizabeth thought.

Lastly, the costumed and wigged lads who would play the women's parts curtsied and lay small, ribboned boughs of sharp-scented pine at the Lady Mary's feet. "So keep your spirits evergreen, e'en as these fond fantasies we strew at your feet for your favor."

Elizabeth was surprised to see that Ned, who had supposedly saved Harry's life, was not the senior member of the troupe. That position was apparently taken by the one called Wat, and the almost effeminate Randall held a loftier place too. Still, as the hour flew by, she thought the young, rugged-faced Ned the most glib and clever. He knew, as they used to say, which side his bread was buttered on, for he played directly to her cousin and aunt with only an occasional glance her way and never a look at the benches. 'S blood, she'd been used to being overlooked like that for years during her brief stays at court. But someday, God willing, all the players in the realm—including this sharp fellow with the well-turned leg—would bow and say their pretty speeches for her.

"And now," Ned was declaiming as the others took their temporary leave to reenter with some new piece of costume or prop, "we shall present a few speeches and scenes from the new and fashionable Italian comedy *The Potion of Pleasure.* Drink up and dream you are in sunny Florence and have found such a magic liquor there as to make anyone who drinks it fall in love with you. . . ."

He was, this so-called Ned Topside, rather a good-looking rogue with his black curly hair and green eyes. Elizabeth noted that a hundred expressions plied his face. His eyes could sparkle with a range of passions from mischief to malevolence. He could speak volumes with the mere lift of a sleek eyebrow or tilt of lip. She noted well he could ape a lordling's pompous demeanor or a cowherd's lumbering walk. And most fascinating, he had the ear and tongue for all types of speech, court or country, familiar or foreign.

Though her heart was heavy with her aunt's imminent demise and the murder of Harry's man, she found herself smiling more than once. How grateful she and Harry both felt when Mary Boleyn smiled too.

ELIZABETH HELPED HER COUSIN tuck her aunt back into bed and said her final farewell. Though she and Jenks must leave before midnight, she was swaying with exhaustion. At last she gave in to Harry's pressing her to take a brief rest in an extra bedchamber.

But she didn't think she slept. . . . She must not be asleep because there it was, clearing through the fog, the stone Tower of London with the gray Thames rippling by it when the queen's guards rowed her in through the iron jaws of Traitor's Gate.

She walked the Tower's dank, dark corridors, looking for her mother. Anne Boleyn had been imprisoned and beheaded here. She was buried under the cold floor stones in the small chapel of St. Peter in Chains, so the place horrified and haunted Elizabeth. Yet she went on, step by step, looking, calling for her.

"Mother! Queen Anne Boleyn! Mother!" she shouted bravely.

She saw her form, all in flowing white, standing on a parapet within the Tower confines. Her mother held to the banister and leaned over it and called down to her, "Elizabeth, my dear Elizabeth." Her voice echoed off the walls, off her tomb. "He poisoned my love. . . . Your royal father poisoned my love long before he took my hand, my heart, my head. . . ."

Over Elizabeth's head Queen Anne held a heart with an arrow stuck right through it. Blackest blood made a huge spot where it pierced the heart. "Dig me up, and you'll see," she called as her form and voice drifted away in the fog. "Poison . . ."

Elizabeth jerked straight up in bed, her heart pounding, her body drenched with sweat. At first she didn't know where she was, but then it all came tumbling back. Wivenhoe . . . her aunt ailing . . . Will's death . . . those stolen arrows.

She got up, seized her cloak, and swung it around the boy's garb she had already donned. Wishing Kat were here to help, she shoved her feet in her riding boots. Still shaking, seeing the dark corridors of the Tower before her, she went down the dim hall to Harry's chamber door and knocked quietly on it.

She heard his feet hit the floor, heard him coming. He opened the door, fully dressed, prepared to see her off. "Already time?" he asked. His hair was mussed from his pillow, with a cowlick standing straight up. When he stared closer into her face, he whispered, "It isn't Mother?"

"Not yours."

"What?"

"Never mind. We must find out if those arrows that

killed Will were poisoned. I've got to see those black spots on him. We can retrieve the arrowhead you said you left in him. Send for my man Jenks, and we'll dig him up ourselves posthaste, then put him back."

He gaped at her as if she were speaking some barbaric tongue.

"If they used poison, mayhap we can trace it," she explained. "I don't want to do it, but we must have answers. Now."

He nodded jerkily and disappeared. Within a quarter hour she, Harry, and a shaken Jenks had taken a lantern and two spades from the garden shed, unlocked the graveyard gate, and begun to delve.

Chapter The Fourth

S HE LOVED THE NIGHT BECAUSE SHE DIDN'T have to wear the veil. It suited her, the blackness, the very void of it, like the deepest reaches of her soul.

She stood in the shadows of the church, watching the trio digging across the small graveyard. At first she thought it must mean Mary Boleyn had died, for her lass said it was almost time. Her burial would be in secret, since she had been officially dead nearly twenty years, but they would surely inter her beneath the church floor with her lord. So they must be digging up the man her little band had killed when the simpletons should have executed Henry Carey.

She shifted slightly closer and peered around a big tree. They were so intent, they would not see her. She realized they had come through the gate she had planned to slip through to meet her girl, using the copy of the key she'd had made. They were too close to it for her to risk entering the grounds of the manor now. A curse be on them, for she would be delayed. If this was to be the night Mary Boleyn died, she wanted to be under her window, staring up, knowing one more Boleyn had been dispatched to the fiery bowels of hell.

The tree limb creaked overhead, and the breeze danced dry leaves through the frosted grass. Autumn had come early this year, as unnatural as the summer disasters that had plagued the kingdom because these wretched Boleyns still were drawing breath, waiting for one of their ilk to take the throne.

She strained to hear what the two cloaked men and the lad digging for them said. The lad's face, too, was hidden, for he had some sort of handkerchief tied over his nose and mouth. Then the wind shifted, and she caught their words.

"The poor wretch been in the ground near on four days, milady," the digger said. "Best pinch your nose, 'cause I know how a dead horse is after that time, 'less it's in the deep of winter."

A servant, but not one Essex-bred, the eavesdropper thought. Off and on she'd been in these parts enough to hear the way the local rustics slurred their words. But who was that lady the lad addressed, and one garbed like a man? Mary Boleyn was too weak, so perhaps this was the Lady Cornish her lass had mentioned. But if they were digging the man up to rebury him somewhere, why at night? Or were they exposing his corpse for another reason?

"Just dig, Jenks," the lady said, "then I'll slit the winding sheet."

The watching woman spun to press her back against the tree trunk; she covered her mouth with both hands. They

suspected something about the corpse. But let them be puz-
zling over it, she thought, let them find her hellebore and
aconite on those tips and shafts, if congealed blood and
earth and worms had not annihilated the deadly concoction.
Before they could try to trace her, she would have Mary
Boleyn dead and then be on to her real passion, her royal
victim, that she would—

"Oh, 'S blood!" the cloaked lady cried and turned away,
retching loudly on the grass near the grave in scraping,
gasping sounds. The watching woman peered back around
the tree. The lady still held the lantern but jerked it so
quickly it threw sharp, tilting shadows of the trio on the
brick manor wall. She wiped her face on her cloak and her
hands on the grass. But she came right back to the grave,
even bent over it, one hand now covering her mouth and
nose. Whoever she was, the watcher had to admire her
mettle. In form she resembled Meg the herbalist, but her
voice was a far hue and cry from hers. She wished she'd
shine the lantern at her face inside that hood. And why was
she garbed like a man?

"Wait!" the lady said in a voice both men obviously
heeded. "I said I'd cut the winding sheet myself, and so I
shall." The watching woman saw her put her lantern down
and kneel, leaning into the grave.

For a moment all seemed silent. Then the sheet ripped in
a long, screaming tear. The wind sighed. The lady spoke
again.

"You did not tell me he was so fair of coloring and face,
Harry."

"And of heart," he added with his arms crossed and head bent as if he were in prayer. So that man must be Lord Henry Carey himself. Such piety from a Boleyn almost made the watching woman vomit too. "He never sought profit or preferment," he went on. "Jenks, help me turn him to get at that arrow that went clear through his middle. We will have to cut it out his back. Can you hold that lantern up now?" he asked the lady.

As wan light leapt into her eyes, the watching woman instinctively pulled her veil down over her face. She crept back to become one with the shadows of the church. Leaning her shoulder against the cold stone wall, she wondered who the lady was and waited.

THE STAB OF SORROW—and the stench—made Elizabeth's nose run and her stomach continue to churn. It wasn't so much the slick, writhing worms that were already at the corpse but the white, fine, velvety coating that covered its skin—and how that contrasted to the dreadful black puddles of flesh. There were dried blisters where each arrow went in and even where the one poked out his back. Because Henry had only one good hand, Jenks worked quickly with his dagger to cut that broken shaft and tip loose. They were all wearing gloves, so those made Jenks a bit awkward, but Elizabeth had insisted on them. She had dreamed of poison, and poison this black festering mass could be.

"Harry, do you think," she said, her voice nasal because

she held her nose, "it went so far through him because he fell on it, as you did your sword?"

"I saw him flat on his back, and he didn't look as if he rolled over onto it."

"Then perhaps the person who shot this arrow was especially strong," she said, her voice faltering, "or else . . ." She began to shake so much the lantern light trembled.

"Or what, milady?" Jenks asked, as he freed the arrow point and broken shaft and held them up to her.

"Or, else," she said, reaching for it, "when they came across the road to look for Lord Harry, someone drove it deeper into Will. But we need not know that to realize we are dealing with cruel or desperate men."

"Take that arrow and go on in," Harry urged her. "Jenks and I will finish up here, and we'll talk before you leave."

"I need to hold the light for you."

"Go look in on my mother," her cousin insisted, tossing his cloak off and helping Jenks awkwardly shovel soil back in, one-handed. "We've enough light here for this."

But to examine the arrow she held up the lantern, which threw light on it and full on her face. "Please go on, Elizabeth," Harry said, his voice annoyed.

Elizabeth was certain she heard someone's swift gasp, but it was neither man and hardly poor Will. She set the lantern down and blocked it with her legs and cloak to scan the darkness better, but the light had temporarily blinded her. Was there sudden movement there, over by the church? Perhaps someone had heard them digging and come to see. But the wind was rustling leaves, and the spades were scuffing soil into the grave. Yes, she would go look in on her aunt one last time before they rode out. But then she thought of it.

"Wait," she ordered and they both halted their spades. "You said he was loyal to me, cousin, that he would have served me. I want to give him this, though he will never know how truly he has pleased his future qu—I mean, his princess." She reached inside her shirt and took off the crucifix that swung by a delicate chain. Her sister had given it to her one yuletide, long before their father died.

"Someone else will find it when they dig him up and put his bones in the charnel house," Harry said, and she thought he would protest further. "But I tell you, Will would be proud of it—and mayhap he knows, eh?"

Elizabeth nodded, but whatever prayer she meant to say caught in her throat. Despite the fact Harry had told her to take the lantern, she left it for them and hurried through the gate. Her eyes soon became accustomed to the dark, then light from the distant house illumined her way. She clutched the arrow in her gloved hand; she would wrap and place it in her saddle pack. Later she would examine it carefully, perhaps find someone who knew about poisons to look at it.

Nearing the back door, she saw a girl going in ahead of her. She had not slipped through the back gate, so she must have come around from the front. Elizabeth did not recognize her from her silhouette. It was just after midnight, so why would someone be up but Glenda, who was sitting with her aunt? Elizabeth crept closer. She could tell that the lass looked young and slender. In her hand she had a bunch of flowers or maybe herbs. That reminded her she had meant to tell Harry she must meet Meg Milligrew. Perhaps this was she, but she seemed much shorter than he had described. If she could but glimpse her hair or coloring . . .

Elizabeth watched as the girl first poked her head in the door, then disappeared inside.

Elizabeth went to the single back kitchen window and peered in. The place was deserted but for this strange girl lighting a rush taper from the single fat tallow candle on the table, opening what looked to be a cellar door, then disappearing down the stairs. All this time Elizabeth had seen only her back.

She looked around to see if Harry and Jenks were coming yet. Nothing. Silence and darkness, and she dare not shout for them. She went to the kitchen door and in. She removed her gloves with the long wrist guards she had borrowed from her aunt and placed them on both sides of the broken arrow shaft to protect it. She stooped to lay it in the corner of the room behind the hearth spit wheels and chains, where no one would see it and she could retrieve it later.

Straining again to listen for the men, she heard nothing but muffled noises down the cellar stairs. *When in doubt, do nothing.* But she had to be sure that the intruder was not lighting a fire or doing something else dire down there.

From the table Elizabeth lifted the candle impaled in its flat brass holder and started down the uneven stone stairs, trailing her free hand along the dank wall. She could tell the girl must have gone deeper into the vaulted darkness, unless she'd snuffed her taper and was hiding down here behind those barrels.

When Elizabeth heard her farther in, she left her candle on a step and edged carefully forward, her hand still along the wall. However much the cellar was used, spiders still ruled here. She grimaced and blinked rapidly as she walked through a web that clung to her eyelashes and damp face.

She came to an arched door and saw the girl just beyond. Positioning her nosegay carefully, she was hanging it up on a string that held many other herbal bouquets. Then she pulled something—a vial—from her bosom and uncorked it to pour a tiny stream of liquid into a wooden firkin. This girl was most certainly not Meg unless everyone was blind: Coal-black hair peeked from her cap, and her nose was pert instead of prominent.

"What are you doing there?" Elizabeth demanded.

Her voice startled even her. The girl jerked around, wide-eyed. She dropped the vial. It shattered between them on the floor stones. Then she lifted the firkin from its wooden cradle and heaved it at Elizabeth.

She ducked. The girl snuffed her taper. Elizabeth felt her flee past.

"Hold there!" Elizabeth commanded, spinning to chase her.

The girl did not stop, but the candle on the steps etched her silhouette quite clear. Elizabeth lunged and caught her. She swung the girl around by one arm.

"Halt, I tell you!"

Elizabeth felt as astounded as furious. She was used to being obeyed by servants, but not now, not by this wretch. Whoever she was, she fought like a fishwife, trying to kick, punch, and scratch. Rage drowned Elizabeth's control. That this chit would sneak in at night . . . that she would not stop when bidden . . . that she would try to assault her person . . .

She pummeled the girl, boxing her ears soundly, getting in cuffs and kicks. She snagged her long fingers in that black hair, however greasy it was. If she had lice, she'd skin her alive. The girl landed two kicks and one punch to her shoulder, but never got the best of her. The more they struggled, the wilder Elizabeth became, as if this rage had been building in her for years.

Harry and Jenks thudded down the steps, the lantern still in Jenks's hands. Harry pulled the girl away and slammed her back against a pile of barrels, which bumped and rolled; he pressed her to the wall. Still, the girl did not cry out or say a word.

"What in creation?" he demanded, as out of breath as if he'd been in the fray. "Who in the deuce is this?"

"You don't know either?" Elizabeth shoved back her hair, which streamed loose from her boy's cap. "I caught her sneaking down here and pouring something in a firkin. Bring her over here," she ordered and took the lantern from the astounded Jenks to lead them into the next chamber.

She cast light upon the glittering, wet shards of broken

vial—thin-blown venetian glass, it looked to be—then found the firkin where it had rolled into a cobwebbed corner. "This is what she was tampering with, corrupting for all I know," she told them, putting it back in its wooden cradle. Half filled with liquid, it was heavy.

"Speak up, girl!" Harry demanded. "We've got you now. Who are you and what mischief was here?"

"And she hung this up with the herbs," Elizabeth said and plucked down the single nosegay. She shook it close to the girl's face. She flinched as if it would burn her but still said naught.

"Maybe she can't talk—she's dumb," Jenks put in.

"One way or the other, she's dumb," Harry intoned and gave her another hard shake. Her head jerked and her limbs moved like a rag doll's.

"Jenks," he said, "go up and knock quietly on Lady Boleyn's door and ask Glenda to send Meg Milligrew down here straightaway. I don't care if she still claims she's puking her insides out."

Jenks nodded and hurried away. Elizabeth could tell the girl was terrified, and yet she did nothing to ease her situation. No explanation, no pleas, just wide-eyed, sullen, or even stupid stares. Perhaps she had been drugged, but she had fought like one demented or under some spell.

Elizabeth's lower lip dropped when Jenks swiftly returned with Meg. Though wrapped in a rough wool coverlet, her strawberry-hued hair wild from her bed, her face pinched and pale—yes, but for the wench's broader face,

Elizabeth had to admit, at least to herself, it was like gazing in a looking glass. Meg just gaped back, her mouth open too. "Good gracious" was all she managed to say.

Elizabeth forced herself to think again. "I am Lady Boleyn's friend, Lady Cornish, Meg. Since you are her herbalist, tell me what this is the girl tried to put among your hanging herbs. These are the herbs you hang here like in the garden shed, are they not?"

"Yes, milady. Could I have the light on this one then, an' you please?"

Jenks took and held the lantern for her. She frowned intently at the cluster of limp leaves on the stalks, then felt and sniffed at them. "Why, 'tisn't true saffron like I got hanging here to make the mistress's favorite honey saffron cakes," she declared. A frown furrowed her high brow. "It's got much simpler leaves and not sharp-edged, see? And they're longer and darker, but when they get mixed in and dried, Cook might not know the difference. Meadow saffron, milady, that's what this is."

Elizabeth just frowned, but suddenly Meg looked aghast. She drew in a sharp breath, then launched herself at their prisoner. "You mean you been poisoning her?" she screeched. "By mixing with my herbs? Meadow saffron's poison, you whey-faced bitch!" Meg's hands, still holding the herb, spread like claws around the girl's neck as if she'd choke the very life from her.

Harry cursed and, with Jenks's help, pulled the two apart. Elizabeth seized Meg's arm and shook her once. "Listen to me," she said, putting her face close to hers. "If someone is poisoned with meadow saffron—maybe put into honey cakes—what would be the signs of it?"

"Don't truly know, but could be gradual—not a big dose that way. All I know is, someone must have told me not to get them mixed, 'cause it's a poison for sure," Meg insisted, hanging stiff and still in Elizabeth's strong grip. Meg seemed suddenly cowed by her. They were eye to eye. The girl even had freckles sprinkled across her nose and cheeks, just like hers that Kat had worked so hard to whiten with lemon and buttermilk.

"I just work with simples for cures," Meg insisted. "Don't know much about poisons. But I'll tell you if she was tampering with that firkin there, that's the Lady Mary's privy cask of honeyed mead."

Elizabeth knelt to feel what had broken on the floor in that shattered vial. It was golden and sticky. "It *is* honey," she said. "Can honey be poisoned? Can it?" she shouted, first at Meg and then at their captive.

"I've heard of it happening natural," Meg put in. "You know, if the bees feed on something harmful 'fore they make their honey. But I s'pose someone could do it a-purpose too."

Harry sagged against the wall, loosing their captive. She was blocked in by all of them, but that moment's freedom was all she needed. Not moving quickly to cause alarm, she took another, smaller vial from her bosom and gulped its contents.

"She'd kill me if I din't," she mumbled her only words in

a slurred voice. Then she dropped the vial and covered both eyes with her hands and pressed herself back against the stone wall as if to wait for death.

Elizabeth yanked the girl into her grasp. "So you can talk. Speak, and right now. Who put you up to this? Jenks, get a cup and pour some beer in it. We've got to make her drink it, dilute that venom. Listen to me, girl," she said, shaking her, "I am the Princess Elizabeth, the queen's sister, so you must tell me directly."

She'd forgotten Meg didn't know, and at that revelation the girl evidently swooned against Jenks. Elizabeth made no move to help her. So what if she'd been ill? She was in charge of these herbs and should have kept them safe. But what sickened and infuriated Elizabeth most was the memory of herself just this evening lifting that tankard of mead to her aunt's lips. At least now Mary would have no drink or cakes that were not inspected.

"Who sent you here?" Elizabeth demanded of the poisoner. "Help us, and we'll take care of you. Do you know anything about men attacking his lordship here with poison arrows?"

But the girl said nothing else and wilted right before them, soon so weak she couldn't stand. They could get no beer down her. She spit it out, and they stood in the puddle of it, mixed with the girl's own urine that wet her thin skirts. In a quarter hour she clutched her chest and gasped for air. Her pulse faded.

"Though this is no ruse, stay with her, Jenks," Elizabeth ordered. He had gone back to fanning Meg's face with his cap as she, at least, recovered. "We'd best look in on the Lady Mary, in case she has any of her favorite drink or cakes by her bed at night."

Followed by Harry and Meg, she hurried up the steps, then the stairs above. They tiptoed into Mary's chamber, amazed the cellar walls were thick enough that no one on the second floor had heard them shouting. Glenda was dozing, but she woke with a start.

"Thought you been long gone, milady," she said to Elizabeth and struggled to her feet to dip a deep curtsy, as if she'd been practicing—or somehow knew her real identity. "Is aught amiss? Oh, there you are, girl," she added to Meg. "Come to take your turn here at last, I hope."

Elizabeth snatched the familiar tankard from the chest at the bedside and sniffed at it, then handed it to Henry, who gave it to Meg. As the four of them stood by her bed, Mary Boleyn opened her eyes.

"Oh," she said, her voice soft but her words very distinct. "I thought for one moment my lord was come late to bed. I always told him to wake me. Meg, dear girl, I'm glad to see you well and to have you back at my side." Her heavy gaze slowly swung to Elizabeth. "And my dearest Catherine has come home at last," she announced.

Elizabeth sucked in a sharp breath and glared sideways at Meg. She understood now why others resented and mistrusted the girl. Harry had even said she was not a local lass and had been in the household only a year. Yet Mary's deep affections for her seemed to rebuke them all. Even in her sleepy state she recognized a mere servant but not Elizabeth. She would tell Harry to cross-question this Meg more closely. If, as he said, the girl had tried some dosing tonics with Mary before she herself took—or played sick—she could have had the chance to harm her.

"And my dear boy, whatever is that bandage for?" Mary Boleyn interrupted Elizabeth's agonizing. Now Harry looked surprised.

"But, my lady mother, do you not recall . . ." he began, but his voice tapered off. They all stared down at Mary Boleyn.

She did not close her eyes, but they seemed to glaze over. She exhaled a deep breath and smiled and died.

Chapter The Fifth

T HE MEAGER BAND OF MOURNERS FELT THE floor shudder when the four men shoved and dragged the big paving stone back into place. It rumbled, then thudded to silence on the central aisle of the small church. In the vault beneath it, Mary Boleyn, Lady Stafford, now slept with her husband for all eternity.

By the light of the four funeral torches, Meg stepped forward to strew dried rose petals on the carved double epitaph, which had borne Mary's name for many years. She sniffed hard and wiped her nose on her sleeve, while Lord Henry Carey blew his on an embroidered handkerchief. Their eyes met before Meg stepped hastily back to her place in the circle of servants. He cleared his throat, then spoke so softly that they shuffled closer to hear his words.

"Needless to say," Lord Carey began, "I am grateful for your faithfulness and loyalty these years to my mother. Some of you have been with her almost from the beginning, when she came to live willingly in exile and then when"— he cleared his throat again—"my family fell from royal favor and fortune. You have heard her written words read to each of you and have received the coins or plate she bequeathed to you so that you might begin new lives."

Meg shifted sideways to see him better around Glenda's broad shoulder. She knew several of the servants—maybe his lordship too—resented her being included in the bequests. After only a year with the Lady Mary, she had eight gold crowns sewn in the hem of her inner petticoat. She wore every garment she owned, and not to keep out the chill night air. She had orders to leave Wivenhoe and head for the Princess Elizabeth. Though she was sore afeared of horses, she had bought one and was going to ride it clear to Hatfield House.

"I am hoping you will be allowed at least a fortnight in the manor house," Lord Carey went on, "before word of Lady Stafford's passing must be reported to the queen and someone comes here to claim it." His voice got bitter as rue when he said, "Like all Boleyn holdings, Wivenhoe is forfeit to the crown. . . . King Henry secretly decreed only that the Lady Mary might have this for the rest of her life, so . . ."

He didn't finish that thought. Some of the servants bowed their heads, some sniffled. Meg bit her lower lip hard and concentrated on that mere physical pain to try to stem the other.

"And lastly," his lordship said, his voice croaky as a frog's now, "should you be asked, I must beseech you to keep my presence here concealed as best you can. But should someone force you to it, say merely I came to comfort my lady mother on her deathbed and have gone back to the continent, parts unknown."

He began to turn away, then whirled back so his short black cape belled out. "And should anyone inquire about Lady Cornish's brief visit, say as little as you can, for we need not cause trouble for one of the Lady Mary's friends. Meg Milligrew, I would have a privy word with you," he said, fixing her with a baleful eye just when she was about to make her quick departure. She could only hope he had seen that she had dug up roots from the herb garden and would scold her only for that. "The rest of you are excused," he added, to make her stomach twist even tighter when everyone stopped and stared at her.

He took her elbow in one hard hand and steered her out the side door into the windy graveyard as if he'd march her back into the manor through the postern gate. But he stopped just outside before the first row of graves. She tried not to look at them. The whole place made her teeth clench and her knees knock.

"Milord, if'n it's about the herb starts I took—"

"That garden looks like a tiny graveyard at the Second Coming," he muttered. Before she could ask him what he meant, he went on. "I want to know what you dosed the Lady Mary with, thinking to help her woes. Do not look at me like that, as I am not accusing you of being in league with that girl we buried in unhallowed ground out there beyond the paupers' place." He gestured to indicate the far side of the graveyard wall.

Meg took a deep breath. "There's something I gave her I

didn't tell her about," she admitted, shifting from one foot
to the other.

His eyes were in shadow, but she could just tell he narrowed them. "Say on," he ordered sternly.

"A concoction of lavender to lighten her grief. See, herbs
can help heal the mind and heart just like the body, though
she was beyond mere simples then. But she liked it and my
raspberry tonic, milord. For my bellyache I took that too."
She tried to tug back from his grip, but it was futile, so she
stood stock still.

"Could that tonic have made her worse?" he demanded,
leaning closer as if to study her face in the darkness. "Is it
what made you sick to puking?"

"Oh, no, milord. I had the greensickness afore I took it. I
think it made me better. But sadly not till that evening she
was gone. I never would harm the Lady Mary. She took me
in and saved my life when I didn't know who I was."

"You mean, when you didn't know who *she* was."

"No, milord. Myself. They found me on the road, her
stable man and Coll, the gardener. Kicked by a horse in the
head and knew nothing but my name, not where I lived or
what happened. Even with her lord sick then, she took me
in and nursed me, and later it come to me I knew all 'bout
garden herbs and strewing herbs. But as for dosing with
infirmary herbs, I remembered only what came back to me
about some simples and nothing about poisons, I swear it on
the Lady Mary's grave."

She saw he scowled at her. The moon had sprung itself
loose from above the big tree and lit his face in all its fur-

rows. She was scared he wouldn't believe her, wouldn't let her go. Maybe he'd even turn her over to the local bailiff or to the king's man coming to claim the manor.

" 'Tis true, milord," she insisted. "And I can't bear it I was ailing when she took worse, 'cause she nursed me so fine when I was going to die. She said it was just like she birthed me herself, gave me life, and I loved her and ever will."

He looked surprised to see he still held her arm. He loosed it and stepped back. "I don't mean to cross-question you so hard, girl, but it's important. Tell me this, then. In the short time you lived here, did you meet anyone about the area who was skilled in herbs? Someone must have sent that dolt of a girl—the someone she mentioned when she killed herself."

"I know, milord. The girl called her only 'she' and had such a fearful look on her face." Meg had plans to talk to that "she," but she didn't let on.

"Well?" he said sharply to make her jump.

"Well what, milord?"

She didn't mean to fret him more, but his voice rose. "Do you know of anyone who could have sent her to the manor? We make our own honey here, so I never would have expected someone fouling it or that meadow saffron that apes the real. Do you know of someone who could have done either? Someone very clever? Is there anything else you can tell me?"

"Only that your lady mother loved you, milord, and always brooded over your safety."

"What in God's name does that have to do with the poisoner?" he exploded. Then he looked about him and lowered his voice, as if afraid he'd wake the dead.

"Nothing, but that's the only message she gave me for you, in case you never made it here on time, she said. That she loved you and always brooded over your safety."

"Yes, all right." As he looked briefly heavenward, she saw that tears glittered in his eyes before he ducked his head into moon shadow again. "We're all distraught," he said, more to himself than her. "But I want to speak to you again in the morn before I leave. I need to go through her things tonight, burn some, keep some. And, Meg, I do thank you for being so loyal to her—and now I do see why, that and perhaps why the others resented how she favored you. Tomorrow then."

He turned and walked toward the manor, not through the postern gate but along the road outside the wall, where the mourners now straggled back toward a cold funeral feast. Meg leaned against the tree and watched them disappear with a big piece of her life. Then she went back into the church, where a single thick candle burned at the head of the flat tombstone strewn with dry rose petals.

She gripped her hands before her and bowed her head to stare at the Lady Mary's name cut in the stone. The flickering flame made the words she could not read seem to waver and leap.

"I don't want to let his lordship down but can't wait to talk to him tomorrow, milady. I got to find your royal niece and take care of her if'n it's the last thing I do."

As she turned away in this deserted place, she thought she heard the echo of footsteps, light, quick ones, and not her own. Her heart thudding, she looked about, staring into corners. But all was silent, shifting shadows, even behind the old vaults with the cold stone effigies staring straight up toward heaven. Tears blurring her way, Meg hurried out the door and ran to where she had her old nag of a horse hidden in the trees.

"YOU'LL HAVE A DEVIL OF A TIME getting back safe inside now it's gone light," Jenks observed as he laced Elizabeth's gown in the thicket beyond the back lawn of Hatfield. It was just shy of midmorning; their return had been a grueling, grief-stricken ordeal. "The watchdog Popes are like to see you sneaking in," he added to rile her temper further.

"I do not sneak, Jenks, no matter what you think you may have seen or been privy to these past two days. Do you understand?" she demanded in a voice that could etch steel.

"Aye, Your Grace. Just bluff your way in, you mean."

"I shall tell them I walked out to get some fresh air. Aren't you done with that?" she said, twisting around to glare at him. "Must your fingers be as slow as your brain?"

She instantly regretted her words. "It is only," she amended, catching his hangdog expression, "I am likely to scream from exhaustion, grief, and distress, Jenks. And to whom else can I show my pain if not those I trust? I could not have succeeded without you these last two days, and I shall not forget your help."

His cheeks flamed like a yuletide candle. "Your Grace, you've only but to ask me ever and—"

"Then go on through the woods to return the horses." She ticked off his tasks on her long fingers. "Be certain you rehearse your excuse before someone sees you. And guard that arrow in the saddle pack with your life until you can get it to me—*to me,* not Kat. Go on now, and I'll be fine."

She knew that last claim was a bold-faced lie, for she was truly desperate. At the last moment she had made Harry promise to flee for sanctuary to her friend William Cecil's country home in Stamford and not return to Europe as he had planned—and as their nameless enemies might expect. He was simply to tell the Wivenhoe household he was going abroad again.

She walked from the forest cover toward the back of the house. A carp pond littered with yellow leaves and a few rose beds gone to autumn legginess were all that lay between her and the familiar house. Hatfield boasted no fine herb garden either. But from here she hoped to get Kat's attention with a few pebbles against the windowpanes. She would have her toss down a petticoat or two so she didn't look like something the cat dragged in. In case someone spotted her, she merely carried her cloak with its lining out so no one could see how mud-speckled it looked.

Please, dear Lord, she prayed as she had much of the endless, sad ride back, *protect me and show me what to do next.*

Though no answer to that prayer, Beatrice Pope popped round the corner of the house with her ever-present needlework in her hands. Her pert face registered shock: Her full lower lip dropped, her tilted blue eyes widened, and she tossed her head.

"Oh, Lady Elizabeth, Mistress Ashley said you were still abed and not eating, and my lord said he's going up to demand that you do." Even when Bea gave a mere yea or nay answer, words seemed to spill from her as if they conveyed the most momentous message to all mankind. "Else we shall have to send to Her Majesty the report that you are ailing and we needs must have her best physician, like the time she sent her own before."

Elizabeth stopped in her tracks. Why had she not thought of that? Her sister had sent the royal physician just after she was released from the Tower following the aborted Protestant Wyatt Rebellion, for which Mary had blamed her. Elizabeth had slowly sickened—with some of the signs her aunt showed—and had publicly protested her fears to all around her that perhaps she was being poisoned. Indeed, when first Mary was queen she had banished Elizabeth after shouting she deserved to be poisoned and claiming that Anne Boleyn had poisoned Catherine of Aragon.

Under the care of Mary's physician and the newly arrived Cora Crenshaw, a cook who still served here, Elizabeth had recovered. There was no real proof of poison. But what if— what if, though Queen Mary dare not have her done away with thusly in the Tower, she had decided to have her somehow gotten rid of here? And what if, when Elizabeth publicly complained, she had bided her time, but as she herself became ill and mayhap would die soon and leave the realm to a Protestant queen . . . Oh, dear Lord, what if Queen Mary Tudor, who burned martyrs at the stake, were the "she" the poisoner had feared when she drank that vial of venom rather than facing her wrath? What if, before she died, Mary Tudor planned to wreak vengeance on all of the Boleyns?

"I said," Bea was repeating, suddenly staring so close into her face that Elizabeth jumped, "are you certain you are well, my lady? You looked as bleached as my linen for this sampler."

Elizabeth glanced at what she held up. The intricate chain stitching outlined rose vines with thrusting thorns and tight buds curled around each other in a mazelike pattern, twisting tighter toward the central space left for the epigram. For a moment she thought she would faint. She took a slow, deep breath.

"I am quite on my way to recovery," she claimed with a forced smile. "My head suddenly cleared this morning, and I could not abide being closed in by the bed-curtains and that stale chamber any longer. I craved fresh air, so I donned a gown while Kat yet slept and took a walk."

"It *is* laced in rather slipshod fashion," Bea observed, with a suspicious glance at her back. "But you really should have put on some petticoats. It's not like you to look so tawdry. And you might merely have stuck your head out the casement for fresh air."

Bea tilted her head and slanted her gaze toward the suite

of windows where Kat Ashley looked out, surprise stamped all too plain on her broad face. Kat could keep a lock on her lips but never, without a veil, hide the feelings on her face.

Kat opened the casement as Elizabeth gave her a jaunty wave. "Oh, there you are, Your Grace," Kat called down. "Best come up and get garbed proper now."

"She's right, you know," Bea said to Elizabeth, her narrowed gaze traversing her mussed gown and tangled hair again. By comparison, Elizabeth realized, Bea's own impeccable gabled hood, coif, and attire only made things worse. Even when Bea had ridden clear to Maidstone to visit her sister's family, she arrived home looking both comely and kempt.

"I'll bring the Lady Elizabeth right in and sit with her to give you a respite, Mistress Ashley," Bea shouted up to Kat and waved her embroidered piece like a pennant.

"How kind of you," Elizabeth said and linked her arm in hers, holding up her heavy skirts with the other. One thing she recalled her father saying was that the best defense was a bullish offense. "You know, I've missed your company, Bea—everyone's these last terrible days."

"You just do not look as if you feel better." Bea's repeated words buzzed in her ears. "You had best go straight back to bed."

"Nonsense. Those head pains just drain me, that's all," Elizabeth insisted as they strolled around and went in the front door, where Thomas Pope confronted them with arms akimbo and face aghast at the bottom of the staircase. She'd never let on, but her head hurt indeed, almost as badly as her heart. So she forced another smile, squared her shoulders, and held herself erect. It was the first time she realized what she might have to do to get to the bottom of this Boleyn plot: namely, put on an actor's face, skilled as that Ned Topside. Say next to nothing, as that poisoner had done before she killed herself. Or tell lies. And, as Jenks had put it, bluff her way, or even be a sneak. Yes, Elizabeth of England thought, she could do all of that to solve this and to survive.

She put one step before the other on the stairs, hoping no one noticed she wore mud-speckled riding boots.

ELIZABETH TUDOR RACED HER big black stallion Griffin down the road toward the little village of Hatfield. Sheep cropping the lawn scattered; she rode fast enough so that only Jenks managed to keep up with her. It was the sole place she had felt safe lately, out in the open air, on familiar ground, but with no buildings or forests hemming her in or hiding enemies. What had happened at Wivenhoe still haunted her. What to do about it, kept close confined as she was, tormented her.

She reined in with Jenks at her side. "The Popes are keeping close today," he observed, patting his horse's lathered shoulder. "Sticky as can be since we come back. You don't think they know something, Your Grace?"

"I believe we got away with our venture. And I must admit I stick close enough to them for everything I eat. If I don't see food go into either of their mouths, I avoid it too.

They think," she said with a rueful laugh, "I've become companionable at mealtime."

"Anything I can do, you only need—"

"I do need to send you to some apothecary with that bloody arrow. I want to know what it's been dipped in and its properties. 'S blood, I wish I had two of myself so one could keep them occupied while the other investigates . . ."

Her voice trailed off as the idea flashed through her. It was mad, but it meshed so well with her other obsessive thoughts lately. She had been toying with the plan to send Jenks to find both Meg Milligrew, who must surely need a position now, and Ned Topside, who could feign to be only her clown. But in truth Meg could serve as her double and decoy, and Ned would become many different people—be her eyes and ears to find things out when she could not escape Bea and the Pope, just like this.

"Come on, before they catch up, let's ride!" she cried and spurred Griffin on again.

They galloped down the main gravel road past the vast lawns and then along the dirt lane skirting the village that had grown up higgledy-piggledy, as one always did near a great house. But as Hatfield had faded from proper royal use, the village had too. Its half-timbered homes and shops were tattered or tumbled, and many—

She screamed. The first arrow winged its way close past her head. She could feel its breath. Another followed farther on. She yanked Griffin's reins, and he reared. She held on, tried to turn him, shouting to Jenks.

"Arrows! An attack!"

Jenks charged his mount the way she pointed.

"No!" she cried. "I can't lose you. Not like Lord Harry lost Will!"

But he dismounted and ran headlong, darting, ducking low. He disappeared behind a tall stone wall. As she kept low and sidestepped Griffin away, Thomas Pope and two others thundered up with Bea coming along behind. Blanche Parry rode over, her face white with fear.

"What is it, Your Grace?" Blanche asked. "Why did you scream?"

"Help Jenks," she cried to Sir Thomas, pointing. "Someone was shooting arrows at us."

They would know too much if she told them more. But at that moment Jenks came dragging two ragged-looking boys by their collars out from behind the wall. Both held children's bows made of bent willow sticks and vines. Thomas Pope shouted a laugh and dismounted to retrieve an arrow in the grass, a stick crudely fletched with chicken feathers and no sharpened point at all.

"They didn't mean to be shooting at you," Jenks said, out of breath. "They say they didn't even see you, Your Grace." She noted that Thomas Pope had begun his usual slow burn he suffered each time her people so much as alluded to her royalty, when her sister's staff pointedly called her only my lady. Elizabeth nodded, flushed with embarrassment—and anger.

"Shall we put them in the stocks," Sir Thomas inquired, his voice mocking, "or send them to the Tower, or use the iron-maiden torment, my lady?" His jowls bounced when he laughed; she detested the man. "Yet I cannot help but think," he went on, playing it to the hilt, "that your bridling your own runaway temperament to go riding about hither and yon would solve this . . . uh, childish problem."

Elizabeth glared down at him from her saddle. "Let the lads go with no penalty," she said. "It took me by surprise, that is all."

"But it could have been something, aye, it could," Sir Thomas pursued. "As I said, you'll not go dashing off ahorse without me again." No doubt to show he ignored her pardoning the lads, he broke their bows over his knee and soundly cuffed both before shoving them back toward the village. Elizabeth wanted to protest, yet she sat silent in shock. Though arrows had not struck her, sharp, instant terror had pierced her heart. She was sick to death of living in fear and would have no more of it.

"Jenks," she said out of the side of her mouth as she turned back toward the village and he, as ever, cantered first at her side, "you must go see your father tomorrow, as you have done afore."

"But you heard the Pope," he said, thankfully not turning his head her way as the others came to ride behind them. "We can't go off somewhere else when—"

"Listen," she hissed. "Not us, you. Under pretense of seeing your father again, you will ride back to Wivenhoe and tell Meg Milligrew I need an herbalist and would have her just appear at my door selling some such. And she must not let on where she's been before, never that she knew

Mary Boleyn. And then you must find those Queen's Country Players somewhere near Colchester and tell Ned Topside I have need of a clown and will pay him well. And if you must to convince him, tell him who I really am and that I admire his cleverness. And on your way go by the village back there, for I shall give you a coin for each of those boys and tell them someday I shall want fine archers in my armies and nav—"

She left off midword as Thomas Pope cantered up to her side and Bea appeared on her other to edge Jenks out. "As I said, my Lady Elizabeth," Sir Thomas intoned, out of breath and frowning at her like a schoolmaster, "best you take no other jaunts without me or Lady Beatrice this close at your side. And perhaps you'll keep this as a token to remember why."

He extended to her a crude child's arrow. She took it, seeing instead that other one they had dug from Will Benton's putrid corpse. She gripped it in her gloved hand and swore a solemn oath to herself that she would search out and stop the plot against her family and herself. Then she thrust it in her belt the way soldiers once did to show they were at war.

Chapter The Sixth

I T CAN'T BE SHE. NOT HERE—SO SOON," ELIZ-abeth muttered as she pressed her forehead to the cold window glass of the great hall, where she'd been taking her exercise on this rainy day. But yes, her eyes did not deceive her. "Oh, dear Lord," she whispered as she began to run, "I pray You, do not let that girl say something to give me away."

But after all, she *had* prayed the Lord would show her what to do next in her dilemma. The children's attack with arrows had been one sign to spur her on, but now here in the flesh stood Meg Milligrew on the very day she'd sent Jenks for her. Was that not some sort of miracle—a sign pointing toward salvation? But with Thomas Pope standing between her and Meg, it could mean damnation.

She hurried out and down the hall to the front entryway, where she'd seen Meg ride in—in pitiable style in the driv-ing rain—dismount from her broken-down nag, and nearly slip in a mud puddle. She heard voices and knew the Popes had greeted Meg before she could warn the girl to guard her mouth. Elizabeth had a stitch in her side by the time she reached the three of them at the door. Drenched, Meg stood holding a sodden hemp sack, while the Popes hovered like king's beasts guarding the threshold.

"Come to sell your goods to the Lady Elizabeth from where, wench?" Sir Thomas was saying. At least they had let the poor girl close enough to the door that she was out of the rain.

"From Stratford-Upon-the-Avon in Warwickshire, my lord. Not to sell her things but give her gifts—for protection."

"She is well-protected here and needs no such superstitious nonsense," Bea put in.

"Oh, not charms or amulets, milady, but God's good, simple herbs for cures and happiness."

Elizabeth joined them at the door. When Meg saw her she dropped into a curtsy in the puddle she was making. Water still dripped off her nose and chin. "Herbs for me?" Elizabeth inquired, wedging herself between the Popes and giving the girl a quick wink when she rose. "How very kind. I love strewing herbs and sweet potpourris. Is that what you mean, girl? What is your name?"

"Oh, yes, that's what I mean all right. Margaret Milligrew, called Meg, that's me."

"Sir Thomas," Elizabeth said, turning to face him down, "I believe Christian charity commands that I accept and give this lass a good meal and night's lodgings at least." Though she fully intended to keep Meg here, that must seem to come gradually, naturally.

"Oh, thankee, Your Grace" came muffled from Meg as she curtsied again, making her shoes squeak with water.

"You may rise," Elizabeth said. She noted that even the rain had not seemed to wash the girl's dirty face and clothes. She was afraid Bea would never let her in. At least she did not reek of horse or sweat but emanated the most pleasant flowery aromas, like a wet garden.

"You may go around the side door," Elizabeth went on, "and we shall stable your horse."

"Just hold here," Sir Thomas ordered. He lifted both palms as if to stay poor Meg's onslaught on the house and Elizabeth's hasty invitation into it. "I insist on seeing in that sack, wench. My Lady Elizabeth," he went on, twisting his head about and frowning, "have you so soon forgot that you are not to go off hither and yon—in any way?"

"Oh, my sack," Meg said with a grin. "I've two saddle packs full of herbal starts, too, milord, and I'd be happy to put in a physic or infirmary garden come spring as well as plant your kitchen or cosmetic ones."

"Come spring?" he repeated. "There was no talk of more than one night in the kitchen." He glowered, but Bea seemed curious as the girl opened the sack and fished about in it, from time to time producing a bunch of something at its broad mouth. She kept up a running commentary.

"I've tuzzy-muzzies to ward off winter agues, and rue to make sweet salves—for bee stings, Your Grace," she said, her eyes wide on Elizabeth's gaze again. For some reason the mention of bees made Elizabeth shudder, and she'd never once been stung. When both the Popes peered into Meg's sack, the girl dared to wink at her, in imitation of Elizabeth's earlier signal to her.

"And peony seeds," she went on, "mixed with wine can cure nightmares, and basil for the heart to take away sorrow. And this, my lord, is southern wood. You burn it and drive all serpents from the house, and that would be protection for Her Grace."

As Meg rattled on it struck Elizabeth that she was giving her a message in code. Warding off disease and troubles . . . stings . . . nightmares, a sorrowing heart, and serpents in the house. Meg Milligrew had come on her own to help her with her troubles. And if she didn't cause her new ones first with her sly looks over the top of Thomas and Bea Pope's heads, it was a clever ruse at that.

"SHE RESEMBLES YOU ENOUGH to be a closer sister to you than your own," Kat whispered the moment she led Meg into Elizabeth's bedchamber late that night and closed the door behind the three of them. Kat had fetched Meg from her pallet on the kitchen hearth after everyone had retired. "If she hadn't looked like such a drowned rat, the Buzzard and the Pope would have seen it too."

"I realize that, Kat."

"Is that why you want her here," she asked, "and not just that she served your aunt?"

"More than ever lately, I need to surround myself with

people I can trust—like you, Kat," Elizabeth said and gestured for Meg to sit beside her on the settle they had pulled up to take advantage of the low-stoked fire. No good to build it up when the Popes thought she was snug in bed. Kat pulled up a three-legged stool and plopped on it so they sat almost in a circle.

"I've come to pledge my services and loyalty, Your Grace," Meg said, looking so intent and eager it touched Elizabeth deeply. "And, to tell true, the Lady Mary said if aught happened to her—when she knew she was dying and wanted to die, I think—she said I should go to you and try to serve you and never let on to anyone else I had been with Mary Boleyn. And more than that," she admitted, and her voice took on a hard tone. She looked directly into Elizabeth's assessing gaze. "If someone poisoned that sweet lady to death like you and Lord Carey said—and meant to make it look like it was me—I'm going to make them pay!"

Elizabeth squeezed her hands. Though she had asked Harry to cross-question the girl about what herbs she had given her aunt, such loyalty helped convince her that Meg had no connection to the poisoner they had caught in the cellars. Before she killed herself, that girl had shown real fear of whomever "she" was. The reference could not have been to awkward, endearing Meg—she was certain of it. Still, there was much about Meg she would know.

For one moment they stared at each other in solemn, silent study. Then Elizabeth loosed her hands and said, "I was relieved to hear you realize you must admit no Boleyn

connections here. Your story about coming from Warwickshire today was mere fabrication, I take it?"

Meg nodded, though her gaze and voice softened as she
frowned at some thought. She explained about losing much
of the past from her head injury, which the Lady Mary
nursed her through. "But since things come flying back in
foggy bits, Your Grace, sometimes ideas just come to me,
but I don't know where from or if they're true." She gestured helplessly, then plopped her hands back in her lap.

"Do not fret, because it changes nothing here," Elizabeth
assured her. She lowered her voice even more. "I sent Jenks
for you just today, but he must have passed you on the road.
He'll learn you're gone and go on for Ned Topside—the
dark-haired actor from the players. You see, Meg, I need
some people about me not only to trust but to help me solve
a—poison plot."

"And I can help you," she declared with a decisive nod.
"I done some asking of my own on that, just like Lord
Carey done to me."

"Who were you questioning?" Elizabeth asked, leaning
closer to the girl's avid face. She was fully aware Kat had
not taken her eyes off Meg and that she resented her. She
wondered fleetingly if that would always be poor Meg's lot
in any household she served.

"I questioned a few folks what live round Wivenhoe,
folks might have taken in or bought goods from that girl
you fought with in the cellar."

"Fought with?" Kat sputtered, pressing her clasped

hands to her breasts. "Your Grace, you didn't say you fought with that foul poisoner, only apprehended—"

"Shh, Kat. Go on, Meg."

"And I found out who she was—I mean, part of it. Named Nettie and came from Kent, she told old Widow Willoughby she stayed with. I even paid the widow one of my gold crowns the Lady Mary left me to buy Nettie's worldly goods from her, since she was dead. I had to put up the whole coin when the old hag didn't believe my story I was her kin and to keep her mouth shut about what I been asking."

"What did this Nettie leave behind? Where is it?" Elizabeth demanded. Her heart pounded in anticipation. "And from where did she hail in Kent?"

"Don't know, and mostly it was a few clothes but for this that I thought was important, and maybe you can read it to say where in Kent," Meg explained in one long breath. She stood and reached down into her stiff bodice. She had obviously taken off a layer of clothes from her ride, but she still looked padded.

"Can't read," Meg went on, tipping her chin up to pull something folded out, "or would have told you already what it said, if it was some threat to you or Lady Mary or Lord Carey or some such." Slowly, she drew out a piece of folded, embroidered linen. The back of it with its knotted threads and cross-stitches looked like chaos. Meg sat again, unfolded it, and turned it up in her lap.

The embroidered green leaves and bright red berries reminded Elizabeth of yuletide colors. Kat, who was looking at it upside down, whispered, "My own mother kept those in our garden. Lords-and-ladies, that's what she used to call it."

Meg nodded but kept silent as she passed it to Elizabeth. While Kat craned her neck to see, Elizabeth sat staring at the long-leafed plants, twined in a wreathed pattern that encompassed the elegantly scripted words: *For I see that you are poysoned by bitterness and bound by iniquity.*

"Does it tell where we can find Nettie's place in Kent or who is that 'she' Nettie worked for, Your Grace?" Meg asked when Elizabeth just glared at it.

"It is words from the Bible," she whispered. "From the book of Acts, and act we must. Like a curse, it says, *For I see that you are poysoned by bitterness and bound by iniquity.*"

"Poison!" the girl cried.

Kat leapt to her feet. "I remember now," she muttered. "Mother said we children mustn't touch it."

"Quiet," Elizabeth ordered, grabbing both their wrists. She didn't say so, but the style, though it could belong to many fine needlework hands, reminded her of Beatrice Pope's work. The saying itself—where had she heard it before? Not in a sermon at court perhaps, but somewhere there. Her stomach twisted; her crunching head pain returned with a jolt.

While Meg and Kat hovered over her, standing close to the hearth, Elizabeth examined the entire piece carefully, wishing the many skilled chain stitches could whisper their maker's name. She flipped it over to peruse the other side.

"Another word here," she told them, "only in crude if

tiny block letters, see? No," she said, bending closer and tipping it to the light, "there are two words, almost hidden by these knots and tie-offs. *Bushey,* it says. *Bushey Cot.*"

"There's a Bushey not so far from here," Kat put in, her voice agitated. "You know, that little market town."

Elizabeth nodded. "And that is not in Kent. Meg, is this embroidered plant indeed lords-and-ladies, as Mistress Ashley said?" She turned it to the right side again, and they stretched it between them.

"Looks to be," she said, squinting at it. "Heard it called a wake-robin too. They say the berries taste sweet and the leaves sour, but I don't know who says that because—"

"Because it's a poison plant," Elizabeth finished for her. Wide-eyed, Meg nodded. "What part of it is poison?" Elizabeth demanded, fighting for control as she fingered the outline of the leaves and the bloodred berries.

"Why, pick it early and all of it's deadly, Your Grace," Meg said, and Kat nodded. "Every last bit."

THE INNYARD OF THE HEAD AND CROWN in Colchester was packed to the gills with a rowdy crowd for the performance, though it wasn't to start for a good hour yet. Silently cursing the fact he must play the role of the lecherous, bumbling Ned Topside he'd made so popular—and had come to feel trapped by—Edward Thompson had curled up for a quick bit of early-afternoon dreaming on the cushion in the deep window seat.

He yanked closed the curtain between the seat and one of

the two bedchambers the players had used last night. Here Uncle Wat and Grand Rand had slept, and it served as their prop room. Their tiring-room next door, which he'd shared with the two lads, was smaller and noisier, right over the taproom. At least there would be no more jamming into one bed or pinching pennies for a while. They'd been living high these last two days, flush with fortune from Lord Henry at Wivenhoe.

Now, despite the noise welling up from the innyard, it seemed peaceful here. An autumn fly that would soon be dead bumped and buzzed against the mullioned window-panes, protesting its unjust imprisonment. His fellow players were taking their ease at a meal, lost in the busy distant drone of human voices.

Yet stirred from his sleep Ned heard his Uncle Wat's voice, muted, muffled. At first he just pulled his cloak over his face, wishing he could plug his ears with it. But he recognized the lines from *The Reluctant Lover*. And then he heard that damned Grand Rand doing the girl's part, of all things, when, ever since Ned's father had died, he'd had the choicest men's roles:

> *"Sword point or stinger do I oft fear*
> *But not when you, my love, are near.*
> *Then desire I more than your fervent eye*
> *So eager on this bed I lie."*

"Best not lie down or we won't have time before the others come up," his Uncle Wat said, his voice breathy.

"Here, just stand, lean . . ." Ned heard a rustling, a groan.

"Did I hear those sweet words, *come up?*" Rand asked, his voice strangely thick.

"Just shut up for once afore—"

The moment Ned ripped open the curtain, he knew that he should not have. Better just to hide here, knowing at last why Randall Greene got everything he wanted lately. But Ned was furious and sick of them both—of his whole life suddenly.

He picked up a battle banner and heaved it at them, then a stool. They leapt apart, wide-eyed, scrabbling for cover.

Rand hopped about trying to pull up his hose, then just grabbed a wooden shield and held it before him. His uncle had the gall to yell at him, "Damn you, boy! You've ruined everything!"

"Leave off, you deceitful, whoreson bastard!" Ned shouted. "I've two things to say to you." He was not sure why he strapped on a stage sword as he spoke, though he was furious enough to kill them both. "One is, if I stay— and I don't have the stomach to perform today—I will play the notable men's parts I have long deserved. They obviously can't go to this one anymore"—he nodded dramatically at Rand. "Hellfire, I know I'd never keep a straight face hereafter. And," he added, pointing with a dagger, "I will kill both of you if you so much as touch the lads."

"The lads," his uncle stammered, crimson-faced. "That has nothing to do with—"

"I may be back, I may not—ever!" Ned concluded, thrusting the dagger into his belt. He stomped out, leaving the door gaping. In the next chamber he knotted his long cloak around his meager goods. He dug in the velvet cod-piece in the tiring-trunk, where he knew his uncle hid their treasury. He seized what he considered to be about one-fourth the coins, then dropped a few back, even though it was his saving Lord Henry that had gotten them this bounty.

He went downstairs and out through the crowded common room into the innyard. "Where you going, Ned?" The boy Rob called to him from where he sat perched on the well watching a cockfight that was evidently the prologue to their play. "We got to go on."

"Aye, lad, we've all got to go on," Ned told him and ruffled his hair before he turned away.

No more Ned Topside, he vowed as he shoved his way out into the innyard through the crowd. No more playing seconds to anyone. Though he had sworn to his father on his deathbed that he would help his uncle keep the troupe together, this double betrayal had canceled that debt. He'd find some other band of players, show them what he knew, even buy his way in if he must, but he'd never trust them or anyone. If a member of your own family could betray you, what was left to believe in? Though he felt like a vagabond, he slung his bundle over his shoulder and started off for who-knew-where.

"Ho there, you!" someone behind him shouted. "You, Master Topside!"

He would have just kept going, but the formal address and the fact he'd been recognized made him turn. A tall, gangly man hurried to him, dragging the reins of a good-looking horse through the fringe of the crowd. "Oh, thank God, 'tis you, Master Topside," he blurted, out of breath. "I know you got a fine calling, but I been sent by a person of renown with an offer for your service."

"By whom? What service?" Ned demanded, his hand on the dull sword they'd used in many a fight scene. He wondered just how much that horse would cost.

"I'm to say as a clown, but—"

He turned away and threw back over his shoulder, "I'm done playing the clown. I'm near a quarter century of age and have no home, no hopes, no patron, no—"

Though he was talking to himself—quite a soliloquy, really—the man kept up. "Just to play at playing the clown, I mean, Master Topside," he amended. "A patron—she wants your wits, your help, and she can pay."

Ned spun to face him. "Who wants my help? Who can pay?"

Pride shone so radiantly on the man's plain face—that was what convinced Ned he spoke the truth—as he said those remarkable words.

"Why, the Princess Elizabeth herself. Saw you in secret at Wivenhoe, she did, and in secret asks you come to her at Hatfield and serve her, if you would, so—"

The man stopped his speech when Ned hooted a triumphant laugh to the skies. He dropped his sack and smacked his hands, one on the other, atop his head. "Serve her? The princess?" he said, his well-honed voice cracking like a boy's. Tears he could not stem blurred his vision. "Elizabeth Tudor—Elizabeth of England? Lead on, man. Can your horse carry both of us?" he asked, but he was thinking this was the best *deus ex machina* salvation he had ever seen at the end of a play—or rather, the beginning of another.

But then he thought of an even better *denouement,* one written especially for his Uncle Wat and Grand Rand.

"Will you wait here just one moment, man? Here, tie my pack on your saddlebags, and I'll be brief. I'd best bid a better farewell to my friends."

He shoved his way back into the innyard, and in his deepest upstage bass, standing directly under their window, he shouted, "Wat Thompson! Grand Rand Greene!"

The bastards rushed out and leaned over the railing as if they all played some fond farewell scene. "You've had a change of heart, my boy," his uncle called down to him. "Of course you and Rand can share—can even alternate—the choice parts and speeches."

"He can have them all—have you too. I just wanted to inform you that the Princess Elizabeth—of England, uncle, the Tudor heir—has sent her man to fetch me to present many a sketch and speech. Heard us at Wivenhoe in secret and singled me out."

They gaped at him, then began to shout down beseechments, apologies, excuses. When Ned only shook his head and waved, Rand started to run down the outer hall.

"And so, farewell," Ned shouted to his uncle with a mocking bow. As Rand thundered down the stairs, Ned pushed his way through the crowd to the man waiting with the horse.

"My uncle intends to detain me by force," he told him. "But if you can get me out of here straightaway, I will serve Her Grace body, mind—and high drama."

When he glanced back to see that Rand had actually fallen down—in the dust their fine mount had made—Ned Topside, alias Edward Thompson, knew this was the finest exit he would ever make in his entire life.

Chapter The Seventh

O THAT IS BUSHEY," ELIZABETH OBSERVED, gazing down the hillside at the shallow valley. The villagers had spread their harvest fair on a central green framed by its houses and shops. Beyond the cluster of buildings, the brassy reds, bronze, and gold of autumn trees encircled furrowed and fallow fields, which looked like an irregular chessboard. Though such beauty lay sun-gilded, Elizabeth's mood was dark.

Leaning toward Meg, who rode next to her in the small train, she said, "Since Jenks is not back yet, I'm trusting you and Kat to inquire about Bushey Cot while we are here. Then I will find a way to visit it somehow, the Popes and their people notwithstanding."

After looking ahead at the two guards, Meg twisted in her saddle to glance back at the other two men, the Popes, and Lady Blanche, who rode at the rear with stolid Kat Ashley. "Aye," Meg said, turning back in her saddle, "but I'm having a few second thoughts about that piece of needlework. What if it was meant to send the one who found it on a wild-goose chase?"

"Or meant to snare a silly goose," Elizabeth replied, frowning. She had thought of that possibility herself and was pleased Meg had reasoned it out. It made Elizabeth trust her more. "But we have no other leads right now," she added, "so this is worth the risk."

"But Nettie and that 'she' Nettie was so afraid of and those archers in the woods," Meg countered, "they were after folks at Wivenhoe. So why would any of them have aught to do with a place here called Bushey Cot?"

"Because, I fear, it is close to Hatfield, and 'she'—or they—are also after me. Surely you realized that."

"You, Your Grace? No. But—"

"I said you must learn to conceal your emotions," Elizabeth cut her off. "I plan," she explained, "to have Ned Topside teach both you and Kat to guard your expressions—facial and verbal—if he comes. But meanwhile you must take your cue from me. Now, try harder, because here comes Sir Thomas again."

"Quite a lot of chatter up here," he observed, shaking his head so his jowls bounced.

"I am asking Mistress Milligrew to buy up whatever herbs at this fair will get us through the winter," Elizabeth informed him archly, looking straight ahead. "I've missed the strewing and scenting herbs I've known at court."

"I've no doubt you miss court—haven't we all?" he muttered. "Just see you do not cause a stir at Bushey, my lady, and that no one gets so much as a hint who you are, at least not of your accord. It doesn't endear you to the queen when she hears you've been flaunting yourself about, hoping to incite hurrahs—and more."

"And she no doubt hears from some source every move I make," Elizabeth countered.

Evidently deciding not to challenge that, he rode toward the front of the band. Elizabeth looked back, caught Bea's eye, and forced a smile. After all, she would never have convinced Sir Thomas to visit Bushey if it hadn't been for Bea, who was looking for imported dyes for her sewing threads.

But the more Elizabeth considered it, the more Bea's helpfulness and watchfulness bothered her. Besides that needlework from Wivenhoe greatly resembling Bea's style, she was upon occasion absent from Hatfield for several days at a time, including, Kat had said, the day and second night Elizabeth was at Wivenhoe. It was supposedly to visit her sister in Maidstone, which was in Kent.

Still, Bea had never shown the slightest special interest in flowers or herbs, but to embroider them. And she seemed such an ally. More than once she had heard Bea standing up for her rights and privileges, though, indeed, that could have been arranged to get Elizabeth to trust her.

"Never forget this, Thomas," she had heard Bea declare to her husband last month through a slightly open door when Elizabeth passed by in the upstairs corridor. "Queen Mary is ill, and Elizabeth is not. Queen Mary is hated and Elizabeth favored; Queen Mary is older and Elizabeth yet young. Queen Mary—"

"Is queen indeed and has put us in a position of authority here with our orders!" Thomas had thundered. "And see that you bridle your lips, actions, and fond heart, madam, because who is to say if we watch the princess and report on her doings that others are not watching us."

It had seemed so convincing. She'd felt at least pity for Bea ever since. She had scolded Kat next time she referred to her as the Buzzard.

But it was just then, riding down into that shallow valley, with Bea no doubt looking at her from behind, that Elizabeth felt a chill slide down her spine like an icy hand. It feathered the hairs on the nape of her neck; she shuddered even in her warm cloak and hood. It was as if someone with poison-tipped intent were spying on her as they rode in.

She spun to look back at Bea again. She was watching, but she gave a jaunty wave and spurred her horse to join Elizabeth.

IN THE VILLAGE THOMAS POPE put out the word they were just passing through to London. He gave no names, but everyone stared at their betters as they strolled the aisles of rickety booths. Besides pyramids of apples, Elizabeth saw piles of scarves and tin trinkets that traveling hawkers had spread on ground cloths. They strolled past a fortune-teller's booth and watched a morality play with puppets. Both made Elizabeth wonder if Jenks had found Ned Topside.

Cider, apple tarts, and sausage pies were everywhere one

turned. At first, relieved the food could be not be tainted, Elizabeth ate with relish. But when she realized people were indeed gawking, she had trouble getting the next pie and cider down. Her eyes watered as she recalled her Aunt Mary's saffron cakes and mead. And all this time Meg and Kat were drifting off into the crowd to inquire if someone knew of a place called Bushey Cot.

Yet despite her unease Elizabeth felt proud to be among the realm's common folk, most of whose lives were seldom touched by shifting events on the larger stage. She wondered how she would have gotten on had she been born just plain Bess of Bushey. At least that lass would not have to fear for her very life.

"The cot—I think I found it," Meg whispered out-of-breath as they all took a brief respite before they set out for Hatfield. She showed her some dried and powdered quinces she had bought, in case someone was watching.

"Where?" Elizabeth whispered excitedly, as Meg knelt beside her on a baize cloth spread on the ground in the sun.

"In the deep woods not so far behind us. Didn't see it but heard tell. Used to be a woodsman's cottage, been deserted for a while, until last year."

"Who lives there, then?"

"An old hag, they say. She comes and goes, and they don't know if she's there or not now. No one goes there much. She keeps folks away, and some of the boys been whispering she's—a witch," she added, wide-eyed.

"The point is, it's a woman and could be our 'she,'" Elizabeth said, feeling both relief and revulsion.

"If you try to see the cot, I'm going too," Meg insisted, " 'cause they say she keeps a garden."

"All right, then," she said, frowning, "Kat must be the one who draws them off."

But, despite her excitement to be so close to what she sought, Elizabeth saw it would be foolhardy to try to find the cot now. She'd never get near it without the Popes and these guards sticking to her skirts like burrs. Sir Thomas was already ordering the party to remount and head back. She fumed inside, longing for the day she could order people about with a mere glance or snap of her fingers, let alone a warrant or decree.

As they headed home midafternoon, Elizabeth sent a long glance back toward the thick forest surrounding Bushey Cot. If a garden grew there in the dank and dark, what could be in it?

"WHAT'S THIS I HEAR?" Sir Thomas raged. They all looked up as he rushed into the solar, where Elizabeth sat before the fire at needlework with Lady Blanche Parry and his wife. "First an herbalist and now some itinerant fool added hugger-mugger to your household here, my Lady Elizabeth?"

"That is correct, Sir Thomas," she replied, dropping her work in her lap and placing both hands on the arms of her chair. She hoped she appeared at ease, but she wanted something to grip instead of this man's fat, fleshy neck.

"Ned Topside, however," she went on in measured tones,

"is a versatile player of some repute and deserves better than the sobriquet clown or fool. He'll do all sorts of parts for us, cooped up here this winter all cozy together."

"Do not try to get me off the track. Next you'll be putting on airs to appoint a privy council in exile," he raged, pacing before the rain-streaked windows.

Elizabeth had to fight a smile, for he knew not how close he came to her real plans for her newly assembled little staff. She wanted not gathered herbs but clues, not clever amusements but proofs about the poisoners.

"Her Gracious Majesty will not like this when she is informed, I tell you that plain," he expounded, striding back and forth, his Spanish leather bootheels clicking on the oaken floor.

"Surely," Elizabeth tried to soothe him, as she rose and handed Blanche her sampler stretched on its willow hoop, "my dear sister will not begrudge me a few simple and private pleasures. Indeed, I am going to inform her myself and inquire if I might not visit Kent before winter sets in—to Ightham Mote to see the Cornish family; you remember them?"

"That little place," he said and snorted. "Granted, a family the queen favors for their loyalty, but one that was distantly related to your Howard kin, I recall, so—"

"Her Majesty did tell me I might move about the kingdom if I do so circumspectly, and this would be a brief, private visit. It will give the household staff time to clean out the jakes before winter sets in to keep us here. You, I know, would like a change, too, Sir Thomas. I can imagine how this backwater place wears on a man of action like yourself." He had stopped sputtering at least. He glanced warily at his wife for support, but she offered none.

"If Her Grace gives written permission," he said, "of course I would go, for you are my charge and care." He sighed and leaned on the window ledge to stare out at the vast gray sky. She supposed he fancied he felt the weight of it upon his slumped shoulders.

"Agreed then," she said, moving quickly in for the kill before he could realize how she'd baited and hooked him. "Then I shall send my man Jenks with the request to Her Majesty at once, and we shall eagerly await her response."

She turned to take her sewing back from Blanche but glanced again at Bea's in her lap. The tight chain stitching, the twist of framing leaves—it was so like the style of the other piece. "I hope, Lady Bea," Elizabeth said, "you will be able to join our little entourage if we go to Kent, or will you be seeing your sister at Maidstone again? At least that is in the shire too."

"Her children have been ill—I'm not certain," she replied, glancing from Elizabeth to her husband and looking rather agitated. "I shall have to see."

"Then I shall go up straightaway and write my letter to my dear sister. Sir Thomas, I would count it a favor if you would send my man Jenks to me to ride to London with it."

She swept from the room with Blanche in her wake. In Kent she could search for the poisoner, Nettie's background and her ties to the master herbalist. Unfortunately, to send Jenks with that missive, she'd have to do without him when she went to Bushey Cot. At least he could also get a letter to her cousin Harry at William Cecil's house, because she had some questions for both of them too. And since Meg had not been positive about the dried tincture on the arrow point, Jenks could take it to them to have it studied.

"Oh, it looks like the storm's quite let up," Blanche observed as they made the turn on the grand staircase and looked out the window on the landing.

"I pray so," Elizabeth said only and hurried on.

BY TEN OF THE CLOCK that night, skittish moonlight had replaced the rain clouds. Holding her breath, in boy's garb that was now all too familiar to her, Elizabeth tiptoed down the narrow back servants' stairs. The house lay silent but for a few inward creaks from age and outward moans from the wind, but Meg's and Kat's protests still rang in her ears.

"But you can't go there at night unchaperoned—with just that player," Kat had insisted. "You hardly know the man. Can he ride or handle a sword like Jenks?"

"And why," Meg had chimed in, "must I stay here in your bed? I'm not a player. They'd know it wasn't you if they looked close."

"Hush your caterwauling," Elizabeth commanded, "or I won't have either of you privy to my needs. This is something I must do, for my family—for my own sake. If I cannot trust you and depend on you to help me, I will send you both away." She had even quoted the Holy Word to muzzle them: *"He who is not with me is against me."*

"Or *she,*" Meg had muttered with a scowl. "You just beware of that one we call 'she.' "

THEY TOOK TWO LANTERNS yet unlit. Elizabeth blessed the moonlight, but she had to lead the way because she had just been this route and it was new to Ned. She could tell he was eager to please her, yet this night ride to a place where Meg had prattled a witch might live did not sit well with him.

"A witch? Stuff and nonsense. Village superstitions," she assured the dark-cloaked man as they crested the hill above the village. "Of course I believe in demon possession, but untutored rustics go overboard dubbing any old hag a witch."

"This woman is old, then?" he asked. He'd annoyed her at first with his spate of questions, but he had a sharp mind and it had helped her hone her own thinking. They must search and perhaps seize things from Bushey Cot—the woman herself if they could.

"I do not know if she is old," Elizabeth admitted as they turned their horses to skirt the village itself. "That is hearsay and what we must learn. I can only pray she does not expect a visit—that there is no one in my household who could warn her. That is partly why I wanted us to come tonight, so the woman could not be warned in time even if someone overheard me speak to Kat or Meg."

"Meg," he said, almost to himself as they turned off the road into the fringe of forest. "She seems to live in fortune's star, stumbling on that news about the girl Nettie and that sampler that sends us here."

"It's all logical. I think she's proved herself true. And you, too, have stumbled into this," she reminded him, "by being there to save my cousin and then perform at Wivenhoe. Life is like that, Ned, happenstance."

"And that is why you stand next in line to the throne?" he dared.

"Little things are happenstance," she corrected herself. "The vast, life-changing ones are God-ordained and -guided."

"Aye, Your Grace, as you say."

He had annoyed her now, but this was no time to quibble, as they had to concentrate on keeping low branches out of their eyes. "Can you use that sword of yours if need be?" she whispered as they searched the moon-washed woods for the cot.

"I warrant so," he answered. His deep, commanding voice almost convinced her until he said grandiosely, "But if some old hag tries to get the best of me—witchcraft or not—I will make such a fine sword-fight scene, I'd convince her I was Alexander the Great come back from the dead."

"Very comforting," she muttered. "Pray keep your voice down, Alexander." She had decided years ago, after her adored father had betrayed her by killing her mother and naming her bastard, that she would never trust another man. And yet in these hard times she had found a few with whom she must cast her precarious lot: Cecil, Jenks, and this man. Perhaps.

DESPERATION BEGAN TO DEVOUR HER. In an hour silently traversing the windy forest, they had found no hut or cottage. She would skin Meg if she had believed a folktale or some rural rumor. Time was fleeting before they must return to Hatfield ere the dawn.

Then it emerged before their eyes, as if of its own accord. They could glimpse the shake roof of a cottage with rough, light-hued stone walls. The whole edifice seemed etched with a shaft of moonlight by the darting, skeletal fingers of the trees.

She heard Ned's swift intake of breath. "I thought we were just through here, and I didn't see that," he whispered.

"It sits in a clearing. No wonder it can have a garden, though plants would be shaded but for high noon."

As they walked their horses closer, her heart began to thud beneath her boy's shirt and leather jerkin. For again as if from nothingness, an opening in the wall appeared to show them faint lantern light emanating from a window—surely that was not merely reflected moon.

"Dismount," she whispered, gesturing and pointing in case he could not hear her in the sigh of wind and rustle of dry leaves. "We'll tie up over there."

They double-knotted the reins and took the two unlit lanterns from the saddle packs. Ned had the flint box. Each holding a lantern, they shuffled closer through knee-deep drifts of leaves. As her eyes became more accustomed to the wan window light, Elizabeth could see the silhouette of something draped or perched on the tops of the stone walls, which stood high as a man. She thought at first it might be heaps of cloth, but it was thick, drooping vines. And some strange and fetid smell reached out to suffocate her. . . .

The high-pitched screech stabbed deep into her. She screamed, her voice drowned by the second screech. "Eee-raugh! Eee-raugh!"

Ned scraped his sword out of its scabbard and dropped his unlit lantern. He tried to place himself between her and the wall, but she darted for the protection of it, pressing her backbone hard against its rugged surface. The screech sounded a third time, searing her soul with its hellish pitch.

Elizabeth drew the dagger from her belt. She shook so hard it bounced before her face. Though Ned froze at first, sword raised, he threw himself against the wall just across the opening to the yard from her.

They stayed that way, breathing hard. When nothing else happened and all seemed still, Elizabeth ignored Ned's shaking his head and holding up one hand to warn her to stay where she stood. She stooped to put her unlit lantern down and stayed crouched low. With her dagger held tightly in both hands, she stepped toward and darted through the gaping gate.

Chapter The Eighth

NED SLID AROUND THE CORNER, CLOSE BEHIND her, his sword a dull glint against the inside of the wall across the gate from her. The next thing Elizabeth saw was—she thought—a ghost, rising from the ground with a huge blooming, monstrous head . . .

" 'S blood," she whispered, "a white peacock. They are as good as watchdogs at some great houses."

She heard only his low curse and then a sigh of relief.

They both stayed still as statues, waiting for it to screech again. It only fanned its bounty of iridescent tail and strutted out the gate between them.

"If anyone's inside," Ned hissed, "they're up or fled now."

"Unless there's only one way out of here."

He joined her on her side of the gate, but they still did not step farther into the enclosed yard. They even stopped talking, instead miming their meaning by holding their noses and shrugging at what the mysterious odor could be.

Sickeningly sweet, rank, cloying, it made Elizabeth's stomach clench. When they spoke next, their voices sounded stuffed and nasal.

"We must look inside the cottage. There's no light in the window now—it must have been the moonlight—a mirage."

They nodded agreement and set off with a shuffling slow step. Moonlight flitted in and out to guide them closer to the cot. Irregular flower beds with the frost-struck corpses of plants impaled on wooden stakes impeded their way almost as if they entered through a maze. The door to the cot was not visible from this side with the gate in the wall.

She gestured they should separate: she around one way, he the other way. He shook his head, then—perhaps when the moon caught her expression—obeyed.

She found it even darker around this side of the cottage. The walls were rough and crude; the wind wheezed through some cracks. She tried to peek through a chink, but something covered it inside, just as the single window had a curtain. She wished she'd brought her lantern, but it would make her too clear a target. She edged around a rain barrel that must collect water off the roof and tiptoed on. A moment ago the stench had seemed stronger here, but now it didn't, or else she was becoming accustomed to it. She unpinched her nose so she could breathe better; she clenched her dagger only in her right hand.

The wooden door was just around the next corner and stood ajar inward, so she could see in. She meant to wait for Ned, but she peeked in and gasped.

Someone had just been here. A glass container in a metal rack barely bubbled above garnet embers on a clay hearth. Only that glow lit the small, single room, but it was enough to see sumptuous fabrics on the walls, a deep bed with a satin coverlet, and one fine, carved, high-backed chair and table. Some sort of food and drink was laid out there—no, it was a wooden rack of glass vials, much like the one Nettie had carried with her.

Elizabeth carefully shoved the door the rest of the way open to assure herself no one hid behind it. It creaked, then bumped back into the wall. Mesmerized by the scene, she took a single step in.

Then she remembered Ned.

She edged back out and started around the way he should have come. And stumbled right over his dark, unmoving form huddled against the cottage wall.

"I THOUGHT AT FIRST you were dead," she told him when he came to his senses, propped up against the wall of the house. She had used rainwater from the barrel to wash his face. Already a huge bump rose on his skull above the nape of his neck.

"This your . . . idea of a clown's . . . role?" he muttered.

"Stash the jests for now. Did you see anything?"

"Naught but stars."

"That peacock tipped someone off. I have to go out and

check on the horses to be sure they didn't bolt. Or get stolen."

"Not on your own. Here, I can walk."

She helped him to his feet and steadied him. They retrieved their lanterns and mounts and led them back toward the small yard of the cot. Both horses balked and whinnied at being brought in, and they had to drag them inside by their reins.

"Smarter than us," Ned muttered. "Hellfire, something stinks to high heaven here, in more ways than one."

Ordinarily she would have appreciated his spirit and wit, but she could only nod. "Are you sure you are all right? Just stand guard here and cut a few samples from these plants. I'll get some from inside. We can't stay long."

"That's the best news I've had all day."

She didn't need his chatter now, but then, what did she expect? Her father's jester, Will Sommers, had been the only one who had ever dared impudence with him, but he gave good counsel on the sly too.

They lit one lantern, and she went back inside with it while Ned gathered samples by moonlight. The interior of the crude hut looked like an opulent, draped campaign tent arrayed for a joust, she thought—or a scarlet funeral shroud. It lay flat against the four walls and close in the corners, at least, so no one could be secreted between it and the wall.

Elizabeth boldly shone her lantern under the narrow bed, then went through the small coffer she found there. The

few but fine-made garments indicated a woman shorter
than she, but heavier with larger breasts—but then, few
were so slender, especially there. The single pair of slippers
looked terribly worn and might not even belong to the
"she," as Meg always called her. Her foot seemed long and
narrow. But what disturbed Elizabeth was that this was the
place and inner trappings of someone of means or rank, not
some poor wretch like Nettie. Despite the pigsty exterior,
the inside befitted a queen herself.

She sucked in a breath at that last thought and at what
lined the bottom of the coffer. She could not believe her
good fortune—or had she been led to the next knot in the
noose by someone setting snares? She lifted it gingerly and
stared at a piece of partially embroidered handwork: en-
twined, twisting leaves of some sort and the beginning of
the now familiar curse, *For I see that you are poysoned* . . .

Again the verse haunted her, whispered from her past.
Then she remembered. It was what her sister had screamed
at her that day she had sent her from court. Oh, dear Lord
in heaven, she wanted no links to her sister in all this. She
must not think it.

Rather, this must merely mean that the Wivenhoe mastermind must be the old hag who was here. It had to be
pure chance that the queen had quoted that to her. Quickly,
as she stood, she snatched one of the empty vials—fine,
blown venetian glass—and dropped it in her sack along
with this piece.

Now the array of drying herbs hanging in the recesses of

the room drew Elizabeth's attention. Pulling her gloves even tighter, she plucked down random samples of plants as if taking laundry from a bush. Some of the leaves smelled smoky. Had the hag been preserving them that way, or had the hearth just smoked? She could not stop to be sure, but the hand that had tied the bunches could have been the same that sent that poison nosegay of meadow saffron to kill her aunt.

She stopped gathering herbs at the sight of a long, cluttered bench against the far wall. Slowly, she walked to it, squinting to make out what instruments lay there. But it was weapons: several daggers, their steel blades blackened by some sticky substance. Two iron carding combs with their sharp tines smeared with the same pitchlike mixture. And six arrowheads coated in the same hellish stuff that had no doubt killed Harry's Will Benton.

"It's her!" she whispered. "The hag is the poisoner."

Shuddering as she touched it, even gloved, she took one arrowhead and dropped it in her sack, then, from this vantage point, noted another coffer behind the first one under the table. She knelt to open it. Perhaps this contained the hag's letters, poison recipes, victims, the names of others in this conspiracy . . .

"Ugh!" she cried as the stench stuffed her nostrils. She lifted her lantern to stare down at a jumbled mass of grotesque-shaped roots, mushrooms, toadstools, and fungus in all stages and sticky hues of decay.

Shuddering, she put some in her bag. If Meg could not

identify them, Cecil must have contacts who could. It was then, as the embers shifted lower, she heard muted humming in the corner farthest from the hearth. Slow, drowsy, not a human sound.

She shuffled closer and tilted her head to listen. A buzzing. Dear Lord, not bees? She hated bees.

She recalled the man who had been her royal father's beekeeper for years—a kindly old man who had worked with honeycombs all his life—had been stung to death by them, though their venom had never affected him before that day. It was just after Mary became queen, when Elizabeth was walking in the gardens at Whitehall, that he fell and died in agony. Someone had said it was only because one sting was so close behind his ear that the poison leapt right to his brain. Elizabeth had knelt to hold his hand, until she realized other bees still buzzed about and someone had pulled her away. Mary had said she'd find a new beekeeper; and then there was something else about bees, but Elizabeth could not bear to think of that. . . .

She shook her head to clear it and stepped slowly away from the muted murmuring. Surely bees were not stored in here and kept deliberately dazed by the smoke. They must be on the other side of the wall. All that sat in this corner was a slumped bag with grain in it. The old woman must mill her own for bread.

She began to breathe again. With a swift look back at the room, Elizabeth snuffed out the wick in her lantern, hefted her heavy sack, and hurried out the door.

"Let's ride," Ned called to her the moment she appeared.

"This place makes my knees knock as loud as the pounding in my head."

She nodded, hardly heeding what he'd said. "She's been here," she intoned, "but she hit you and slipped out. She's here, close by, hidden in the dark of the woods, watching and waiting. I—I can feel her."

"But who is she?"

"I still don't know. But I will."

"Could she be armed?"

She heaved her sack up to fasten it on her pommel. "Probably not with more than what she struck you with. We'll make a dash for it. But there's just one more thing. Do you know aught of bees?"

"Only that there's a thatched hive of them set in the nook of the chimney," he said with a nod in that direction, before he put both hands to his head again, evidently pained by the slightest movement.

"Then," she whispered, almost to herself, "they gather their sweet from all this sour. So their stings could be more deadly than most."

"I only know I never heard a hive make such a buzz at night, like we've disturbed them. We'd best fly, Your Grace."

"Yes," she said and mounted before he could help her up. She glanced around the walled yard, studded with plants she knew must be poison. "I know what she's been doing but not why," she whispered, more to herself than him. "And I will have her head, before she can get mine."

"I CALL TO ORDER this meeting," Elizabeth declared as she took her place at the head of the small table in her withdrawing room at Hatfield. "And I dub you my privy and covert council."

Shoulder to shoulder sat Ned on her left, Kat on her right, then Meg and Jenks. It was dark outside, and all but Kat had singly sneaked up the servants' stairs.

"We are not," she went on, keeping her voice low in case someone hovered at the keyhole, "to solve problems of government but of this poison plot I have explained to you. We shall be like those who sat at King Arthur's old round table in the days of yore, where all may speak out equally when we have such meetings. If there ever needs be privy communication among us, I shall be known as just plain Bess."

Kat's eyes widened in obvious surprise, then narrowed to disbelief. She shook her head slightly. Jenks frowned and shifted in his chair. Meg nodded, but Ned crossed his arms over his chest to look watchful and doubtful. It was not, Elizabeth thought, an auspicious beginning.

"Of course, I shall have the final say if there is disagreement," she added hastily. "Secrecy must be our byword in all we do. But in the trust we share, I must tell you I have an aide who has confederates in London, a man privy to my problems, whom I shall not name at this time. And that man is housing my cousin Henry Carey, so he shall be a support to us also, especially since he is of Boleyn blood and was intended as a victim."

"What good, Your Grace," Ned put in, "will it do for us

to have an unnamed aide to rely on if some of us know not his name? Besides, I warrant Kat Ashley knows, and that puts some of us at a disadvantage."

"Whatever Her Grace says," Jenks put in with a fist thumped on the table, "that's the way it shall be."

"Thank you, Jenks. And you are right, Ned," Elizabeth admitted, "that no one must have a disadvantage and we must always trust each other. But until I have this aide's specific permission, I cannot divulge his identity. Now for a report of current discoveries. Meg, tell us what you know about the dreadful hodgepodge of goods we brought back from Bushey Cot."

"Don't know a thing about the mushrooms and fungus, 'cept they stink so they could nearly kill a body that way. Some of the poison plants I did know were the roots of black hellebore with its white flowers. It's got to be dried out of the sun, so maybe that's why 'she' had them strung up inside the cot."

"Are we going to just call her that?" Kat asked. "She? And can't we get a reckoning of women who might hold a deadly grudge against the Boleyns and search them out, Your Grace?"

"Yes, Kat, on both questions," Elizabeth said. "I am working on attaining such a list, and when we find someone suspect we shall, as you say, search them out. And as for She—that will do for a title of that hellish murderess for now."

" 'Course, mayhap," Jenks put in, "She is working for someone else. It's usually men behind plots, isn't it?"

"Not necessarily," Elizabeth said. "We don't know yet who is behind Nettie's work or those who attacked my cousin, Lord Carey, or even if someone is behind this She. Meg, tell us more about the Bushey Cot herbs."

"Wouldn't know a thing about them 'cept a few like hellebore—same thing I'm thinking might have been on that arrow—but the gardener at Wivenhoe used to poison foxes what kept getting in the henhouse with that. After it was dried and pounded up, he used to add honey." Her gaze met Elizabeth's, and Ned cleared his throat before the girl went on. "And add some fat in equal parts to make a paste. He rolled balls of it and hid them in food you leave out to kill the fox—or whatever."

"Say on," Elizabeth said when Meg hesitated. She saw that Ned kept glaring at the girl as if she'd done something wrong. "Go ahead, Meg," she prompted again.

"Other herbs from the cot I knew was nightshade, with its black and purple berries, and hemlock, what's called poison parsley. 'Course, Your Grace, yourself recognized the English yew and meadow saffron—the rest, don't know, 'cause I only work with garden plants and simples."

"Sounds like you know more than you think, Meg," Jenks put in, while Ned nodded as if he'd put him up to that.

"So," Elizabeth said, "I will have you, Jenks, carry samples of the rest of these poison plants to my aide—"

"Jenks knows of this aide too?" Ned asked, swinging back toward Elizabeth. "Only Meg and I don't?"

"But will soon," she said, pointing at him to make him sit

back. "Now, everyone, it is my belief that our enemy—our prey—is a master poisoner, whether or not She has a superior pulling her strings," she explained, looking from one to the other. "At Bushey Cot—and God knows where else— She keeps her poison garden. Ned, I have a task for you, if you will accept."

"Of course and gladly."

"I would have you assume some hail-fellow-well-met identity, just in case the She of Bushey Cot is still in the area and would recognize you from our nocturnal visit there. You must ask about and endeavor to find some further description or information about her. And we must have this before we set out for Ightham Mote in a few days."

"And what shall we do, Your Grace," Meg asked, "Kat and me?"

"Without tipping your hand you must keep a close eye on Lady Beatrice Pope—because of this." She reached behind her on the bench to retrieve the first two pieces of poison embroidery. Placing them on the table, she added between them a linen towel Bea had done for her this year for May Day—a circlet of mixed flowers with the words, *Consider the lilies of the field, how they grow.*

"I'm certainly not saying Bea is our She," Elizabeth admitted, "for I have proof she has defended me to her husband. But she could be an informant here in the house, and for whom, I'm not sure."

"In other words, anyone up to the queen herself," Ned said.

Elizabeth nodded jerkily. She could not bear to think

that, face that. Surely her own sister would not be behind this attack on the Boleyns—and herself. Though Mary hated her, she must surely draw the line at poisoning her heir, however reluctant she had been to name her so.

"And wouldn't," Ned interrupted her agonized thought, "the poisoner She have had such an informant in the manor at Wivenhoe, and Lady Beatrice Pope was hardly there." The question was directed at Elizabeth, but he dared to dart a glance at Meg, who kept staring down at the samplers.

Elizabeth glared at him and deliberately stepped on his foot under the table. He started and drew back. "All things are possible," she said, "and we shall consider them. And we shall meet again soon to lay our plans for tracing Nettie and her employer in Kent. There we must search two places that have ties to my past—to the Boleyns—where someone might have held some kind of long-tended grudge. But till that time I insist we act as a team, pulling toward the same goal. We must learn to trust each other and rely upon each other," she said, staring again at Ned, who finally looked guiltily away. "May I have your word, your hands, on that?"

She grasped Kat's proffered one on one side and Ned's on her other and pressed them together. Jenks and Meg leaned in to put theirs atop.

"And," Elizabeth added, "there is work to be done here that bears on this investigation in a more indirect way. Ned is to teach Meg to mime my carriage and voice—at least my enunciation—lest I need her to stand in for me. And he is to teach Jenks and Meg to read on the sly. Jenks must teach Meg to ride a proper sidesaddle, as well as being my messenger and guard. Kat will stick close to me but also serve as go-between for us all. Are we agreed?"

Each nodded in turn.

"We'll help you find her 'fore She kills someone else, don't you fret, Your Grace," Meg whispered.

" 'Tis damned dangerous business," Kat murmured, frowning.

"But from this moment," Elizabeth vowed, "the hunt is on."

Chapter The Ninth

ARBED IN A COWHERD'S LOOSE CLOTHES, WITH a floppy hat pulled down and the ragged collar turned up, she stood behind a thick tree trunk. She glared at the red-bricked house beyond the broad meadow of brown grass, dying wildflowers, headless clover, and too many rabbits. She watched her informant, cloak rippling in the chill wind, walk toward the manor house, keeping close to the meadow's fringe in the thin shadow of skeletal trees.

When she clasped her hands to warm them, she noticed her fingers were still sticky with honey and hellebore paste. She bent to wipe its remnants on the grass and clover leaves so she would not get it on her horse's reins. She'd wash thoroughly in the first stream she saw along the road to Kent.

As she smeared the tacky stuff over more of the thick clover, she laughed deep in her throat. She plucked a piece of it, a shamrock sure enough, then stood staring at the second-story windows she had just been told were Elizabeth's. She crushed the clover in her raised fist.

"Here I'm standing on your land, and you'll not be the only lass going about as a lad. I was even closer that night in the Wivenhoe graveyard but did not fathom you'd be digging up a corpse. And then you nearly snared me in the cot. But I'll be standing closer yet on your own grave soon enough to pour poisons on the sod so naught grows there, that I will for sure."

The wind ripped her words away and whined through the tree limbs. As she strode toward where she'd tied her mount in the hawthorne thicket, the memory of Queen Mary's bitter voice came back to her from last year when she saw her privily at court: *I was tempted to have her beheaded in the Tower, but my beloved husband would not hear of it. Yet I swear on my mother's soul she is not of royal blood. However red her hair, that one was not sired by my royal father, as my half brother Edward and I were. Her whore of a mother could have caught her from tupping her russet-haired lutenist, Mark Smeaton.*

Ailing though she was, the queen's voice had gotten louder, sharper. *Her pretty Smeaton used to lie about her chamber at all hours.* Dios sabe, *that woman bedded him and others in her lust. It all came out at the adultery and treason trial of that witch woman. . . .*

"Witch woman," the cowherd echoed Mary Tudor's words as she untied her mare's reins and pulled her to a stump so she could mount astride more easily. "Witch woman," she repeated. "Bewitching, more like."

But "hag, witch" was what those rustic fools of Bushey had called her. She wished she had the time to put a poison curse on them. She'd wipe them off the face of the earth just as she would Kentish folk, every man jack of them who ever served or swore loyalty to a Boleyn.

She yanked the reins to halt her horse and swing it back to face Hatfield, though she could barely see the red brick through this more distant scrim of trees.

"I left my curse writ clear in your meadow!" she screamed like a banshee. "Come looking in Kent for me, Boleyn bitch!"

"NOT THAT WAY, GIRL. How oft must I tell you?"

Ned Topside bounced back off the bench under the window in the princess's old schoolroom and rounded on Meg again. Hellfire and brimstone, but this girl was a slow study—or tongue-tied around him. At least this time *he* was the one giving directions instead of being chided and chastised by Uncle Wat and that damned Grand Rand. Ned knew he was about to throw a fit of choler, but, hating that in others, he reined in his voice.

"Now, heed my words, Meg. Her Grace takes more measured strides, with her head up and shoulders back, in this fashion."

He imitated Elizabeth's walk again along the sun-struck oaken floor, past the large window where he pivoted and strode back toward the flustered, frowning girl. He hadn't, he thought, played female parts in the beginning for nothing.

"And her elegant hands," he added, "are either clasped

or carried gracefully—like this. You can tell she's proud of them. If our motley band ever goes to court hanging on her royal petticoats, you'll have to wear gloves when you're digging about in the soil with those hands. Just look at them now."

He seized her wrists and turned her palms up, running the pads of his thumbs over her skin. She gasped throatily as if he'd done something entirely more intimate.

"Calluses no lady would ever have," he plunged on, ignoring her reaction, "and broken nails moated by dirt, though at least your fingers are almost as long as Her Grace's."

Blushing, she snatched her hands back, thrusting them behind her. She backed away several steps, almost coyly. "Can't you find a thing to say I done right this past hour?" she asked, in a voice hurt, not harsh as he'd expected. "Did no one ever tell you honey catches more than vinegar? You think I fancy your making me mimic a fine woman like her, the finest in the land, when I—I—"

He watched her hug herself and spin away so hard her meager skirts belled out. "I meant to say," she went on, lifting her head and straightening her back, "when I know where I come from—"

"Came from," he corrected.

"Came from. Only I don't really have a notion about that. 'Cept—*ex*cept at Wivenhoe, how kindly the princess's aunt dealt with me, and her once a great lady." Slowly, as she spoke, she turned toward him. "All I know is, I'm not made to put on airs, but I'm not made to be browbeat neither." Her voice clipped along faster and she became more animated. "I'd rather be back out in the rabbit meadow gathering dried flowers for winter wreaths and strewing herbs. I found a whole spot of lady's-mantle already dried right where they grew, just waiting for me this morning."

"Another sign of fair fortune's star, under which you must have been born, Meg Milligrew," he said with a sweeping mock bow. He almost regretted his subtly sarcastic tone, but she usually didn't catch on to it.

"Meaning what?" she asked warily, drawing herself up even taller. He certainly didn't say so, but looking at her recovery from the verbal drubbing he'd just given her, he almost dared to hope this girl might find the backbone and pride to carry off looking like Elizabeth of England—if the room were dim or from a distance, of course.

"I mean," he said, one hand on his hip, one gesturing as if he were center stage, "how you so auspiciously stumbled into Lady Mary Boleyn's house and reminded her of her own daughter living in exile or of the princess, so much that she readily favored you. And after someone poisoned her 'twas just happenstance you found all about the poisoner Nettie, which led us to that poison pit of Bushey Cot— which you, Kat says, were the one to locate during the fair in Bushey."

"I heard some folks speaking of her—the old hag witch who lived at Bushey Cot," she protested, her voice rising.

"As the princess keeps her tones well-modulated, why don't you practice the same?" he interjected, narrowing his eyes at her. "After all, Her Grace was born under fortune's star too, so *there* is something else you hold in common besides the face and form the world sees.

"Now, Mistress Meg," he went on, "as I was telling you afore we began, to imitate someone truly you must study them privily, listening to every word that falls from their lips. You do that with the princess, don't you?" he added, trying not to sound as suspicious as he felt about the girl.

"She's good to me, and her lady aunt told me to come to her—a-course I do."

"*Of* course," he corrected.

"*Of* course," she mimicked perfectly.

He nodded again, glad she had gone wide of the mark of what he'd implied but dared not accuse her of—yet. As he had told the princess yesterday, his inquiries at Bushey had revealed that the old hag of Bushey Cot was not necessarily old at all but walked upright and quickly. And she was not of a certain ugly, despite her loose-draped garments and some sort of lawn veil draped from her hat over her face. No one had so much as seen her countenance, so she could have *features fine and fair to launch a vast array of ships*—a line from one of his favorite roles in *The Tragedy of Queen Helen,* in which he'd taken to inserting comments subtly critical of Queen Mary these last years.

And, playing the part in Bushey of a London-born merchant looking for his lost herbalist aunt, he'd discovered that the lady of the white peacock, as he'd dubbed her, had been visited by two rural maids a hunter had spotted more than once. One of the wenches sounded as if she could have been the poisoner Nettie, as Elizabeth and Jenks had described her. The other was taller and paler, but walked with a bit of a shuffling slump.

"Now," Ned said, clapping his hands so sharply that Meg jumped, "let's walk together again, just as Her Grace would if she were here. So this time do not shuffle or slump."

HARRY CAREY WATCHED WILLIAM CECIL cast his favorite gyrfalcon, Nonesuch, to the winds from the leather gauntlet. The brown-and-white bird flapped aloft into the scudding winds, soared, then swooped, the tiny foot bells on its jesses jingling. They heard it hit the slower game bird with a thud and a scream as it bore it to earth. One of Cecil's falconers ran to recover the prey before the hawk could rip it to pieces.

"Raw weather for October," Harry said, hunching his shoulders into his fur-lined cloak and stamping his booted feet.

"A wretched year—ungodly weather on top of this royal mess," Cecil muttered, scanning the sky.

In nearly a fortnight as a guest at Burghley House in Stamford on the edge of the wool-rich midlands, Harry had learned his host was a man of few but well-considered words. The thirty-eight-year-old Cecil had not been high born, but his fine schooling at St. John's Cambridge and his study of law at Gray's Inn in London had prepared him well. He had served the late Lord Protector Edward Seymour and as a secretary in young King Edward's government, until Mary Tudor came to the throne and dismissed Cecil for his Protestant, humanist leanings. Cecil had been wily enough to take the Catholic oath and keep his conscience to himself, waiting for the wind to shift. Now, as a family man—which made Harry miss his own wife and children even more—and as a sheep farmer in the countryside, Cecil bided his time awaiting Elizabeth's ascendancy.

But the wily lawyer had already made himself of great service to Her Grace, not only publicly as the surveyor of the meager lands her father had left her, but privily as her adviser. Just last night Cecil and Harry had discussed a missive Cecil would send her with information she had requested—and with additional advice she had not.

Now, with a sideways glance, Harry saw that Cecil was not watching for the return flight of his hawk but more likely for him to say something more. Cecil's long face looked solemn, older than his years, even more so with his shovel-shape beard. Harry had noted that his mouth barely moved, hardly bounced his beard when he talked. His eyes were a piercing brown, quick as a falcon's swoop of wing.

"I know the times here have been terrible," Harry said, propping one boot on a rock fallen from a stone fence. "I hope you do not think I acted in a cowardly fashion to flee while others stayed. I try to keep up with events here while we all wait for the tide to turn in the princess's favor."

"About the weather you mentioned," Cecil countered, as if a host of royal spies hovered nearby. "In July a windstorm in Nottingham knocked down houses, and the River Trent flooded to wipe out two small towns. Quartan fever raged like the very plague during the dog days, hailstones fell, and the wind—marry, it stunk from London to the shires with the charred flesh of the queen burning men and women she insists are heretics."

"But in God's truth are really martyrs," Harry added grimly, shaking his head. "The poor people. I heard inflation is the highest ever recorded in the kingdom," he added, hoping to show Cecil he'd tried to keep abreast of English affairs. "And that some unemployed laborers are grinding acorns to make their bread."

"Aye, that too," Cecil said with a sniff.

Suddenly, he lifted his arm and Nonesuch came swooping back, fanning his great wings for balance before folding them tightly to his sleek body. His talons gripped the leather glove, and Cecil skillfully turned to keep the bird's beak pointed into the stiff wind. If it got its feathers ruffled, its powerful wings could beat Cecil black and blue. The falcon's eyes looked keen but expressionless, rather like its master's.

When Cecil had its leather hood back on, Harry said, "I've been on edge in Europe too. Mayhap distance makes waiting even worse." Cecil nodded, and Harry followed his lead back toward the copse where they'd tied their horses.

"You know," Harry added, his voice rising on the breeze, "I've been wishing like hell I had some great gauntlet to throw down in their smug Catholic faces to champion the princess at all costs."

"We all have hoods over us, just waiting to fly—to attack if need be, eh, my lord?"

"Exactly."

"But, marry, even this bird knows to sit patiently till he is cast, till the prey is ripe, and the time has come."

"Aye, but I keep hearing that cry of those assassins who would have killed me in the woods." He glanced about nervously, though only two of Cecil's men waited at a distance. "I heard them talking while they stalked me, but I was so shocked by being attacked and thrown that their words did not stick. But that curse on the Boleyns one man cried—I have been trying to place the regional origin of the assassin. If the princess is so sure that girl Nettie, my mother's poisoner, had ties to Kent, I ask myself, could it have been a Kentish brogue? But the wretch's voice was rather lilting, singsong in a way I cannot place."

"You've heard King Philip's people at court, have you not?" Cecil asked. "You know," he prompted, "the way their Spanish tongues dance and lisp over their words?"

Harry halted dead in his tracks, so Cecil stopped too. "Heard it but only briefly before I left the court. It could be—not just some rural English speech, but foreign. And who hates our Elizabeth and ever the Boleyns more than the Spanish?"

"You may write an addendum to my letter in your own hand when we send her man back to Hatfield on the morrow," Cecil said. "Who more than the Spanish indeed, though that can hardly be news to Her Grace. But that is much of what I mean to write to her—and to remind her that the two places she intends to seek this master poisoner

KAREN HARPER

in Kent have ties not only to the Boleyns but to dangerous and hostile foreign elements."

As he mounted, despite hearing of new dangers to his royal cousin, Harry felt better than he had in days. They would send a key clue and warnings to Her Grace. And, finally, clever Cecil had trusted him enough to speak of something else besides the weather and sheep, farming and falcons, though every time he did there lurked second meanings there. He spurred his horse harder to keep up with the older man.

"NO, I CANNOT TAKE YOU TO KENT with me tomorrow," Elizabeth told plump, flat-faced Cora Crenshaw, one of the Hatfield cooks, in the corridor outside her chamber door. Kat and Blanche had gone down to air sheets and bolsters on the bushes.

"I tell you, cook," Elizabeth went on, "I shall regret it, too, for I shall miss your fine pigeon pies and that carp in orange sauce. But I cannot offend Lady Cornish by bringing my own kitchen staff to that small country house."

The woman bowed her covered head, and Elizabeth thought that would be the end of it, but she had not spoken to her recently and had forgotten her stiff backbone. Clasping her flour-dusted hands, Cora spoke the next words to their feet, but her voice was still strong.

"But e'er sin' I come to you, my Lady Elizabeth, you had nary a stomach complaint nor fear of tainted food, not from my hand. And in these times—"

132

"In these times, aye, but my answer is no. You must not gainsay me more. But should I ever be called back to court—my sister's court, I mean," she amended hastily, "you have my word I shall take you with me there so that—"

A woman's shriek shredded the air. Elizabeth pressed her back against the wall and glanced both ways in the corridor. Had that been Bea? Blanche, Kat, or even Meg? From the courtyard or outside?

When no one came running for her, she gestured for Cora to follow and ventured down the hall toward the grand staircase, glancing into every room that had an open door. Strange, but the memory that bombarded her was that one time she had heard the midnight scream of her cousin Catherine Howard's ghost at Hampton Court years after her beheading. She was begging for her husband king to listen to her pleas, not send her to the Tower, though she had been unfaithful. She was shrieking for the Great Henry to show her one shred of mercy. . . .

Goosebumps shivered Elizabeth's flesh. She hurried down the stairs to find the front door wide open but empty.

Cora close behind her, she stepped to the side and peered out. Bea was dragging Sir Thomas by his wrist across the drive toward the meadow, pointing, shouting, as demented as a bedlamite. Several grooms and stableboys came running, their feet spitting gravel. She wished Jenks were back from taking her letter to court and a quick dart up to Stamford to Cecil and her cousin Harry, but she'd have to face this without her favorite man. At least, ever curious,

Ned appeared with Meg from another secret schoolroom lesson, even as Kat and Blanche dashed out from the side of the house.

Elizabeth strode out. Long tendrils of red hair sprung loose to whip her face in the wind. She blinked in the bright sun. Whatever were they looking at? Pray God, not a body they had found in the tall, dry meadow grass, which they didn't let the stupid sheep crop lately since it was a rabbit warren of holes to break legs.

Her stomach clenched. Bea had covered her eyes and Pope was pinching his nose as they peered down at something in the blowing grass.

"What's amiss?" Elizabeth's bell-clear voice called out.

At first no one looked at her. The wind shifted, and she caught the stench. She shook off Kat when she tried to pull her back. Elizabeth stepped closer. She had to see what it was—who lay here. . . .

She went past the Popes and gasped. Scores of rabbits lay dead or twitching at their feet. And one moaning, bleating sheep on its knees that must have got through the hedgerows somehow. At first her mind could not encompass what she saw. Then Meg spoke close behind her.

"Poisoned—I seen foxes go down like this with hellebore."

"Have you now?" Ned said much too quickly, before Elizabeth lifted her hand to halt more he might say.

"Poisoned?" Sir Thomas bellowed, swinging about to glare at Elizabeth and her little band of people. "What evil intent is this?"

"Look," Meg added, pointing, "pasty balls here and there in the grass they may been licking or eating. Pasty balls someone's been rolling in her—or his—hands."

"And some shiny vile stuff smeared on the low clover leaves the frost hasn't got yet," Kat added and stooped to point at a clump of grass that ants had covered in a writhing, black mass. It reminded Elizabeth of poor Will Benton's wounds. She almost dry-heaved but put her hand over her mouth and quelled the impulse.

When Kat looked as if she meant to examine the stuff closer, Elizabeth shrieked, "Don't touch it!" and yanked her back. "Any of you, don't touch it. Sir Thomas, get someone to dose that sheep with purgative, but bury the dead rabbits."

"I'll give the orders here to keep you safe and sound," Thomas insisted, his voice booming. "Now, you just go on, my lady, get back in the house. I'll order some men to take care of things, ride circuit to question folks. It's a blessing in disguise we'll hie ourselves to Kent tomorrow. But for now, none of you ladies are to leave the house till we are ready to ride. My lady"—he addressed his wife now—"see to it that no one goes out. No one!"

Elizabeth glared daggers at him. He shouted as if they did not stand close enough to see the veins pop out like ropes on his florid neck. Despite his tirade, she dragged her gaze away from the pitiable carnage to scan the meadow and the rim of trees beyond to look for—for whoever had committed this cruel outrage, as if she did not know.

Her pulse pounded in her head. She clenched her fists so

hard at her sides her fingernails bit into her palms. She fought to control herself. At this moment she could have thrown things, shoved people—kicked down the bricks of this house. In moments like this she knew she was her father's heir indeed, no matter what some traitors had dared to accuse at her mother's treason trial.

As she turned her back on the Popes, her dark, narrowed eyes in her white face met Ned's, then Kat's, and finally Meg's. They fell in behind her, striding pell-mell to keep up.

"I'll see her soul in hell," Elizabeth hissed, "if She fathoms I'm the next dumb beast she'll torment and kill."

Chapter The Tenth

HER RETINUE'S JOGGING, JOLTING, THREE-DAY progress toward Kent was an ordeal she and Jenks, hard riding, could have covered in but one, Elizabeth groused silently. Her flesh crawled as they entered the thick woods of the Weald, for she could not shake the feeling that poison arrows could fly from the trees. Frustration, fear, and fury obsessed her. And a wretched toothache bored into her jaw and patience, though Meg had dosed it twice with periwinkle and rosemary in wine.

All the way she had felt that she was being watched. Not just by the Popes, nor by stolid fellow travelers gaping at a passing party of their betters. She didn't mind the common folk gawking as they picked walnuts or gleaned the last of the rye harvests with huge rakes or pruned the hop vines. She was watched by someone she could not see or identify. Someone who stooped low enough to poison rabbits and dared reach so high as to poison—

"Lady Elizabeth," Bea Pope's voice interrupted her frenzied thoughts. She sidled her horse close to Elizabeth's Griffin to nose out her own husband's, who dropped back for a bit, while the ever watchful Jenks rode on Elizabeth's other side.

"Did you not hear me?" Bea said, twisting in the saddle to peer at her. "I said, we are almost there. No wonder ordinary travelers never stop at Ightham Mote, and Her Majesty gave you permission to visit such a godforsaken part of Kent."

Elizabeth ignored the insult. The fact that the manor was tucked deep in this maze of tunnellike lanes between the two main roads was part of its allure for her right now.

"You know," Bea chattered on, not daring to look at her now, "I believe I shall soon make a sampler 'broidered with a knot of these dreadful vines that keep snagging my hat." She reached up to rip at one. "My work shall bear the saying *Abandon all hope, ye who enter here.*"

She laughed musically, as if she had made some brilliant jest. "I believe," she went on, when Elizabeth did not deign to reply, "your fool, Ned, said that's from a speech he did in *The Tragedy of Aeneas in Torment* or some such when he was with The Queen's Country Players. The knave's frightfully clever, you know," she added, gesturing behind them with a flutter of gloved fingers.

"Someone told me so. It's why I took him on, of course." And why, Elizabeth added to herself, I told him to keep a watch on you. With the slightest nod of her head to Jenks, they kicked their mounts to leave Bea riding alone in their wake before she could think to inquire *who* had recommended Ned.

But Bea, like an apothecary leech, was not to be deterred as she caught up and clung. "And did he tell you why he took the sobriquet Topside?" she asked with a chortle, as if she caught naught of their snub. "Because the groundlings took to heart his braggadocio naval captain of that name, who insists he always be topside when he goes to sea or beds a wench." She dissolved in gales of laughter again.

It was all Elizabeth could do to keep from hanging Bea Pope with the next noose of vine they rode under. Her chatter was the least of it, for as far as Elizabeth was concerned, Bea had been topside in Cecil's warning letter.

'S blood, she wished she could have reread it several more times before they had to set out, but Jenks had been delayed getting from London to Stamford and back. She'd had time to skim the epistle only twice, then burn it, but its message was burned in her brain.

Sui bono, he'd written and underscored, her wily lawyer, for the letter was entirely in Latin. It mattered not: She could have read it in Italian, French, Spanish, or Greek. Though Kat Ashley had been her first teacher, she had spent years under the tutelage of two brilliant scholars, even during her exile from court. *Sui bono* was a Latin law phrase meaning *Who will profit—who is to gain?* It was the way lawyers delved for motive in a crime. *Sui bono*—cold and calculating, but clever. The very way she would have to act to save herself so she could get the throne and then bind such men as Cecil and Harry to her as advisers.

Always—*semper*—Cecil had written and underscored also, look for who will profit monetarily, politically, or even passionately in affairs of the heart—including vengeance.

Vengeance is mine, sayeth the Lord. Elizabeth recalled the biblical warning, but she had known a hundred believers who had not believed that, including her royal sister.

However, in this instance of the so-called poison plot, Cecil had written, he had concluded that Mary Tudor's consort, King Philip of Spain, as well as his courtiers, his Catholic church, and his country had the most to gain if Elizabeth died. At least Cecil had not dared treason to include Queen Mary as the puller of strings behind the plot. Yet in the dark of night and those places in her own soul, that was Elizabeth's worst fear—and best guess.

Cecil had listed as possible suspects some Spaniards currently in power who would lose all influence should she ascend the throne, names from the Count de Feria, the Spanish ambassador, to others—names she had not had time to learn by rote.

But he'd written and underscored that since the poison victims included Boleyns of the past as well as the present, they'd best look first to those who could lose much now but were also tied to Catherine of Aragon—a sort of double *sui bono.* And so that second detailed list was of some members of Queen Catherine's household. Though several of them were dead, they either had offspring or retainers who were fanatically loyal to the Catholic queen, daughter and wife of Spanish royalty:

*Miguel De la Sa was C. of A.'s loyal personal physician. The
man was with her during her darkest days and was overheard to
vow vengeance on Anne Boleyn and her rapacious family—
rapacious, a direct quote, not my term,* Cecil had carefully
added. *And, of course, as a physician, De la Sa knew something
of lethal herbs. He is dead, but he could have passed on his
hatred—and knowledge of the herbs, so I shall look into that.
His heirs have much to lose should you rule.*

De la Sa, Elizabeth thought. Yes, she remembered him,
another stale old fellow from the past who had not lived
long in Mary's reign. Had he not been of such lofty age
when Mary took the throne, she would have probably ap-
pointed De la Sa as her own royal physician in her mother's
honor. But he had often visited and had pronounced Mary's
old beekeeper dead on the grass at Whitehall that day Elizabeth was there. Queen Mary had buried one old beekeeper
and one physician and replaced them both with younger
retainers that first month of her reign.

Secondly, John de Scutea, Cecil wrote, *who lived to a ripe
old age in London, passionately dedicated to the Spanish cause
and Popish religion, was once Queen Catherine's apothecary,
working closer with De la Sa. Dr. Scutea had a daughter named
Sarah Scottwood—whether she had wed a Scottwood or taken
an Anglicized approximation of her father's name for anonym-
ity, I am not sure. Sarah also knew the herbs, and the queen,
and upon the event of her father's death last year, disappeared
from London and could not be traced.*

Elizabeth had made a mental note to herself to have

Cecil pull some strings to find out what this Sarah Scott-wood, *née* Scutea, looked like. And if any of De la Sa's heirs were women.

He had included other names on the list, but it was his final item that most angered and alarmed her. *And you know, do you not,* he had written, *though I see no herbal connection here, that Maria de Salinas, faithful lady-in-waiting to Queen Catherine to the bitter end, who had publicly claimed that Anne Boleyn's people had slipped poison to her predecessor, was foster mother to Beatrice, Lord Thomas Pope's wife you have ever with you. . . .*

Not ever with me, Elizabeth fumed, for she finds excuses enough to visit her sister in Kent. But she bears thorough watching, even if she goes off to nearby Maidstone again.

Just as upsetting, Cecil had warned her that both Kentish houses—Hever Castle and Leeds Castle—where she intended to pursue Boleyn connections were linked to dangerous foreign elements. He would send her word posthaste on these if she did not already know of this herself.

And Harry, in his own hand, had written of his loyalty and devotion to her. She stopped rubbing her sore jaw and let her lips rest in a smile at the memory of her dear cousin. He had explained he was more certain than ever that his would-be assassins had shouted their cursed battle cry with a foreign accent. He and Cecil had discussed it, and it could well have been Spanish with its lilt and Castilian lisp.

"Are you quite well, Lady Elizabeth?" Bea interrupted again. "This journey was all your idea, yet you have looked pained and pale all the way. And your testy temper and refusal to converse civilly tells me it is more than a tooth-ache."

"I am certain," Elizabeth declared, staring straight ahead, "the company in Kent will much improve my disposition. Ah—look there through the trees. How I love these old moated manor houses. They once knew how to keep the enemy out."

Bea only sputtered as Elizabeth spurred Griffin to ride at the very vanguard of the group.

"NOW, REMEMBER, JENKS, your story is that you are my body servant, and we've been living abroad," Ned said as the two of them rode into the little town of Edenbridge late the next morning. "Since our personae don't know much of what's going on and are heading for London, we need some information about the tenor of the times from the towns-people. And don't stand agape or clap me on the back this time when I assume an educated London accent."

Edenbridge was the only decent-size village near the Princess Elizabeth's ancestral home of Hever Castle and about ten miles from Ightham Mote, where everyone else was settling in and resting today. With its row of crooked, half-timbered shops downstairs and living chambers up, all overhung with drooping thatched roofs, the place looked like a hundred other hamlets Ned had seen on his theatrical tours. A small church with a graveyard at its skirts, a few scattered wattle-and-daub houses, and only one place with pretentions crowded a narrow, rutted lane.

Several people stopped and stared at them but gave no greeting. Though their horses' hooves came not near, a woman yanked two children back into an open door and slammed it. Several people peered from second-story windows until an old woman with a wrinkle-webbed face shut hers with a smack and the others followed suit.

The two men reined in at an ivy-fronted public house probably called the Queen's Head. No words named the place, but a weathered sign of a crowned woman squeaked in the breeze. She had hair so black she must be either Catherine Howard or—in these parts, where it could not be Catherine of Aragon—Anne Boleyn.

Jenks began to look as nervous as Ned felt. Usually rural folk were friendly or at least curious about strangers. Jenks's eyes kept darting about to watch their flanks, but it didn't keep him from continuing their conversation.

"But Her Grace said I can ask round what they think of the Boleyns, too, Ned. I heard London talk lots of times. But I'll follow your lead like I done hers at Wivenhoe."

Because Ned liked Jenks's openness and honesty—and deferential nature—he nodded instead of shaking his head in disgust. Meg, at least, would have never made the doltish assumption that anyone could summon up someone else's speech at will, especially that of their betters.

"Just remember to listen more than you talk," Ned encouraged him. "I'm going to play this to the hilt. I'll do a version of Lord Henry Carey's voice, for he's been abroad and has now come home. But no—that doesn't mean I'll use his name," he added hastily, reading the next question the man would ask before he opened his mouth.

They tied their horses, and Ned gave a dirty lad a groat to watch them. The boy had begun to back away, but the glint of the coin stayed his feet.

Ned was impressed with how reasonably clean the common room of the Queen's Head smelled compared to other such places he'd been. The rushes on the floor didn't reek of dog or manured boots.

Though the Princess Elizabeth had come to Kent to probe the plot against her, she was inordinately eager to visit her mother's girlhood home nearby. Her plans were to take a small party out riding and just happen to stop at Hever. Their hostess, Lady Cornish, had told them that Queen Mary had sold the place last year to a Sir Edward Waldegrave, who had been an officer in Her Majesty's household. Not exactly the strong Spanish connection the princess was expecting because of Cecil's letter, but one that bore watching. That was why she planned a surprise visit rather than one announced—just as they did here today.

The six patrons and tapman in the common room bore watching, too, Ned noted. All talk stopped when they entered. No one sang out greetings, inquiries, not even insults. The hair on the back of his neck prickled as he ordered two tankards of beer. He could sense when he introduced himself and said he was just passing through from the Kentish coast to London that he'd somehow said the wrong thing.

He could tell from their frowns, hardened gazes, and shifting stances that they were not impressed.

"Back to London, eh?" the tapman muttered. He was bald with a bull neck so short that his head seemed to sit directly on his rounded shoulders, as if it could topple off. Out of the corner of his eye, Ned saw three others sidle up to the row of hogshead casks, which meant three others were still somewhere behind him. He slowly pivoted to lean back against a big tun. Jenks shifted his free hand to his sword hilt. Whatever in creation's name was wrong here? He was usually skilled at reading strangers. What had he missed?

"But we're not on court business or anything like that," Ned added hastily, addressing everyone now. "Just hoping for a little catch-up on the latest happenings hereabouts." To his chagrin, one man closed the door and leaned against it, cross-armed.

"Meanin'," the tapman drawled, "this be an unofficial visit, just to gather more information, like you said. Been employed at Bloody Mary's court afore, I'll bet. Maybe, lads, this fine lord left the country like a rat off a sinkin' ship, but now he's scurryin' back with more news from the shires for Her Majesty, eh?"

"News from the shires?" Ned echoed. "No, not the way you imply—"

"Curse her filthy Catholic soul, an' you can tell her that next time you see her—in hell," the tapman cried and spit into the rushes at his feet.

That seemed the sign for a general melee. The tapman

swung a pewter flagon, catching Ned on the upper arm as he tried to draw his sword. The others rushed them in a big blur of shouts and bodies.

It was then Ned learned why a brilliant woman like the princess could abide someone as thick-headed as Stephen Jenks. Before Ned could so much as draw his sword, Jenks thrust Ned behind him so hard he bounced off the wall. Jenks scraped his sword out and, with a battle cry that would have done a Turk proud, swung it in a broad arc back and forth to keep the first barrage of rogues off them.

When the tapman ducked low and came at him, Jenks kicked the rogue in the groin, then shoved him at the others so they went down like ninepins. He darted sideways to roll flasks to pen them in a corner. Somehow, the two plank tables got upturned to hold them there.

Ned had his sword and dagger out and was ready to run for the door when Jenks bellowed, "We're queensmen, aye, but of our next queen! The Princess Elizabeth sent us to greet you, living near her people's home at Hever."

Though shaken and astounded, Ned saw that was the right thing to say. Their burly attackers froze where they stood or sat, wiping bloody noses. The tapman, bent over in pain, retched on the floor. One lout spit out two teeth before he lisped through a cut lip, "God's truth, man?"

Jenks motioned Ned out of the corner with two jerks of his sword point. "You go ahead and talk now, Lord Ned."

"Yes. I—it's—it's God's truth indeed," he began, cursing that he sounded like a stutterer. His upper arm began to throb where the tapman had laid into him, and his shoulder stung from Jenks throwing him back into the wall.

"Heard she's hunkered in at Ightham Mote, our princess," Cut Lip said. "Come home to us Kentish folk loves her best, ain't she—waitin' for that Cath'lic she-wolf to die?"

"Aye," the tapman agreed, getting unsteadily to his feet and wiping his mouth with his sleeve. Another man rolled a barrel out to give them some room in the corner. The tapman gave Cut Lip a hand up as he talked.

"Bloody Mary's royal arm reached out right o' a London—to loyal little places never done naught to her," he explained as he shuffled closer. "Burnt to death our schoolmaster, Alexander Walton, in front of the old church just for holding to his belief the communion host stood for Christ but wasn't his real flesh, that's what She-Wolf's London men come here and did." He spit blood again but no more teeth.

"A burning here?" Jenks said, finally sheathing his sword. "Heard tell the queen hauled heretics—martyrs— off to London or Oxford for that."

Ned wanted to say something, to take over, but for once words wouldn't come. Besides, it seemed these bumpkins thought Jenks was the spokesman here. He didn't know whether to laugh or cry.

"Naw, like in other little towns, burnt him here when he wouldn't recant. And when some folk protested, her men whipped every one of us so much as spit," the tapman said and quickly shed his jerkin and shirt. He turned his back to them to display the ugly patchwork of red welts across his skin. "Every man jack here can show the same," he said, wincing as he gingerly pulled his shirt back on.

"So then," Ned said, and his voice broke with emotion, "strong loyalty for the Princess Elizabeth and her Boleyn family still flourishes here?"

"We'd all go to the whippin' or the burnin' stake for her," a younger, thinner, freckled lad said. He stepped out from the makeshift battlement of barrels to peer past Ned, so he could address Jenks. "Bless you for servin' her, man. Keep her safe for us."

"KAT MENTIONED YOU CRIED OUT in your sleep again, Your Grace," Meg said to Elizabeth as she prepared to ride out to Hever Castle with a retinue the next morning, though everyone but her privy plot council thought she was merely taking a ride in that direction.

When she appeared to have a whim that they stop at Hever for a respite, it would give her an opportunity to meet, assess, and carefully question Sir Edward Waldegrave, whom she had learned in Cecil's second letter was an ally to the queen and friend of the Spanish ambassador Feria. Hopefully, Waldegrave would give her a tour of the place. No use taking the risk of slipping in there secretly at night if one could be taken inside openly. Besides, like Ightham Mote and many manor houses in Kent, Hever was moated with a working drawbridge that would be difficult to breach unless one were welcomed in.

"No doubt my unrest was from a nightmare, my Meg, but one I don't recall." Over Kat's shoulder Elizabeth smiled at the girl as she helped her don her fox-lined cloak over her russet riding gown.

But her bravado was not quite the truth. She had dreamed that bees were buzzing her, bombarding her. Bees from Bushey Cot, bees from the hives beyond the knot garden here at Ightham Mote, bees from Queen Mary's Whitehall Palace. The dreams were warnings to beware of danger, of course. Her dreams always meant something, like portents of—

"You're gone pale as a ghost, Your Grace." Kat's concerned voice cut through her thoughts. She reached out to gently rub color into her cheeks. "Not the toothache again?"

"No, I'm fine, my Kat, just a bit excited about today," she said, reaching up to pinch her own cheeks.

But she knew she must stop lying to those closest to her, those she trusted. Lies must be told to the others, but not her little poison-plot council. For if she looked as if she'd seen a ghost, it was because the past still haunted her. That dreadful dream—she'd had it more than once of late—had made her flee for comfort and courage to the Lord. Again and again today she had silently recited to herself parts of her favorite Psalm: *The Lord is on my side; I will not fear: what can man do unto me? . . . Therefore shall I see my desire upon them that hate me . . . They compassed me about*

like bees . . . Thou hast thrust sore at me that I might fall:
but the Lord helped me . . . I shall not die but live.

"But from somewhere," Meg pursued as Elizabeth took
her riding gloves from Kat and sallied out and down the
upstairs corridor, "I recall a real fine cure for nightmares. I
tell you, afore you go to bed tonight we could try rosemary
and peony seeds in wine, Your Grace."

"Wine with toothache tonic and for that too? Perhaps
that is your secret ingredient, my Meg: wine, wine, wine.
But the pain in my jaw is much better today. I shall see you
when we return."

She gave Meg a gay wave. She knew the girl wanted to
accompany her, but she was riding out only with Blanche
and Bea as ladies-in-attendance, for the rest were men.
Even here—especially here—she must do things for safety's
sake.

She tugged her gloves on before she went downstairs so
her hands were free to lift her skirts and grasp the banister.
Ah, she could not wait to see upstairs and down in the place
Mary Boleyn had described to her, the childhood home her
mother had known, where King Henry had come calling,
hunting for game and a new love in the forests of Hever.

She was hunting, too, today, but for answers to who in
Kent could be connected to the master poisoner and why.
She would not let that damned woman and whoever was
pulling her strings ruin this jaunt. To be there might be
almost like touching her mother again, and she had not
done that since she was three. But it was to the bold Anne
Boleyn she owed her right to wear England's crown, for she

had gone to the block rather than declare her babe a bastard. And so, she thought, pausing on the bottom stair, this is a pilgrimage I make today.

The princess's host and hostess, the Cornishes, awaited her at the door to the courtyard. "At least it is dry today and not so brisk as of late," Penelope Cornish said, taking Elizabeth's proffered hands. Sleek silver hair pulled back in a dated gabled coif framed Lady Cornish's plump face. Her slashed velvet overgown and brocade kirtle also reminded Elizabeth of her father's days, but what did it matter when the Cornishes never went to court anymore? After all, it was keeping clear of royal politics for decades that had made Queen Mary believe they were yet loyal to any Tudor on the throne.

Thin and tottering, Lord Neville Cornish bowed and escorted Elizabeth outside to the central courtyard, where her party waited. He had offered to ride along, but Elizabeth knew he was not up to it, nor could he give her any sort of entrée to Lord Waldegrave, as their separate past loyalties kept them from being friends.

Outside, she noted that Thomas Pope was not yet among her retinue, though Bea was present—and pacing. The day was brisk and bright, but Elizabeth felt as if a cloud had cast itself over her expectations. When her eye caught Ned's across the cobbled courtyard, he pointed toward the front of the house and gestured something to her she could not decipher. At least he did not seem sulky, as he had yesterday after the near disaster at Edenbridge he testily admitted Jenks had bailed him out of.

"Is aught amiss with my plans for a ride today?" she asked Lord Cornish.

"I suppose both good news and bad, though Lord Pope is likely to chew rocks and spit them out too," the old man told her with a thin smile. "A rather goodly size crowd, Your Grace, especially for this place hidden away in the Weald, has gathered at the front gate, hoping for a glimpse of their princess. Word has spread like wildfire, you see—"

"A hostile or friendly crowd, my lord?" she asked warily, cocking one eyebrow.

"Why, this is Kent, Your Grace." His smile widened to display crooked, darkened teeth. "It might as well all be Boleyn land, instead of none of it anymore."

Exhaling a sigh of relief, she could not help but smile back at him. While Jenks held her horse, she climbed the mounting steps and sat, hooking one knee over the sidesaddle, putting the toe of her boot through the stirrup, and settling her skirts. While her retinue scrambled to get astride their mounts, she took the reins and riding whip Jenks handed her and tried not to look as excited as she felt.

"But we're not to ride out until my lord re—" Bea Pope began.

Pretending she did not hear her, Elizabeth clucked Griffin on. She had to see and hear English folk who set no tricky political or religious plots in motion but who truly cared. Men like those Ned and Jenks had met at that public house. People who were proud of her Boleyn blood and didn't want to poison it.

Sun glinted off the diamond-shape mullioned windows

of the inner courtyard as Jenks, a few Cornish retainers, her two ladies, and three of Pope's men fell in to funnel through the narrow tower entrance. Elizabeth craned her neck to glance up at the barrel-vaulted roof adorned with carved Tudor roses. The spikes of the iron portcullis were raised into the stone ceiling. Outside, bridges spanned three of the four sides of the square moat, fed by springs and a waterfall Elizabeth could hear from her rooms if she opened her windows. Horses' hoofs clattered on cobbles behind her.

She heard the buzz of voices before she saw the crowd, nearly twoscore folk strung out along the far edge of the moat. Thomas Pope was haranguing them to go home. When they caught sight of her, wild hurrahs drowned him out. Caps flew and someone threw dried rose petals into the air.

Tears stung Elizabeth's eyes. She smiled and lifted her hand to wave—but then she felt it again, the fear.

Someone in the crowd . . . she was being watched by someone who might be cheering . . . but hated her. She reined in Griffin and narrowed her gaze into the sun, squinting to peruse their faces. Sir Thomas strode to her across the patch of grass and seized Griffin's bridle.

"Her Majesty will not be pleased to hear of this, my lady. You are not to be showing yourself to crowds—flaunting yourself to incite unrest."

Elizabeth tore her gaze from the women's faces in the crowd. She looked down her nose at the man. With her other worries he suddenly seemed a pesky fly she could crush under her boot, yet she had to heed him. His words found their mark. Her temper flared, though she fought to stem it.

"I have hardly summoned these few folk, nor have I incited unrest, my lord. I would merely ride out—"

"I am now dead set against it, because the queen would be likewise. And when she hears of this in her delicate state, she will no doubt rescind her permission for you to be here in this hotbed of . . . of misguided loyalties in Kent from which your . . . some of your . . . people sprang."

She blinked back tears. How foolish she had been to expect she could act openly here, she who had no power but dangled by a thread hoping for safety in the future. But she had to act now against the poisoner, and evidently in secret. She nodded to the crowd again but did not dare to wave. Still they cheered as, stony-faced, she wheeled about and rode back in through the iron jaws of old Ightham Mote.

Chapter The Eleventh

T HANK GOD—AND PENELOPE CORNISH— that Sir Thomas and Bea's rooms are around the other side of the quadrangle."

Elizabeth's voice came muffled as Kat helped her tug the man's shirt down over her head and laced it for her. Since Jenks was so much bigger, she had borrowed Ned's good one—besides, it didn't stink of horses. Elizabeth shoved the tails into her boy's breeks and cinched the whole thing in with a broad belt. They tied her heavy hair back in a tail and shoved it up under a black felt cap. Lastly, Kat swirled her fur-lined cape over her, for the night was chill.

Kat stood back, tapping one finger against her pursed lips. "If someone sees you three about after dark with extra horses, they're likely to think smugglers came up from the coast again with fine Frenchie goods," she observed. "Lady Cornish's maid Bett's been telling me this area used to be full of them before the Tudors put wardens in the Cinque ports on the channel."

"We *are* smugglers," Elizabeth declared. "We're going to

somehow smuggle ourselves into a moated, gated—mayhap guarded—manor house and discover exactly why the queen gave my ancestral Boleyn home to Sir Edward Waldegrave for a pittance last year, as Cecil put it in his second letter. Since Waldegrave's so tight with Ambassador Feria and her Spaniards, he's doing something special for her here, or why would he live away from court? And that something could be to give sanctuary to a nest of poisoners who are targeting me. If that girl Nettie came from Kent, the mastermind behind the poor wretch probably did too. Oh, where are the others? I told them ten of the clock!" she said, smacking her palms on her breeks.

Kat returned to wringing her hands, but Elizabeth was relieved she had given up arguing. It had not been Cecil's second secret missive about Waldegrave that had convinced Kat. Rather, it was her intimate view of her royal mistress's face when she had ridden back into the courtyard earlier today after her first aborted attempt to get to Hever. Besides, poison clover and dead rabbits in the front meadow of Hatfield had finally persuaded Kat that Elizabeth might not even survive to become queen if she didn't fight back somehow.

A flurry of light knocks sounded on the door, and Kat flew for it. Meg entered with Ned hard behind.

"Jenks holds the horses beyond the moat," he said, out of breath. He wore a thickly padded jerkin and a cape, but carried his cap and gloves. "And may I present to you the fair Princess of England—at least for the night," he added, nodding at Meg.

The girl was dressed in one of Elizabeth's night rails and robes. She nodded slowly, almost elegantly, without shifting her stance or slumping her shoulders. Some progress here at least, Elizabeth thought. It was much like gazing in a looking glass.

"Your Grace," Meg said solemnly as if she spoke set words, "I vow I shall not fall to pieces if Sir Thomas comes insisting he speak to you while you're gone and it's me in your bed."

"I in your bed," Ned interjected.

"Kat will see that doesn't happen," Elizabeth assured her. "You are here only for a surety that someone like Bea doesn't cause trouble. If she does, pretend to be in a foul temper, keep your head covered, and moan that your toothache has come back with a vengeance."

"But then they'll send for me, and I'll be you, so—"

"Hush," Elizabeth insisted but gave her shoulder a quick squeeze. "We must all pray that our risks will be worth the rewards. Meg, this is your maiden voyage impersonating me, and I believe Ned has launched you well."

She turned quickly to hug Kat farewell, but not before she saw the look of longing Meg shot Ned. He missed it, fiddling with his dagger in its sheath.

'S blood, Elizabeth swore to herself, all she needed in this maze of problems was for Meg to be yearning for *that sort* of regard from Ned. But no, she only wanted his approval, as any scholar wants to please a tutor. Anyhow, she had no time for such maudlin tripe from her people, not now, not ever.

She and Ned tiptoed down the servants' stairs that led to the back hall with its pantry, buttery, and bolting room. Though only dogs dozed by the low kitchen fire and no one worked this late, it seemed to Elizabeth that a fine flour dust hung in the air. She jammed her finger under her nose to stop a sneeze. Then they were out the back door, through an autumn herb garden, and across the eastside bridge where Jenks, already mounted, held five horses.

As they mounted, Elizabeth glanced back. A second-story window showed the silhouette of a woman's shape. She sucked in a breath of crisp air. That would be at the top landing of the central stairs, wouldn't it? Had Kat or Meg come round to this side to see them go? If it was Lady Cornish or Blanche, she could probably deal with it, but if it were Bea . . .

"Let's ride," she said.

THEY SPELLED TWO HORSES each hour on the way, a good fifteen miles wending through roundabout roads. Elizabeth's heart thudded faster than their hoofbeats. The forest floor was dark, but Jenks had done a good job getting directions, and she hardly feared they'd meet someone abroad this late. Few could be so brazen or desperate as she.

When pale moonlight revealed the painted, faded facade of Hever Castle, tears wet her lashes, she who never cried but deep inside. Not even, she thought, suddenly awash with emotion, when she lost Tom Seymour in his betrayal, not even when she faced Traitor's Gate at the Tower over the Wyatt plot.

She fought for a happier thought so she would not lose her resolve. After all, this home had seen glad events and bold endeavors. One time, her Aunt Mary had said, Anne insisted she was ailing and dared to stay in her chamber the entire time her parents entertained their increasingly frustrated sovereign. If only she herself, Elizabeth thought, had that much power over men, to make them dance to her tune. But then, disaster oft came hard upon the heels of passion and power. Sometimes they seemed much the same to her, all twisted up.

"I said the drawbridge is up, just as you feared, Your Grace."

"Yes, Jenks. But no more 'Your Grace' here, remember. You shall call me Robin in case we are overheard."

She had hardly pulled that name out of the air, but she hadn't explained it to them either. Robert Dudley, nick-named Robin, had been her friend, and in his brown eyes she had tasted a man's adoration and first sensed a woman's power. His family had fallen hard, too, when his father led a rebellion against Queen Mary's right to the throne. Robin's father had illegally crowned Robin's young sister-in-law and Tudor cousin, Jane Grey, as queen. Their rebellion had lasted only nine days before Mary and her Catholic loyalists put it down, beheading some Dudleys and sending others to the Tower. Robin had still been there when Elizabeth was imprisoned. He had sent her flowers he'd picked on the parapet, and—

"Robin," Jenks's voice cut in again, "you sure I can't go in with you and not just Ned?"

She was grateful the darkness hid her flushed face. "No, Jenks. We need you to defend the horses, for if we lose them when we create a stir, we're trapped. Ned and I will be fast and light on our feet, once we can dart inside. Ah, I see what our diversion shall be to make them open the drawbridge and rush out so we can slip in." She pointed toward the barn in the sprinkle of farm buildings outside the moat.

While Jenks sneaked out of their forest cover to set the fire in the sole hayrick that stood outside the barn, Elizabeth's thoughts drifted again. She was in the strangest, detached mood, when she knew she must concentrate on everything here. But this place lured her so sweetly—

"Sit tight," Ned muttered. "The flame has caught. If someone doesn't see it soon, I'll yell. I've got the Kentish talk down flat."

"You'll not make a peep until Jenks gets back here to hold these horses. And not until you and I get in the shadow of that other outbuilding, away from where they will gather round the fire."

Jenks ran back; she and Ned fled to their post. "Do it now," Elizabeth urged him, breathing hard. Her heart seemed to pound in her ears. "We'll need all the time we've got to get inside and look around. Yell like it's doomsday."

"Fire! Fire!" Ned bellowed, his hands curled around his mouth like a trumpet. She could see his breath puff white in the night air. "The barn will burn. What ho, the castle there. Help afore it spreads!"

"Enough," she ordered, gripping his arm. "I asked not for an entire prologue."

Voices. Noises. People ran from the outlying warren of buildings. Several rushed close past where they pressed themselves against a stone corner of the stable block. They saw a single lantern shining in an arched window of the castle. Someone shouted orders out another window. Then, after an eternity while the flames crackled higher, the drawbridge creaked down, its old chains rattling. House servants streamed out to join the others, finally followed by a big-shouldered, tall man wrapped in a huge robe, giving orders in a commanding voice. Another man and then a woman bundled in cloaks hurried out to watch as servants began to pass buckets of water hand-to-hand in a line from the moat.

Elizabeth noted that the lantern had finally disappeared from the corner upstairs room. A servant who had stayed behind or an elderly family member? She felt better when several others came shuffling out, robed and in nightcaps.

"Now or never," she told Ned.

They strolled behind the clumps of onlookers—a baby wailed nearby—then darted across the bridge into the castle. As Lady Cornish had mentioned, Hever was built much like Ightham Mote, with a quadrangle of buildings around an inner courtyard. Elizabeth wished she had asked her aunt to explain the layout of the first-floor rooms better, but of course, there had been no time for a full description as she lay dying. Elizabeth's belly cramped in foreboding.

"This way," she threw back over her shoulder. "And pray all Waldegrave's men and servants have gone out to see or fight the fire."

The timbered entrance hall lay in silent shadow, but six suits of armor standing at attention gave them pause. Crossed swords and pikes adorned the whitewashed walls. A board creaked underfoot.

Here, she thought, her grandparents had greeted guests; here her mother and father—but there was no time for that now.

Assuming that any dangerous information of a poison plot would be secreted in a privy chamber or bedroom above, they felt their way up the staircase. When the household returned to bed, they could search the downstairs—if there was time.

Aunt Mary had told Elizabeth the original placement of the rooms on the inner side of the upstairs quadrangle. She wondered who had those rooms now. She was both relieved and disconcerted to see several fat tallow candles burning on a tall chest at the top of the stairs. They each needed to carry one, but they threw such shifting shadows on the walls and into doorways that Elizabeth could almost see ghosts here.

But not her mother's at least, she tried to buck herself up. If she haunted any site it was the Tower in London, where she was betrayed and beheaded—and the chambers of her daughter's heart.

"Which side do you want?" Ned asked. She jumped at his voice.

"The inner courtyard," she whispered. "That means you must be the one to glance outside now and again to see if they are heading back inside. Come warn me if we must secrete ourselves until they are back in bed. Go now."

She took the inner rooms because her aunt had told her those were the family chambers in her mother's day. The first one she entered, which had been her Uncle George's as a boy, was evidently now nothing more than a guest room, currently unused. The bed was not disturbed, and no items of clothing lay about. Still, she opened the heavy lid of the big, carved coffer at the foot of the bed. It smelled of common wormwood and pennyroyal to keep out fleas and moths. She thrust her hand down through old furs and velvets to be certain no correspondence was secreted here.

The next room had been Aunt Mary's—smaller than George's, but then he was the male heir. How could her grandparents have known that the destruction of the third child and youngest girl, Anne, would pull George and the entire family down too?

Here, for the first time, Elizabeth felt shame at what she and Ned did this night. Destroying property and invading someone's privy chamber—their lives. But that's what She and whoever sheltered and supported her were daring to do to a royal princess, and Queen Mary had no right to give this heritage house of hers away to her own Spanish-loving lackeys. With a vengeance, Elizabeth stepped farther into the room and lifted her candle high.

The bed linens were pulled awry, for someone had slid

off the high mattress quickly. A half-drunk goblet of wine winked crimson in the light of her candle. Trunk hose and a shirt on the chair and padded jerkins and cloaks in the coffers revealed it was a man's room, but surely Waldegrave would not sleep here alone. Cecil's second letter had said that he had wed his wife, Francis, daughter of Sir Edward Neville, only last year. Perhaps this house had been their wedding gift as well as a bribe so Waldegrave would help She rid the kingdom of a hated, Protestant royal sister. Still, sometimes Elizabeth could not believe Mary would stoop to such treachery.

This room had a writing desk under the windows. Elizabeth plucked a pile of letters from a cubbyhole and thrust them in the bolster cover she had brought along as if she were a common thief. She had not time nor light to read them here.

She forced herself on. This next chamber, she knew, with the big oriel window, was the master's suite, where her grandparents had bedded—and that was no doubt now Edward and Francis Waldegrave's.

She breathed fast and hard. Trembling, she went through the desk first, set under the window as the other had been. Only a few letters, but one with such a large wax seal, it could be from the queen. She stuffed them in her sack and looked around again. The room boasted a fireplace of its own. What conversations had it heard late at night over her grandfather Thomas Bullen's plans for his children? And had his ambition to rise far on the popularity of his daughters made him easily accept the fact that Anne had changed the old family name of Bullen to Boleyn, a spelling that the French-educated girl thought far more grand?

She ran her hand down into the black depths of coffers, fearing she was taking too long. She could not let anyone come back before she had visited her mother's girlhood room next door. But before she could close the lid, tallow from her candle splattered onto a brocade, fur-edged robe. She regretted that some poor servant would probably catch Cain for what a princess had done.

As she hurried to the last room she glanced down the dark corridor, hoping Ned would change chambers when she did, that she could catch a glimpse of him to ask him how it went outside. How long had they been here so far? A quarter hour? Eternity?

But her candlelight caught only the solemn, disapproving stare in a man's portrait from an olden day—perhaps even one of her ancestors' painted faces, if Waldegrave hadn't burned them all like the queen burned martyrs.

She noted that there was one more door beyond this one, but surely this was the room Aunt Mary had said had been her mother's. Biting her lower lip, holding the bolster cover with her booty close to her breasts, Elizabeth stretched out her hand toward the big brass door latch. She would feel closer to her mother inside; she would feel safe and not afraid.

An odd floral scent wafted out as she drew open the door. It creaked. A chill draft from inside gutted her candle out. She jumped back as she blinked at light from inside—a single lantern and wan moonlight. Had she stumbled on someone still here?

But silence reigned, and the bed in the center of the room bore the familiar telltale signs of someone who had quickly thrown off bed linens, counterpane and all, and slid out. Still, she stepped no farther in. A set of sleeves lay on the counterpane, both the clothing and the pane gaily embroidered with twining vines and flowers of slightly different patterns.

That made her hesitate the more. She pressed her eye to the hinge side of the door. No one behind it, and she could only pray the occupant was not behind or under the bed.

She saw the room boasted a big bay window with its slightly vaulted roof set higher than the ceiling. Moonlight washed in to etch everything in tarnished silver, despite the steady flame from an oil lamp. Finally, Elizabeth stepped inside and closed the creaky door behind her.

Then she saw what adorned the wall over the bed, strung high up from plaited cords. She gasped and pressed back against the wall. Herbs and flowers hung behind her too; she crushed and crinkled some. Just as in the cellars at Wivenhoe, nooses dangled dry and dying plants.

She jumped away from the wall. Though she wanted to flee, at least to get Ned, she seized control and forced herself to search the two coffers, one at the foot of the bed, the other in the far corner. Despite decent light here, she shuddered as she plunged her hand inside the depths of the first one. She kept seeing that dreadful coffer at Bushey Cot with the sticky poison fungus.

It was full of dried flowers of all sorts. She took several handfuls at random, hoping they could link them to their finds at the cot, mayhap even the deadly meadow saffron from Wivenhoe.

In the second coffer her hand touched only heavy garments near the bottom, but fine, light ones lay atop. She picked one up to examine it in the crosslight of moon and lantern. Just a veil with hand-rolled hems and delicate needlework along the edge. She squinted to discern the pattern.

A decorative coil of some sort of leaves, greatly reminiscent of the designs in the previous embroideries they had as clues—and in Bea Pope's creations. Were these leaves some sort of poison herb? They looked a bit like clubs on playing cards, or . . . like clover, three-lobed. She wished Meg were here to identify this. And something else in each corner—a tiny heart pierced by an arrow dripping blood.

She began to shake harder. Though she was drenched in sweat, her teeth chattered. It all meant something, something just out of her reach. If the veils were for disguises and not mere modesty or fashion, She must be someone people would know bare-faced. Ned had reported a veiled woman came and went at Bushey Cot. The poisoner She must live here where Waldegrave sheltered and supported her. If so, she had defiled Anne Boleyn's bedchamber as part of her revenge. But revenge for exactly what?

As Elizabeth thrust the single veil into her sack, the toe

of her boot stubbed something under the bed. She fell to her knees and tugged out a leather and brass-nail studded box, narrow but as long as her arm. She tried to lift it, but it was heavy. Glass or pewter clinked inside when she shifted it. And then she heard the chamber door creak open.

Chapter The Twelfth

LIZABETH DROPPED TO HER KNEES BEHIND the bed. The brocade counterpane draped to the floor, but she lifted it and started to slide under, dragging her sack of pilfered goods. The scent of the drying things she'd disturbed—or just dust—assailed her. Flattened on her back, she could not get her finger up under her nose.

Her sneeze exploded. Surely she was snared. She'd have to fight her way out as a lad or reveal her identity and risk—

A whisper of a voice. "Robin, are you in here?"

She sneezed again as she slid back out and stood with her eyes watering.

" 'S blood, Ned. Why did you not sing out right away? I thought I was trapped in this second Bushey Cot."

"What? She's here?" he said, gaping at the hanging herbs.

"She's been staying here and is no doubt coming back."

"If we don't fly we'll be staying too. They're coming in, all of them."

As she kicked the leather box to send it back under the bed, she heard the distinct clink of glassware again. More vials, she thought, as she followed Ned quickly out the door.

"This room has no one staying in it," Ned explained, pulling open the door directly across the hall. It, too, creaked. "We'll hide out here till they settle, then get downstairs and out before they—"

But as he ran across the small chamber and opened the single window to look out, they heard the unmistakable groan and rattle of the drawbridge going up, then banging to echoing silence. She quickly closed the door behind them and joined him at the window.

"The whoreson poxy Spanish lackey bastard traitors," Elizabeth muttered over Ned's own curse. "I thought they'd but keep watch outside, but they've closed us up."

They heard voices in the hall and knelt behind the bed, just in case someone opened the door to peek in. She whispered close to his ear. "I thought sure we'd at least be able to hide downstairs if they closed the bridge. And then we'd get out a window there. If they linger in the hall or leave a servant up, we've got a long drop to the grass inside the moat from here."

"There had better be a rowboat on the inner-moat side, like at Ightham."

"I told you to keep an eye out for them so we'd have time to get downstairs."

"By hell's gates, Lord Robin, you also told me to search chests and coffers. You're making a fine fool of me indeed."

She ignored his sarcastic wordplay. "I've letters and such here I don't want sopped in the moat—not to mention myself."

"And since, of course, this entire hugger-mugger scheme was my idea from the first—"

"Shut your smart lip and listen!"

The authoritative man's voice sounded in the corridor, hard by their door. Obviously, she thought, Sir Edward Waldegrave. And perhaps his wife's voice too—a woman's—almost musical and much more muted.

Though she kept bent low, Elizabeth got to her feet and tiptoed toward the heavy door. The man's words carried; the woman's did not.

". . . mayhap deliberately set by Kentish Protestants again, knowing we're loyal to the queen."

The woman's murmurs.

"I doubt it. I don't care if she is staying with supporters at Ightham. I'd wager this castle it was local louts."

Elizabeth gripped her hands together and pressed them under her chin. They were talking about her. This woman had evidently thought she might send someone—or come herself.

"Her Majesty Queen Mary," the man went on, his voice increasingly agitated, "had best burn the lot of these Kentishmen. They forswore their Catholic oath and lurk about, hoping for the Boleyn whelp to last long enough to have the throne fall right into her pretty little lap. By the rood, if Philip and Mary only had a child!"

The woman spoke again, something mayhap about the fire tonight. Elizabeth ached to crack the door and peer out, but it would creak and they would be caught. She yearned to rip it open and declare herself, accuse them, but that would be far more foolhardy than what she'd already done tonight.

She dipped her head to try to see through the keyhole. The key blocked it, but on this side. Slowly, she slid it out to give herself a view.

Maybe the woman was not his wife at all, but the master poisoner, for she stood in the door to Anne Boleyn's bedchamber. Devil take the man, his big shoulders blocked her view. Hoping to hear the woman's voice better, Elizabeth pressed her ear to the keyhole just as Waldegrave's voice leapt through it in answer to whatever she had just said.

"Aye, that sort of purging flame will do just as well as the queen's burnings. St. Anthony's fire, you say? I can see it now," Waldegrave went on, his voice becoming more expansive. "Bodies strewn about like those Hatfield rabbits you described, as many as swarms of your bees, but this time Boleyn loyalists . . ."

Elizabeth pressed her hand over her mouth to keep from crying out. Her stomach twisted so she thought she would dry-heave. Her frenzied fears drowned his next words until she caught control of herself.

"But just you take a care," Waldegrave added, "that our

farm workers here at Hever are spared. Over by old King Henry's beloved Leeds, eh, that will be a warning to the rest of them. Sleep well on that thought then."

Elizabeth silently damned him again for his complicity—and for standing in her view and not using the woman's name. When he stepped away, the door across the hall creaked closed. She saw no one now, so at Waldegrave's next words she jerked so hard she cracked her nose into the iron door latch inches from her face.

"Ho, men! If you've searched the first-floor chambers well enough, start down here at this end, but stay out of this last bedchamber of our guest."

"They're coming," Elizabeth whispered to Ned, though hovering, he had heard Waldegrave and was already half-way across the room.

"Come on," he whispered, digging in his sack. "I lifted a brace of men's hose just in case we needs must tie and gag someone—or get out these windows on a rope."

She jammed the key back in the lock and turned it to give them more time. As she hurried back to Ned, she fingered her painful nose. Already it was swelling, and she had to breathe through her mouth.

She soon saw that Ned Topside was good for more than a fast mouth. He had four knitted silk hose knotted together before she grabbed some from his pile and followed suit.

She tried to keep from admitting that the next queen of England—God willing—was trapped like a rat in a trap in her mother's home, praying for even so much as an igno-

minious escape. Again she had stooped to illegal entry,
theft, and now peeking through keyholes like some old gossip or scullery maid.

But she had learned this poison plot was more far-reach-
ing than she thought. Not only were she and the Boleyns
the target, but common Kentishmen loyal to her. She could
not help but think, though, as they desperately knotted the
slippery hose, that if she'd only brought a weapon—and
Jenks—she might risk facing that poisoner here.

Someone in the hall rattled their door latch and cried out,
"This one's locked. Shouldn't be. Been empty. Ask his lordship if'n we can break it down."

"Make haste, Ned."

"I would send you down first," he said, yanking on their
cord to test the knots, "but don't know if this will hold." He
bent to tie the makeshift rope to the leg of a heavy chair. He
had trouble with the knot; she saw that his hands shook.
She seized and tied the knots herself. Even if the chair lifted
off the floor at their weight, it could never follow them out
the window.

"As soon as I drop off, you follow," he ordered.

"Fine. Go. I'd not make it across the moat without you if
there's no boat there anyway."

"Can't swim, Robin?"

"Can you?"

"Like a fish."

"Go!"

Despite their banter, his face looked frenzied as he hiked

himself over the wide wooden window ledge, grasped the cord, and descended. As black night swallowed him, she felt so alone.

Waldegrave's men began to batter something against the door. *Dear Lord, help me,* she prayed, though she didn't close her eyes. She had her hands clasped though, tight on the bolster's neck as if she would strangle it. *Please Lord, my refuge and strength, my very present help in trouble, do not let me be taken by my enemies. Do not let me be poisoned by their iniquity—*

The wooden door shuddered and cracked, rattling even the open windowpanes against their lead frames. At the next hit the door splintered but did not break. She sat on the ledge, pulled her knees up, and peered out and over.

As the chill breeze cooled her hot face, she realized Ned was so close to the walls she could not clearly make him out, but the line was still taut with his weight. Whether it could hold both of them or not, she had to go now. Else when they broke down the door, she would be silhouetted against the sky. They would turn her over to Waldegrave, who would let that witch poison her, then . . .

As Ned had done before her, she dropped a bolster out the window and tried to seize the slippery knotted hose. But his weight kept it too taut to the frame and outer stone wall.

Suddenly, the rope slackened, and Ned cried out, "Robin!"

She held to the rope and went over, bumping and dangling before she began to inch down. Above her, it sounded as if the door splintered to shreds. She scraped her knuckles against the stone wall; her nose throbbed. She slipped, but only from knot to knot before she could stop herself and slide to the next, her legs alternately dangling or scraping the walls.

A downstairs window, fully lit, went by, but she, praise God, saw no one in the room. A long carpeted table. Chairs. An arras with a hunting scene on the wall.

And then Ned's hands were hard on her ankles, her legs. The sensation of being seized so firmly by a man jolted her from her fear. No one had touched her there at all, not since Tom Seymour—

"No more rope, Robin. Let go. Drop."

She did, half into Ned's arms, half against him as her knees buckled. He thrust her bolster back into her hands, and ducking under windows, they darted away, even as men must have run to the open window above. Their voices came clear now.

"Look, lads, a knotted cord. Someone been here and escaped. Fetch his lordship."

Elizabeth and Ned dashed around one corner on the sloping grass between the walls and the moat. Then, while she held their bolsters, Ned tore around another corner before coming back, breathing through his mouth more raggedly than she. Even on this side of the quadrangle, more windows both upstairs and down were showing lights.

"No boat, the bastards," he muttered. "I'll try to heave these sacks across, then if you just get in the water and float on your back, I'll try to pull you over—"

"Listen!" Elizabeth cried, grabbing his arm at the muted

sound. "They're putting the drawbridge back down. If we can get to it before they do . . ."

But the muffled creaking was coming not from the bridge but from the moat itself. From rusted oarlocks that moaned each time Jenks pulled hard on the oars to span the fifteen feet of water to get to them in time.

SHE OPENED THE DOOR to her chamber after the worst of the banging and voices in the hall subsided.

"You there, sirrah," she said, gesturing to one of Waldegrave's men. "To me."

He was the last man in the hall as the others ran down the corridor toward the stairs. Even through the fine lawn of her veil in the dim light, she could see he wore his blond hair shaggy and a stubble of beard gilded his cheeks; his shoulders looked broad and his waist narrow. Yes, he would do quite nicely, that he would. She hoped he didn't smell of sweat, but she had aromatic remedies for that.

She could see him hesitate. Despite his size and bulk, the familiar look of fear glazed his features as he stared at her. Finally, he found his tongue.

"But, good madam, his lordship says we're all to haste outside and find the intruders what mayhap lit the rick too."

"Did they now? But they were in here, too, that they were." She gestured again with one white hand that emerged from the sleeve of her sky blue robe. Her veil moved against her mouth when she breathed or spoke.

Sometimes she thought she should go only half veiled, as the women of Araby, to show her eyes. She had fine emerald eyes, her father used to say, and a bounty of hair black as the bog of Tralee. But the skin around her eyes—

"I'll tell his lordship straightaway," he said but didn't budge.

"I must show you the evidence they were here," she insisted, her voice soft and silky. "And you must search under my bed to assure me your lord's enemies are no longer in my chamber."

"Oh, right, then. Just a quick look, then," he agreed and shuffled in. He jumped when she closed the door behind him. She knew she made men nervous going and coming alone as she did, and the veils, of course, though some found them utterly intriguing—until they peered beneath. If only she could find one man, of any rank, both clever and strong, she'd keep him for a while instead of trying out something new on him and being well rid of him by the next day.

"And who might you be?" she asked.

"Owen, good madam. Want me to look under the bed, then?"

"I have not a doubt in my mind they were here, Owen— see?" she said as she walked slowly closer and pointed to her leather box of concoctions, shoved halfway under the bed to catch the counterpane.

He hunkered down to look, as if handprints and embossed names of the intruders would stand out all over it— though she doubted he could read.

"And," she said, "someone has gone through my coffers, there's no deny that."

"I'll fetch his lordship, so he can come up to look," he said, obviously fearful to glance at her again. She had sat on the coffer at the foot of her bed and let her robe split open far up her bare, crossed legs, though he kept peering under the bed, which was obviously too dark to see a thing. "They'll miss me down there, and we gotta catch—"

"I'm afraid they'll be gone by now, with all that shouting in the hall. Rather like the little people—the fairies—who do their naughty deeds in the dark but flee before they can be caught. So now we've settled that you've volunteered to protect me the rest of the night—"

"Eh?" He jerked to his feet like a puppet, then began to sidle toward the door. When she rose, slowly and sinuously, he stood stock-still but snatched off his cap and rotated it in his big, square hands.

With a predatory smile he could not see, she said, "I know his lordship would be wanting you to help me, just in case they do return."

"But you said you thought they were gone, so—"

"A spot of wine then?"

She silently cursed that she'd gotten a man who was acting more like a nervous squirrel than a lusty goat. She began to lose her hard-won temper after being bested by the Boleyn forces once again this night, even though she'd known they could be coming. But breaking into a moated castle? When others forced her to turn choleric like this, she always slipped back more into the brogue of home.

"Just be having a bit of wine with me then, and you can go tell Lord Waldegrave you deserted me in my hour of need."

"Oh, no, didn't mean that. I wouldn't do that."

"Good. Very good, Owen," she said, her voice almost a chant.

She crossed to the small table in the corner by the door and poured spiced and drugged wine into her own goblet from the ewer. She used valerian root herself to sleep sometimes, but now, her back to Owen, she added a pinch of nightshade, always good for quick drugging of victims for robbery or even murder.

He took the wine and gulped it down. "Much beholden."

"And I too. Now, let me tell you," she said, lifting a hand and stepping forward when he made for the door, "the list of things I think might have been taken from here, so you can be telling his lordship. Here, man, just sit down on the mounting stool by the bed for a moment, will you? You're worn out, I'm sure, fighting that fire and then guarding the castle."

"Nary a bit, good madam, and don't want to be a bother."

But he sat heavily, hunched over, his elbows resting on his spread knees. She took the empty goblet from his unresisting fingers. His words and breathing were already slower. He'd not get up again till morn, and that was certain. The fine thing was, the potion didn't put a man clear out but made him able to be coerced and plied to one's will yet recall not a thing.

She locked her door and lighted a gillyflower-scented candle. Though the night was chill as one in Carrick-on-Sur, she removed her robe and even her cap and veil. In her thin linen night rail, she turned down the wick of the lantern until it gutted out. She'd just be letting the moonlight do its work, she thought.

She did not wonder if Waldegrave had caught whomever the Princess Elizabeth had sent—if, as before, she had not come herself. But she could afford to be a bit patient now. She knew she was destined to face and deal with the royal Boleyn in person, for there was no denying destiny. That would be God's justice for all she and the queen—and their sainted mothers—had lost.

By the time she was ready to return to her big bed, the man was slumped half on the stool, half on the mattress. She wrapped her strong arms around his flat belly and, grunting and groaning, hoisted and dragged him up the rest of the way to lay him the length of the bed.

He flopped where she put him, muttered something, and began to snore.

Methodically, she stripped off his garments, threw them in a corner, and washed him in rose water with lavender. The sweet scent of that lingering tomorrow would be enough to make him keep his mouth shut about what might or might not have happened this night. He was well-endowed and would react well when she rubbed up his thighs and stimulated him with the oils, but she was suddenly exhausted and didn't bother. She only wanted to pretend—to drift away, drift back.

"You know, me lad," she said, kneeling over him while he slept on, "me mother was the mistress of a grand man, a wee bit taller than you but just as golden-haired. Slept in her bed every night, all night, couldn't leave her alone. She held him nigh on seventeen years, my da, and he gave us all sorts of fine gifts. He loved us both till it got ruined, that it did."

She heard herself slip more into the brogue of her childhood again, but it didn't matter. This man would never give her away. He would be loyal. And if she chose any vial from under the bed, he would never, never leave her.

Suddenly, fearful of the whole, horrid memory of her father's loss, she cuddled desperately beside him, one bent knee draped over his slack thigh. She threw her top arm over his hairy chest and wedged her forehead in the crook between his chin and shoulder, settling closer, shutting her eyes, pretending that he held her.

She wanted to make it all come back, the safe, sure times. She wanted to be her mother as she'd seen her many a summer night when she'd sneaked in behind the arras to watch her lying in her handsome father's arms in those happy days before King Henry had her father poisoned.

Suddenly enraged, she sat up and half-shoved, half-kicked the man out of her bed. He hit the floor with a crack that could have been his arm bone, groaned, then shifted to snore again. She yanked the bedclothes up to hide her face and sobbed wretchedly until she could barely breathe.

Chapter The Thirteenth

ARY A WORD IN THIS ONE ABOUT WALDE-grave being in on the poison plot," Kat observed as she, Ned, and Elizabeth skimmed the last of the letters taken from Hever.

Elizabeth had called the second clandestine midnight meeting of what she had dubbed her privy and covert counsel. So far, Meg and Jenks sat silent, as they could not read more than the alphabet Ned had been slowly, secretly teaching them.

"But these letters do prove that Waldegrave is Spanish Ambassador Feria's spy in Kent," Elizabeth noted. "The wretch has been fingering key anti-Catholics whom Feria and Mary have ordered burned at the stake. And Waldegrave's been harboring a poisoner. He knows, at the very least, that She is planning to murder hundreds of my loyalists near Leeds, so whether he knows She wants me, too, is a moot point. 'S blood," she added, smacking the epistle with the royal seal down on the table, "I shall send him to the Tower for his treachery someday."

Her foul temper at what she'd overheard at Hever had not been one whit improved by the fact they'd made a clean escape. Thank God, Jenks had seen Ned and her dangling on their rope before that lighted window and filched the boat to rescue them.

But she had not gotten off scot-free. Though her nose was not broken, it was badly swollen, and her left eye had gone black and blue. She had told the Popes that she had run into a door and that Meg was rubbing it with plantain paste. All of that, at least, was true.

But she hated looking like this and feeling as if she had the most wretched cold. She had to breathe through her mouth like the village simpleton. And she had nearly bitten poor Meg's head off this morning when she'd tried to tease her by asking if she should start learning to talk as if her head was all stuffed up too.

"So we know a great deal more than we did," Ned was saying.

"True," Elizabeth concurred. "We may have no written proof linking Waldegrave—nor my royal sister—to the plot to poison me, but . . ." Her voice snagged, but she'd finally said it aloud. It was what she feared, that the queen herself—

"Don't think it, lovey," Kat protested, reaching out to pat her hand as if she were but ten years old. "All the ups and downs the two of you royal half sisters have been through over the years, despite your differences—well, she is fond of you. Deep down, she is, I know it."

"And deep down afraid of me and what will come after—if—she is gone," Elizabeth said, wiping under her nose with her scented handkerchief, which she could not even smell. She jumped to her feet, paced back and forth, then sat back down. Everyone's heads turned in unison, like at a tennis match, to watch her. "She no doubt," she said more quietly, "has night terrors that I will undo her holy work, expel her friends, turn on her Spanish husband . . ."

"And won't you?" Ned challenged, one dark eyebrow gone atilt.

"No theoretical questions," Elizabeth evaded him, stopping her steps to rap her knuckles on the table. "We must deal with the here and now. And that is this heinous plot, which has spread like wildfire from my aunt and cousin Harry to me and now threatens loyal English folk. I overheard Waldegrave try to bargain with her—with She—to spare his workers at Hever in the mass murder she has planned, but I warrant she'd just as soon kill every last one of them who would back me for the throne."

Kat clucked and shook her head. Ned sat grimly staring at his folded hands. And Jenks, damn him, was studying Meg and not paying the slightest heed to his royal mistress. But what she had just said about a wildfire plot reminded her of something else.

"Can any of you think of a way She could use fire to kill a great lot of Kentishmen near Leeds?" Elizabeth asked them. "Waldegrave said She would use some sort of holy fire, and he mentioned a saint's name I cannot recall."

"I heard him say that—St. Anthony, I think," Ned

chimed in, looking up. "But why would a master poisoner suddenly switch to using fire, and in rainy Kent? And what edifice could be large enough that she could try to trap and burn that many folk?"

"I don't know," Elizabeth admitted, "unless she means she'll burn Leeds Castle itself. I've never seen it, but I hear it sits in a lake, so even a huge conflagration would be contained there. But hundreds burned?"

"Mayhap," Kat put in, "you misunderstood what you overheard, and they were talking of giving more names of men around Leeds for the queen's burnings of martyrs. Hurrying to wipe out hundreds more during her last days if the belly tumor is really eating her up like they say, so—"

"Speak not of that," Elizabeth insisted, wrapping her arms around her own flat belly. Though it was the only way she could ascend the throne, she was uncomfortable with talk of her sister's death, even among these people she had gathered for herself and trusted.

"I agree, Ned," she went on, "the poisoner must not mean she would actually set a fire. I believe, however, she could place poison in a well near Leeds. Meg, can you recall any sort of deadly herbs that have a name with *fire* in it? Or anything to do with St. Anthony?"

"Nothing with fire, not herbs, 'least—at least, best I can recall," she said, sitting up straighter, as she always did these days when Elizabeth or Ned spoke to her. "Still, with saints' names, there's St.-Benedict-thistle, St.-John's-wort, and St.-Joseph's-wort—that last one's same as sweet basil."

She ticked them off on her fingers, which looked much cleaner these days. "And something with St. Mary I can't remember. But nary a one's poison."

"One more question, then we're off to our beds," Elizabeth said, before she saw that Jenks meant to contribute something. At least now she had his attention.

"Yes, Jenks."

"I thought we'd be heading for Leeds Castle, after what you said, Your Grace."

"We are, but not quite yet. We shall find out more and lay plans. It is slightly farther from here than Hever, so the risk increases. Mayhap they would expect us at night this time, so I am having second thoughts about that. Besides, a lake is more of a challenge than a mere moat." She glared at Ned as he dramatically rolled his eyes, but Jenks did not change expression. "Also," she went on, "we shall have to have a more clever entrée than setting a fire. . . ."

Her voice faded and she frowned before plunging on. "Besides, the master poisoner evidently tried to tell Lord Waldegrave I sent the intruders to Hever. They may try to verify my presence here. Worse, I saw someone staring at us from the staircase window in this house when we headed for Hever—a woman, I am sure. Meg or Kat, did you watch us ride out?"

They both shook their heads solemnly, almost warily, as if waiting for some explosion from her.

"Then it could have been Blanche or Lady Cornish or even a servant," she mused, staring down at the broken wax of the royal seal of Queen Mary of England.

"Or the Buzzard herself—Bea Pope," Kat intoned what Elizabeth dreaded to admit.

Elizabeth looked up, meeting the eyes of each in turn. "Exactly. She's always watching me, but now especially we must continue to watch her. Should I hazard a guess, I would say she is tied to the poisoner somehow, and she does make occasional visits to her sister in Maidstone in Kent— or so she says."

"And if she's in the thick of it, his lordship could be too," Jenks said.

"Yes, but—"

A sharp rapping rattled her chamber door. Elizabeth shot straight out of her chair as Thomas Pope's voice resounded, "A word with the Lady Elizabeth. A messenger came for her, and this late too."

"Get down," she whispered to her people, gesturing. "Hide."

"Coming," Kat called while the others scrambled to roll under the bed or dart behind curtains.

Were his words a ruse? Elizabeth wondered. Had they made too much noise? Or had the Popes looked for one of her people and found them missing, and two nights in a row? Her heart thudded, for messages in the night were rare and fearful. Or could the rumors be true? Could the queen's cancer have claimed her?

Kat had the good sense to pull her robe over her gown and muss her hair. Elizabeth did the same and poked her head around Kat's wide shoulder as she opened the door. Kat had smoothly slid the bolt out so he would not hear that the door had been locked. Elizabeth set her feet solidly and lifted her chin. No way Thomas Pope was getting into this room even with the door open.

"I thought I heard voices inside," he began, trying to dart a look past the two of them. He was in his night-robe, so perhaps he'd even been to bed. But Elizabeth knew instantly her sister lived. He was his usual brusque, meddling self, and he'd not dare that—not if Queen Mary had died. Unless, Elizabeth thought and her stomach cartwheeled, he believed Mary's half sister would never live to claim the throne.

"I can't sleep," she told him before Kat could reply. "Can't even breathe well with this swollen nose, my lord, and Kat keeps me good company talking of happier days. The message then?"

"Hmph. From your lawyer who oversees your estates clear from Stamford—William Cecil."

Her heart leapt, but she kept her voice even. "Is he well?"

"I warrant so, my lady. His man brought word that he will be here in the flesh to report on the state of your estates—rent rolls or some such—by midday tomorrow, and he hopes you might receive him. Always good to see a fellow exile, is it not?" he dared to add with a mocking grin that did not reach his eyes.

Elizabeth held her tongue but set down in her memory another mark against Sir Thomas Pope. Yet she was so relieved—thrilled—she would see Cecil that she even smiled at Pope before Kat firmly closed the door in his face and silently reshot the bolt.

"We're having a toast to the first good news I've heard in weeks," Elizabeth whispered to her little band as they emerged from hiding. She whirled once as if she were pirouetting in a pavane, her hands clasped together. "Kat, my favorite canary wine for all, but everyone must whisper till we're sure the queen's second-most favorite Pope is not lurking about in the halls. To Cecil coming to give us sound advice," she said quietly, lifting her goblet. She touched its rim to the one that the others, smiling, passed from hand to hand.

It hurt her nose every time she smiled, but it was worth it.

ELIZABETH TUDOR DRESSED FORMALLY in her second-best gown of blue brocade with embroidered underskirt and narrow neck ruff to greet Cecil and his two companions in the courtyard at midday next. She so seldom had visitors and wanted to let the loyal Cecil know she honored him. Besides, she had to do something to make up for a fat nose and black eye, which Meg's paste and Blanche Parry's oyster powder could barely conceal.

She knew the moment Cecil bowed low over her hand before he greeted the Popes that he would be the man for her as principal secretary when—if—she went to court as queen. His expression did not alter even when he saw her bruised countenance. She had learned many a wily political move on her own, but it was Cecil's counsel she trusted over that of anyone else, even through the blackest times of the Seymour scandal and the Wyatt mess. And now.

She knew he was concerned for her safety and that was really why he had come. She fully understood the rent rolls and the way he handled her business for her. So, not a half hour later, after he had refreshed himself and changed garments, she had Blanche, Lady Cornish, and Kat buffer the two of them. Standing before the big oriel window in the solar, she and Cecil turned their backs on the Popes as she pointed out the gardens while they quickly, briefly talked.

Without moving his head, his voice kept low, and his lips hardly moving, he asked, "Your face, Your Grace. That brazen bully Pope has not taken to striking our next queen?"

"This is the least of my problems. I ran into an obstacle—or two—at Hever."

"Hever? More news of poisoners there?"

"I must talk to you. My women will keep off the watchdogs after we dine. There is much to tell."

"Lord Carey was right to suggest I come. We shall make much of my meager report of your estates."

At dinner she went to school again, watching William Cecil. She reveled in the way he replied to each of Thomas Pope's inquiries but told him nothing, though she knew—Pope probably did too—that the lawyer had many friends and kept close ties with London doings. Cecil claimed that clear up in rustic Stamford he had heard naught but prices for wool and his young son Robert learning to talk, and he certainly hoped the queen's health was good. They drank to it.

And then, just when Elizabeth was about to make her move to get him alone, Cecil said, "I do hope Lady Cornish would not mind if you gave me a brief tour of her gardens, Your Grace. Late as it is in the season, I see the brick walls have sheltered a few of the last roses. Rather as they always did at Hampton Court, all those red and white roses, do you recall, my lord?" he asked Pope. But they were out of the room and down the hall with their servants sweeping cloaks around them and their entourage falling in behind before Sir Thomas could reply or Bea could so much as send for her cloak.

"Admirably done," Elizabeth told him with a smile. "I know you usually eschew such long speeches—about gardens and roses, at least."

"Right now we must both eschew any sort of talk but of this plot that threatens you."

"First, how does the queen, in truth, my lord? I cannot believe what I am told here."

"She fades and is delirious at times. Her belly tumor and pain grow. She has named you successor but refuses to send you the onyx coronation ring from off her finger until—until she can at least accept that she will die."

"We must all accept that we will die, Cecil."

"Aye, but I'll not have talk of it for you. Not at age twenty-five, on the cusp of your destiny. No damned poison plot shall sully or stop you, when so many of us rely on you to save this chaos Bloody Mary's made of England." His voice was more dark and bitter than she had ever heard it, but he shook his head as if to cast off his melancholy. "Now, tell me straight what you know."

They walked the grounds, pretending to admire an occasional late, leggy bloom. She saw Cecil become more and more disturbed—though he managed yet to look pleasantly bored—as she hurriedly told him what she had learned about the poison plot, and how. Farther back from the house, they walked Lady Cornish's knot garden, and Elizabeth pointed out its intricate patterns of box edges entwining designs of colored gravel and plants the frost had blasted while she talked of much else. They stopped but one moment to peer at the brass sundial, then moved on.

"I cannot believe my ears," he said, his voice as quiet and contained as hers. "Not only the risk, but that you would—and could—take it upon your person to ride out like some freebooter to Bushey and then Hever."

"I had to know. To stop it before it is too late. And somehow I must get to Leeds too."

"Too damned dangerous. When I wrote you of Waldegrave's Spanish ties, I did not fathom he was her spy there. I smell conspiracy."

"It was because it all began to add up that I had to act. I know you used to tell me 'When in doubt, do nothing,' my lord, but—"

"Hang what I used to tell you. You are on the threshold of ruling this realm, Your Grace, and they are desperate to stop you at the last."

"But who? *Sui bono,* as you say? Who is this woman, and why does she bear such deadly hatred for the Boleyns and those loyal to them? And I can hardly run to my sister for help. Last time I so much as hinted at poison in her presence, she exploded and accused me—and my mother . . ."

"I can imagine."

"And then, my lord, I know it's treason," she went on, her voice ever more passionate, "but what if Her Majesty herself stands behind this woman?"

She saw him shudder. He quickly pulled his cloak up tighter around his neck and beard, but he did not respond to that.

"Dear princess, the other reason I came was to warn you that Leeds, too, has dangerous foreign ties, as Catholic and convoluted as they come."

"The Spanish again, of course."

"The Irish. Sir Anthony St. Leger, Leeds's owner, is English, but he served your father as lord deputy of Ireland. King Henry gave him Leeds as a boon payment—a reward for his services."

"My father? And the Irish? Now there are two wild cards on the table when I have not yet discerned the rules of the game."

"But Anthony St. Leger was underhanded," he went on with his explanation.

"St. Anthony—that is part of his name?" she questioned, remembering the clue of St. Anthony's fire.

"What?"

"Nothing—not now. Say on."

"St. Leger somehow played both sides. Aye, he convinced the rebellious Irish to accept the occupant of the English throne as the Irish monarch. But he set himself up well in the process, double-dealing with the Tudors, becoming a true ally to the Irish, it was said—"

"Ah, finally we can join your conversation," Thomas Pope called out, as he and his lady determinedly plunged through Elizabeth's women, bouncing wide skirts and furred cloaks out of their way. "What is said, my Lord Cecil?"

"I was just musing aloud, Sir Thomas, about beehives like the fine-looking wicker ones Lady Cornish has in the corner," he said, pointing. "They are run just like the court, with a queen and busy, buzzing servants. But those servants need remember not only to honor the queen but the one who could be queen someday."

Thomas Pope stopped dead in his tracks and sputtered. Cecil stared him down. Elizabeth drew herself up short. Not only did she want to throttle Pope for interrupting them, but she had been so intent on Cecil's words she had not noted they had come this close to the hives. However cleverly Cecil had set the Pope back on his heel, she was piqued that he had so much as brought up bees and queens.

For the rest of an interminable quarter hour, Thomas Pope and his Lady Beatrice walked between her and Cecil. But Elizabeth knew when she bid her guest a good evening, he would not depart until he had told her the rest of what he'd come to say.

Chapter The Fourteenth

EMON JUICE, MILK, AND ANTIMONY," CECIL whispered to Elizabeth the next morning. He swirled the pale, green-hued ink in a small bottle he'd produced, literally, from up his sleeve.

The two of them sat side by side at a wide table in the solar, supposedly to review her rent rolls from Hatfield and Woodstock, two estates her father had left her, both of which had served as her rural prisons in her sister's reign. Sir Thomas and Bea sat in the room; she and Cecil made certain they could see them. Bea was embroidering, while Kat, Lady Blanche, and Lord and Lady Cornish cast hazard dice at a small corner table and Sir Thomas watched them—all of them.

Elizabeth took the quill Cecil offered her and used his ink. 'S blood! She watched while the air dried each word she wrote to make it quickly fade to nothing.

Invisible ink. She bit back a smile. If she ever needed advice on spies, she'd go to William Cecil too.

But how does one read it later? she wrote.

Heated against hot metal plate or shovel, he wrote back. *But just write fast.*

"Now, Your Grace," he said so all could hear, "let me take you step by step through the process of my men collecting the rent from your tenants, first at Woodstock and then Hatfield."

Frowning, Kat looked up at them, then quickly back to their game. She had taught Elizabeth to do her first sums, and no one knew better that the princess already kept a sharp eye and tight hand on her financial affairs. This chitchat was a bald ruse, but at least Sir Thomas didn't know it and Kat was getting clever enough not to show it.

"I'd like a look at the Hatfield figures when you get to them," Pope put in, making a big show of peering over Lord Cornish's shoulder at his throws of the dice on the painted board. "Just to be sure no one's cheating the Lady Elizabeth while she's in my charge."

"Fine. I'll let you know," Cecil said, but he was watching as Elizabeth swiftly sketched a clover and a heart with an arrow and two drops of blood. Then she wrote, *On She's veil. Could tie to poison arrow through Harry's man near Wiv. and poison clover at Hat.*

Clover could be shamrocks—Irish good luck, he wrote back.

"Are you following my percentages so far, Your Grace?" Cecil asked. "You do see if you are not careful, your Woodstock profits could take a tumble?"

"I see that. Let me copy some of these figures out for myself instead of having you keep the only set of records."

But, she wrote, *there was no one on your* sui bono *list to me who was Irish. And no Ir. tied to Queen C. of A.*

He responded, *Did I not have her old chamberlain, Sir Edward Ormonde, on that first C. of A. list? But he's long dead and left no direct heirs.*

Had to skim and burn letter, she wrote. *No doubt some Ir. hated Boleyns or fear a Prot. queen.*

"You've got the figures right," Cecil said, "but now we must plan to protect your future interests. Why don't you copy these rent rates down?"

Remember the Ir. Butler family? Elizabeth wrote. *Twice, Bols. offended them. My father took a Butler's title away from him, then after Anne Bol. was promised to a Butler, she caught the king's eye and betrothal broken.*

In both cases, James Butler, he wrote, *9th Earl of Ormonde. He inherited title of C of A.'s Ormonde, but was only distantly related. Can't be the Butlers. J. dead and his daughter—bastard daughter—went back to Ire.*

Another dead end, Elizabeth thought, masking the stab of disappointment that came all the sharper following a moment of exhilaration. Then she recalled what else she must ask Cecil.

Did you find out what Sarah Scottwood—Scutea—looked like? she scribbled. *Span. ties—the herbs—her father's desire for vengeance for C. of A.—all fit.*

"Are you on the Hatfield reckoning yet, Cecil?" Thomas Pope asked.

As intense as they had become, neither of them had seen him coming. Elizabeth slowly slid her ruffled wrist over her last words to blot whatever might remain. She was not certain if Cecil had time to read them or not. She reached for the sheet with the columns of numbers Cecil had first sat down with.

"Nearly so, Sir Thomas," Cecil muttered, smoothly switching pens and ink while he shuffled papers.

"The Lady Elizabeth has gone white as a bleached sheet," Pope observed. "I warrant your steep lawyer's fee has unsettled her, Cecil." Pope grinned to show his yellow teeth.

"Nonsense," Elizabeth countered, gripping the edge of the table with both hands in her frustration at Pope's eternal butting in. With him hovering this close, any further talk with Cecil was hopeless, so she'd have to make another plan.

"I do have a slight headache," she said, "from staring at all these numbers in the bright sun. My Lord Cecil, why don't you go over the Hatfield figures with Lord Thomas and I shall get them from him later? I will take a brief respite upstairs, then join you before you must ride out later."

Cecil rose to his feet with her. Her ladies and Lord Cornish stood. Bea's embroidery tumbled to the floor, and she stooped to retrieve it. As if they yet spoke invisible words between them, Elizabeth's eyes met Cecil's. He nodded—or was that the hint of a forbidden bow?—as if to promise a final conversation before they parted. But with everyone swarming them again, Elizabeth feared it was up to her to be certain it was a privy conversation.

"THIS TAKES SHEER GALL," Kat muttered as she helped Elizabeth and Meg switch garments with each other.

"It takes sheer gall to hope for the throne—and to survive to get it," Elizabeth replied, but Kat wasn't to be dissuaded.

"It's one thing to have Meg attired like you—behind the curtains under the covers at night," Kat continued, "but *you* becoming her?" Kat shot Meg a swift, sideways glance. Though she had the more intricate task of donning elaborate garments, they were puddled at her feet while, in just her shift, she, too, helped Elizabeth.

"Don't fret," the princess insisted. "I have played many a part, and this will have to work if I'm to see Cecil alone. Just be certain he gets the note and that the Popes don't see it. And don't you be whispering to him, Kat, or you'll give us all away. I'll just go down the back stairs and out as if I'm gathering the last of the herbs. There," she concluded, flouncing wrinkled skirts, "that will have to do."

Over Meg's best smock they had laced and pinned her other garments: a russet kirtle, a sleeveless, front-laced blue bodice that still gaped a bit, a pair of sleeves, and a brown doublet that buttoned up the front. The petticoats seemed thin and light, as if she went half naked, but she'd get used to them. All that was covered by a grass-stained work apron.

As she bent to regarter drooping stockings and shove her feet into the girl's blunt-toed, scuffed shoes, Elizabeth noted that her legs and feet must be longer than Meg's. She silently vowed that one of the first things she would do if she ever went to London as queen was to buy her household decent garments—not to mention herself after having to wear last season's mended pieces all these years in exile.

"All right," she said with a nod, "fetch Ned from the hall."

Meg scrambled to cover her shift with a big shawl, but he did not so much as look her way when Kat let him in. He seemed speechless at the princess's transformation, but he soon found his tongue.

"Kat," he began, walking around Elizabeth in a tight circle, "it will take more than that broad-brimmed hat to pull this off. Her red hair's got more gold in it than Meg's. We'd best cover it with a kerchief."

"I don't do that," Meg protested.

Ned still ignored her as he took the kerchief Kat extended to him from one of Elizabeth's coffers, balled it up in his hands, then rubbed it on the floor in the corner of the room. He displayed it with a flourish, wrinkled and dirtied.

Elizabeth saw Meg's face become a thundercloud; the girl's fists shot to her hips. "You just listen here, Master Topside—"

"Do not start anew, any of you," Elizabeth interrupted. "Kat has to go down to tell Cecil my headache is not better and slip him the note. And I—that is, Meg—must be clear out to the edge of the forest when he tries to find me. Ned, is Jenks ready?"

"Aye," he assured her, as he dared to knock Kat's and Meg's hands away from Elizabeth's hair to handle the kerchief himself. Now both of the women were hot at him, but he went on blithely. "I used to make the lads in the company look like lasses, so this is easy as pie." He flapped the kerchief open, halved it neatly to a triangle, and tied it around Elizabeth's long hair, which the fuming Kat lifted off her neck and shoulders for him.

Elizabeth glanced in the looking glass Kat held and nodded at what she saw. A strange, even shocking, sight, but necessary. Clapping Meg's broad-brimmed, floppy hat on her head over the kerchief, she grabbed the herb basket and made for the door.

Downstairs, she dare not go through the kitchen but ducked out the side entrance and went out back through the gardens she had walked with Cecil yesterday. Bending here and there to pull up a dried flower in case anyone was watching, she made her way through the postern gate, still inside the moat. At least most of the household would be assembling in the courtyard to see Cecil ride out and should not pay a bit of heed to Meg Milligrew.

Jenks, good man that he was, had positioned the rowboat for her and was waiting directly across the moat with his horse. She tossed her basket in the boat and, awkward at having do this for herself, rowed across to him, cursing under her breath when the oars went askew and she got a splinter in her ungloved hands.

She almost ordered Jenks to help her, but she had told him not to emerge from the fringe of trees unless someone tried to stop her. As she tugged the bow of the boat up on the edge of the grass, her appreciation of Meg's independence grew. Indeed, what would it be like to be one of her people, a commoner, just plain Bess Tudor, the herbalist? As Ned had hastily suggested, she stared at the ground as she walked, slightly swinging her basket, and shuffled through dried leaves.

"Pretty good," Jenks observed, "but Meg can row that boat like a seaman."

Elizabeth narrowed her eyes at him but said only, "Do you think I have time to walk to the fork of the road? I can hardly be seen riding with you or taking your horse."

"I took Meg on a ride afore," he admitted, standing stiff as if he expected her to scold him for that. "If we go through the forest—"

"Mistress Meg!" a voice behind her called.

'S blood, caught already? Keeping her hat brim pulled low, she turned to see Sam, Lord Cornish's chief groom, beckoning to her from across the moat. Since Jenks stood in the shadows, perhaps Sam didn't see him.

"Saw you go out," Sam shouted, "and I'm free for a bit, since the guests are riding off without an escort. Just give that boat a bit of a shove back, eh?"

Elizabeth held her ground, though her instinct was to move farther into the forest. When she did not answer straightaway, he went on. "I told you next time you went out in the forest for mushrooms, I'd go along. The princess's man there's not going with you, is he?"

Elizabeth cursed under her breath again. He could see Jenks. And Meg had been out in the woods? Gathering mushrooms? And with all her duties had the time to lead this man on, a man she could not have known before last week? She must be on her way before Cecil rode out. Worse, she had not intended to have to talk like the girl.

"Aye, Sam, walnut gathering, we are," she called across the moat and waved the way she had seen Meg do, all limp wrist and quick motion. "The princess sent us both, and quick, she said."

She knew she sounded wrong, but she wasn't sure just how. Before she ever tried this again, she'd pay more heed to Meg, get Ned to tutor her too. She turned in a flurry of skirts and darted into the forest with Jenks pulling his horse behind her.

CECIL ROLLED THE NOTE KAT ASHLEY had given him into a tiny ball between his thumb and first finger. He had managed to skim it, then surreptitiously dropped it in the moat as he rode out, grateful he could trust his own people—if he could. And he had wanted to see Her Grace privily to ask if she could trust hers. At least now, as foolhardy as this scheme seemed, he would have the chance.

A few minutes later, when he spotted the dead chestnut tree at the fork in the road just beyond the first big bend, he told his three men, "I need a few moments alone here." He drew his horse up hard and dismounted.

"Your nervous stomach again, my lord?" his man Givens called to him. They were all obviously surprised and trying not to seem so.

"Just hold the horses—and off the road should anyone else come through. I shall be back directly."

He walked west, as the princess's note had said. If she was not at the clearing by the brook, he was prepared to wait till doomsday. But he was not prepared for the common lass who emerged from the deeper forest, until he saw the tilt of the pointed chin and the flash of those dark Boleyn eyes. So, he thought, relieved, perhaps this scheme was not so foolhardy after all, if she could pull off this ruse.

"My princess," he said, trying to control his lawyer's face not to show either astonishment or amusement at her appearance or the rude basket on her arm. With a sweep of his hat, head bowed, he went down on one knee in the sodden moss. He had seen her man, holding a horse, but he kept his watchful distance. At least she had not come out here alone. She might be daring and desperate, he thought, but never broken.

She came closer and touched his shoulder lightly with her free hand to indicate he should rise. "In these times—in this attire—my Cecil," she said, as he stood, "between us, let there be no ceremony. I have so yearned to speak freely with you."

"I am ever at your command, Your Grace. But should we be interrupted again somehow, let me first warn you of something that both your cousin Harry and I have been concerned about, and I did not find an opportunity to write before or tell."

"We were interrupted when I was asking you to describe Sarah Scottwood's countenance."

"It all, mayhap, ties in. I glimpsed your Meg Milligrew only from afar when Ned Topside pointed her out to me, but—"

"But what does Meg have to do with it? And you sought out Ned? He said naught of that."

"He spoke with me rather. Your Grace, as best I can discover from contacts in London who have described Sarah Scottwood's countenance and form, as you instructed," he began carefully, then just let it all tumble out, "Meg Milligrew could actually *be* Sarah Scottwood, *née* Scutea, an herbalist tied to the old, loyal Spanish party that vowed vengeance on your mother and you, no doubt all the Boleyns."

Her head jerked up. He could see she struggled for control. "But—but, then, I resemble Sarah, too, my lord. Ned told you why I really took Meg on—because she can counterfeit my presence should I need a decoy—or the other way around, like today?"

He nodded. "A clever chess move, Your Grace, but perhaps on your girl's part too. Ned says she has a mysterious past and just arrived at your aunt's and keeps conveniently discovering helpful things so you come to rely on her. Lord Carey told me he was to question the girl again at Wivenhoe before she disappeared. But my point is, you must be careful, very careful, because someone you cannot trust could have been planted close to you."

He fingered the meager dried herbs she had laid in Meg's basket, before emphasizing, "Planted by someone who does not wish you well."

She dropped—or threw, he was not sure—her basket on the ground. "But it is Bea Pope I believe has been planted, and by my sister. Meg has helped me again and again, even as she did my aunt."

"Your Grace, I am going to admit something to illustrate my point. I pray you will not be out of sorts over this. Cora Crenshaw, the cook at Hatfield—"

"You accuse Cora too?"

"Only of being my eyes and ears there to be certain you were safe and to keep a good watch in the kitchens that no one does—did—to your food and drink what happened to your aunt's. I still pay Cora Crenshaw to keep a watch over you, for such like reasons."

"Ah," she said only, assessing him anew with those sharp eyes. "For such like reasons—*sui bono,* master lawyer." Her expression made him want to fidget or back away, but he did neither. Still, he swallowed hard enough to bob his Adam's apple as she went on, "Then, my lord, I shall keep an eye on Meg and others I tend to trust because they serve me well—yet without them, I am so wretchedly alone."

Her voice broke on that; he knew he included him in her mistrust now. Still, he dared to plunge on. "And I believe the others who have been assembled to help you years ago"—here he glanced at her man in the distance—"should be scrutinized closer too. Even once-loyal folk can be pushed or priced."

"Jenks?" she demanded. "And Kat Ashley, of course? Dear Kat?" she taunted sarcastically, hitting his shoulder with a balled fist so hard he had to step back. "What about

Ned Topside, the wily actor? And the list must include you, of course, who has stood by as my adviser I trust enough to meet out here."

She began to pace and gesture wildly, just as they said old King Henry did when he was vexed—before he got too fat and his leg too full of gangrene to move. Cecil swallowed hard again.

"I regret, Your Grace," he said, feeling he was in the docket at his own treason trial, "that I stand here like a harbinger from hell to croak bad news, but in your tenuous position, especially now so close to the throne as Queen Mary weakens, you can trust no one. The time is too ripe, the odds too high."

"Lecture me then, master lawyer, and quickly," she ordered, flinging out an arm as she paced past him again. "Build your case against Jenks—who can dissemble nothing and would die for me—and Kat, who is like a mother to me. And against you, of course. Say on."

"Jenks came as a mere lad to you, I believe, from the household of the Lord Thomas Seymour, who was nearly your destruction."

Her skirts swung as she halted before him. Her porcelain complexion blanched, then flushed. Cecil had long suspected she had actually loved the seductive, traitorous Seymour.

"My Lord Seymour is long dead," she said, her voice harsh with barely leashed passion. "What in heaven's name could Jenks have to do with all that now? You refer, I warrant, to the fact some men fanatically loyal to Tom Sey-

mour thought I deserted him and let him go to the block?
Well, he deserted me first, and I had to save myself. There
was no help for it. So Jenks is innocent, master lawyer, of
whatever dire, convoluted motives you ascribe to him. You
have no case against the lad. And Kat? What crazed thing
will you say about my loyal Kat? Well?"

"When your enemies had Kat Ashley in the Tower during the Seymour situation, they merely threatened to torture
her—merely showed her the instruments—and she con-
fessed everything about her being a go-between for Tom
Seymour and you."

Her nostrils flared. He was walking on eggshells now, he
knew it. But she had to be made more cautious, protected.
He had long advised her just to sit tight, hold on, and her
destiny would come to her. In this treacherous poison plot
that reached, perhaps, clear to the palace, he knew she had
chosen to act, but it was deadly dangerous. He wanted to
scare her into being more defensive, not going on the offen-
sive.

She stood, hands on her hips, staring at him down her
long nose. Her voice came at him dart-tipped, but entirely
under control now. "And you fault her for that? I do not.
The Tower is the most fearsome place on earth, my lord. I
can testify to that."

"But I am only saying, Katherine Ashley gave you up
quickly to Queen Mary's men and hurt you as a result.
What else did she promise them, under duress, to be so
quickly freed and released back to you then?"

"Hardly to report to the queen what I do in secret—and

never to let someone poison me years later. She's had a hundred, nay, a thousand chances to betray or dispatch me and has done nothing but protect and coddle me. If Kat's guilty, my lord, it is of worrying overmuch and scolding—treating me as if I still toddled about in leading strings. And Ned Topside? He only saved Harry's life."

"Oh, I give you that he came along on that road and appeared to save Harry's life, but what if he did that to ingratiate himself with Harry and the Boleyns—then you? Or mayhap he expected to find—or deliver—a corpse to your aunt and then have access to her. He either did not know it was you at Wivenhoe or learned too late to get to you— or to make a second attempt on Harry's life. Then, when he would have found a way to get to you again, you actually summoned him. He in turn tries to throw doubt on the others, like Meg—"

"You are demented. Ned has been alone with me twice and done naught but help me when he could have handed me over to the enemy or done me in."

"But your earlier letter gave me the impression you feared that this She was enjoying tormenting you—playing with you cat and mouse—until the time she prefers to strike. So she might have told her informant or liaison to string you along—to bring you to her. I will find out more information about the Irish ties, but until I do you must not continue to trust your people so wholeheartedly and under no circumstances go to Leeds."

"Master Cecil, I shall do now—and ever—what I must do."

He merely made a stiff half bow, though he wanted to shout and pound tree trunks at her obstinacy. "I am glad to hear you can vouch for all your privy plot council, Your Grace, for that is clever and careful, as you must be. Marry, you must!"

"And you, clever Cecil? Should I not trust you either?" she goaded, pointing her finger nearly in his face. "I believe I asked you to give me evidence against yourself too."

"Very well, Your Grace. I am vaunting ambitious—I plead guilty to that—ambitious for myself, my house, but most of all for the rightful queen I want to serve. This is why I came to Ightham, why I bide my time with my family and farm in the countryside—to wait to serve you."

His pulse pounded. He could barely catch his breath; he knew his usually well-modulated voice rose and quavered. Before he knew he would say more, he blurted, "And I will not have some vengeful poisoner attack you at the last minute and snatch my dreams away."

Tears stung his eyes, blurring his vision. He was aghast he had lost control. But, with her, perhaps it was that moment that saved him and strengthened their unspoken bond.

"Then we are agreed," she declared, "for She will not snatch my dreams either!"

Though afoot in the dank woods in stained, common clothes, she had never looked more a queen to him.

Chapter The Fifteenth

I MUST GET TO LEEDS CASTLE," ELIZABETH told Kat when she returned from her covert meeting with Cecil. "It's a risk, but one that must be taken, and soon."

Kat's forehead clenched and her lips pursed hard, but she said naught as she helped Elizabeth divest herself of Meg's garments.

"Cecil says that Leeds's owner, Sir Anthony St. Leger," Elizabeth went on, "has tight Catholic and Irish ties. Like Hever, Leeds was a place my mother loved, for my father once brought her there in great triumph. The poisoner revels in defiling places dear to the Boleyns. And since I overheard at Hever that She is intent on destruction there, St. Leger might be housing her at his castle. She must have gone to Leeds!"

"Gone to sit there like a spider, just waiting for you to get snared in her web," Kat muttered, as she gathered up the garments.

"But nothing risked, nothing gained, even if that risk must be in secret—even if I must appear to be doing nothing. The poisoner must be stopped for good."

Despite her brave words, she felt her resolve waver. But she could not hide or hunker down here or even back at Hatfield like some scared rabbit—a rabbit She could probably poison if she put her mind to it. This plan was perilous, considering only Ned and Jenks would be with her, but that could have advantages too. She must depend on the few faithful people she had gathered about her. Suddenly, she hated Cecil: He had made her feel more beleaguered and alone than ever by throwing suspicion on her staff, even Kat. Elizabeth studied the older woman through her eyelashes and slitted lids, then decided to trust her.

"New, more-bold tactics will throw them off guard at Leeds, my Kat," she rushed on as if she were trying to convince herself. "I will not enter the enemy camp at night this time. I'm going to have Ned write a short play, and he, Jenks, and I shall invade Leeds in broad daylight, yet disguised, a small company of players to perform for them. Well, do not gape at me like that. All players' companies have girlish-looking lads for the women's parts."

"Your success garbed as Meg has gone to your head!" Kat declared as she bent over to fan out Elizabeth's petticoats for her to step into. "And now you'll be a woman grown, playing a lad, playing a lass? Who would believe it?"

"Exactly." She put her hand on Kat's back and stepped

into her garments. "They will never suspect. But I'll still let Ned talk our way in so I can keep in the background."

"You?" Kat grunted, lacing her petticoats. "You, in the background?"

"I did so when I visited my aunt."

"Only till you took to digging up the dead and scrapping with a wench who killed herself. Lovey, you've had to do too much thinking and agonizing over this, and it's addling your wits. Queen Mary's keeping you in rural exile these years has hardly kept you in the background. I've heard," she whispered with a wink, "that true English courtiers are just waiting for the final downturn of her health to flock to your side."

"You've heard such from whom?"

She looked guilty, the cat with the cream on her whiskers. "Why, Cecil, of course," she blustered. "You think you are the only one can corner him for privy talk?"

Elizabeth put her hands to her forehead to massage away hovering head pain. Her closest people were all protective but sometimes seemed to conspire. They had chinks in their armor, but if she trusted no one as Cecil said, how could she survive?

Dear Lord in heaven, she prayed, *keep me safe and sane. I am going mad with fear and doubt.*

"I admit it, Kat," she said softly. "I feel beset on every side, swarmed and stung." She didn't know why she had put it that way, *swarmed and stung.* A fearsome memory flew at her, but she shoved it back. "But I am going—

somehow—to survive by stopping this poison plot, no matter what others want or will for me. It is *my* will that
matters—mine!" she cried, thudding a fist to her breast-
bone.

Kat had moved forward, arms outstretched, as if she
would embrace her, but at that imperious tone she jerked to
a halt. She looked uncertain whether to curtsy or cry. For
one moment they stared at each other like strangers.

"Help me finish dressing," Elizabeth ordered, her voice a
cold command. "I must find Ned. Meanwhile, you will
fetch Meg here to wait for me. And tell her, I do not want
to see Sam from the stables hanging on her petticoats."

"What? Sam, the groom? I don't believe it."

"Nor do I." Elizabeth's voice came muffled from under
her bodice as Kat pulled it down over her head, then began
to lace it the rest of the way up the back. "I don't know
when she found the time."

"Nay, 'tisn't a question of time. Meg doesn't give a fig for
anyone but Ned. Pity, since it's cow-eyed Jenks been hanging on her every word, so that's a pretty pickle you've got to
solve—"

Elizabeth pulled away and spun to face her.

"I am going to solve *nothing* that petty but will command
them all to stop it, just stop it," she cried, pacing and gesturing with both hands. "Ned cares naught for Meg but to
teach her to ape my speech and bearing, and Jenks—Jenks
cares only for horses and me. This is a time for logic, not
wild emotions, especially personal ones!"

Kat gave her that all too familiar squinty stare, as if to

ask who was the pot calling the kettle black. Elizabeth knew her moods swung and her temper seethed, but she could not rein them in. But she alone had a sound excuse. No one understood her, and she might as well just face down that poisoner alone. Yanking her snood from Kat's hands, she fastened it in her hair herself as she stormed from the room.

ELIZABETH HAD CALMED HERSELF by the time she found Ned in Lord Cornish's library downstairs. She followed his voice along the hallway, for he was declaiming a speech her grandfather, King Henry VII, supposedly gave at Bosworth Field when he seized England for the Tudors to end the War of the Roses. The monologue was from a drama called *Triumph at Bosworth,* which he had done sections from the other night for the Cornishes as well as Sir Thomas and the overly impressed, applauding Bea. Now he evidently did not even hear Elizabeth when she opened the door, stepped in, and quietly closed it behind her.

She hated to interrupt a man so intense, so possessed, but as soon as he went down on one knee to pluck the crown Richard II had lost in a thornbush, she loudly cleared her throat.

"Forget Bosworth," she ordered. "We're going to Leeds."

"Now? Tonight?" He rose but nettled her by going on with his playacting to pretend to place the rescued crown on his brow with a flourish. When she smacked his elbow, his distant gaze focused on her at last.

"No, but soon," she said, starting to pace again. She could feel ideas and passions boiling in her, rattling the lid of her composure again. "We must get into Leeds to capture and question the poisoner—if She's there. As soon as you can, pen me a brief play our little company of you, me, and Jenks can offer to give for Lord St. Leger there—something, I'm afraid, that must be pro-Catholic and pro-Queen Mary. Of dire necessity, we shall be walking into a bed of vipers, anti-Boleyn Irish who may be tied yet in loyalty to Catherine of Aragon or even the Butlers, whom the Boleyns insulted twice—"

"Whoa!" he interrupted, mimicking pulling back on the reins. "You've left me in your dust. What of all that is to be in the script? And you'll play what part? Mayhap you had best write it."

"*You* write it; I shall amend it," she ordered, coming to a stop so fast her skirts belled out around her. She pointed her finger at him as her voice rose. "And I will brook no scenes where actors go behind their mistress's back to consult with lawyers, nor ones where a princess's staff carry on secret romantic triangles, if you catch my drift, Edward Thompson, alias Ned Topside, alias King Henry the Seventh and whatever other parts you choose to assume."

"Now, that was quite a speech," he dared, grandly sweeping both arms outward.

She spun away, went out, and slammed the door. But he had the mettle to open it and hie himself after her down the long hall.

"Do you want someone serving you who cannot think on

his own?" he demanded, keeping up with her brisk pace. "Do you want a mere puppet show and not a play, Your Grace?"

"Keep your voice down and your damned cocky spirits too."

She darted a sideways glance at him. He looked abashed.

"I shall, truly," he vowed and hung his head.

She stopped to face him, going one step up on the staircase so she could look down at him. She could predict the impudent rejoinder he longed to give: *You have not kept your voice down.* But he was wily enough to bite back those words for some far gentler.

"I did not mean to displease Your Grace."

"Of course I do not want merely to pull puppet strings— not exactly."

"So you once made me believe. I was to play a sort of fool, you promised, but never truly be one."

"Granted."

"Then grant me one moment more and do not scold, I pray you, even if my upbraiding is richly deserved." He kept his voice lowered and touched her elbow beseechingly to steer her back into the library and close the door behind them.

She folded her arms across her bodice. "Say on, Ned."

"I know you have not approved of how—how amusing the Lady Beatrice Pope finds me. I admit I have cultivated that."

"Bea Pope? I was not even referring to Bea Pope!" Elizabeth felt jolted again. But, of course, she had other things on her mind—important things—so she must have overlooked such little *affaires de coeur* in her people.

"You will not tell me," she choked out, "that you have become Bea Pope's paramour."

"By hell's gates, no. Never. I adore but one woman, yet from afar, however much we argue, one above my star, whom I will serve forever if she will allow it, I swear it."

His words rhymed like pure poetry. His warm voice roughened so convincingly, and his eyes were as green as wet emeralds. She nodded to encourage him to go on.

"I must tell you, Your Grace, that the Lady Beatrice has confided to me that she must needs see her sister in Maidstone again soon."

"Ah. When?"

"That is the sticking point, what made me suspect her all the more as the poisoner's informant here in your household, one of them at least. The lady is not certain what day she will leave—when she is summoned, as she put it, but she is packing now. And Maidstone is on the very road and close to Leeds."

"Indeed it is. Well done, Ned. Let me know the moment she leaves. If I had a man to spare, I would have her followed. And, whatever you do, keep our plans for this play and the stage we intend for it a secret from everyone right now."

"To Leeds and soon," he said and pantomimed lifting a goblet to drink a health. He threw back his head as if to quaff it.

"Your new-won Bosworth crown just tipped off your head, sire," she said as she went out and closed the door.

THE WINDOW IN THE BEDCHAMBER and withdrawing room Lord St. Leger had given her surveyed the six-acre lake that surrounded Leeds Castle. Today the water looked as bog-dark as the sky from a storm sweeping in from the Channel. She stopped her preparations to lean her forehead against the cool glass, catching her unveiled reflection for one moment in its makeshift mirror.

She could hear Colum McKitrick and his henchmen's cries echoing from the inner courtyard as they battered each other with their staves to control the leather stoolball. In Gaelic they shouted, making her yearn for her childhood days at Carrick-on-Sur. Ordinarily, she wouldn't care a whit if the lackbrains killed each other, especially after they had made such a ruin of executing Lord Carey, but she still needed them for Elizabeth of England's coming judgment day. Colum—and now he'd probably be a filthy, bruised, sweat-soaked mess—was to escort her to Ightham Forest this afternoon, rain or not.

She sighed, glancing at herself in the wan mirror the panes of glass made. She loved to look at her countenance in window reflections but usually at night. Since it was not a true looking glass, the pits and marks from the pox, the ruination of her beauty, never showed. That made her think of times past again, but she must think only of now.

Still gloved, she returned to kneading the sticky paste of aconite, hellebore, and banewort-tainted honey in a wooden trencher. These pellets must be stronger than those that had felled the rabbits at Hatfield, for the prey was much bigger this time. And red-haired, she thought, and laughed aloud. With the help of her informer who lived so close to the princess, it would bring great joy to leave the corpse lying right in the bitch Boleyn's own bed.

ELIZABETH CAME BACK INTO her chamber so quietly that Meg, staring out the window at the graying sky, one shoulder slumped against the frame, did not hear her. Kat had gone out somewhere, so they were alone. The princess frowned at the girl's back, wondering if she were longing for Ned or tended darker thoughts. But no, though Cecil could be trusted to send her another swift letter as he had promised, he had no right to judge poor Meg.

"A penny," Elizabeth said quietly.

Meg turned so fast her curtsy went atilt. "For my thoughts? I warrant they're not worth even that much to you, Your Grace."

"They are worth a great deal." Elizabeth sat on the bench by the low-burning hearth and patted the cushion next to hers. Looking suddenly wary, Meg came over and sat.

"I suppose," Meg said, using her crisp London enunciation Ned was so pleased with lately, "you mean my knowledge of the herbs. I wish my own thoughts were worth something to me too. I mean, the past I can't recall."

Elizabeth turned to face her squarely. She knew such worries weighed on Meg's mind, but she hadn't expected her to bring it up herself right now.

"That's partly what I wish to speak about," she explained, leaning forward. The girl nodded, wide-eyed, looking totally trusting. Surely such sincerity could not be a sham.

"Do you think, Meg, that if you were asked specific questions, not necessarily about herbs, it might help you to recall your life before you were kicked by the horse and taken in at my Aunt Mary's? For example, has another name ever struck you as sounding familiar, or are you sure you have recalled your real one? And concerning places you've lived—though Ned says you didn't sound as if you came from there at first—have you ever been to London?"

The girl shook her head, then shrugged. "If Ned says no, I guess not. He's so awfully clever. We've agreed now if I work hard on imitating the way you talk, he'll do parts for me in return. He can do voices that sound Italian"—she began to tick off on her fingers—"Froggie—French, I mean—Spaniard, Irish, and Scots, so witty."

"Spanish and Irish too? He's not done those for me. But let's see about names then. Turn your back just as you did when I first came in. Close your eyes and let me say some names to see if any of them . . . well, strike you." She hadn't meant to proceed this way, but she felt guilty setting this up with the girl staring at her so eagerly.

"If'n—I mean, if—you say so, Your Grace." Dutifully, she turned away, her backbone stiff, her shoulders straight.

"Penelope," Elizabeth began, pausing after the name. "Anne, Katherine or Kate. Gwendolyn, Cynthia, Eleanor or Nell. Jane, Philadelphia. Diana. Frances, Sarah. How does Sarah sound?"

"I like it—Sarah."

"Think carefully. Have you ever heard of Sarah Scottwood or Sarah Scutea?"

Meg spun around, her face hopeful. "Scutea's a funny name. And is that two Sarahs or one? I think I knew some Scottwoods once, but I'm not sure. Why are you looking at me like that, Your Grace? Is this a trick? Is that name Scutea Spanish, then?"

Elizabeth sighed and flopped her hands in her lap. "I'll tell you straight, Meg. My Lord Cecil says a girl your age with a similar description was reared by an apothecary in London. A girl by the name of Sarah Scottwood, who used to be Sarah Scutea and disappeared about the time her father died last year and hasn't been seen since."

"God save us! And he—you—think she—that woman is me?"

"Do you think it could be?"

Tears filled her eyes, and she blinked them back to mat her pale lashes in clumps. "And what's the rest of it, then, Your Grace?" she asked. "Is she one of them loyal to Queen

Mary you mentioned—ones with Spanish ties? And if her sire was an apothecary, you think I know the poisons, that I harmed your aunt and now—"

"No, Meg, I am saying no such thing."

"I keep trying to win Ned over, but he's against me, isn't he? Talk about poisoners. Ned tries to poison your good opinion of me, and I'm just trying to please everyone—you, Ned, Lord Cecil too."

"Meg, I do not think you are a poisoner, and Ned has not said such either."

She dashed a tear away and asked, "And Master Cecil?"

Elizabeth heaved a sigh of exasperation and exhaustion. "Cecil advised me to be certain everyone near me was to be trusted. Stop crying this instant. If you are going to act my counterpart—even in London someday perhaps—you must learn to control your damned tears." Elizabeth ended with a sniff herself.

'S blood, all this was getting to her. Even if Queen Mary died, she'd be a ranting, raving bedlamite by then, not to mention that she couldn't sleep or eat well anymore. Her long-tended and hard-won control of her temper had gone to hell in a handcart. She always wavered, forgiving Ned when she meant to rebuke him roundly, believing this girl when she could be someone from the very bosom of the enemy camp. Thank God, Kat and Jenks were beyond suspicion—surely they were.

Meg stopped crying. She sniffled and started to wipe her nose on her sleeve before Elizabeth handed her a handkerchief. She nodded and honked at first, once, before she began to mimic the short puffs Elizabeth made. Elizabeth could not help it; her heart went out to the girl.

"May I say something else, Your Grace?"

"Of course."

"When you said that Sarah Scottwood, I liked the sound of it. But I don't think I ever even saw a big city, and I'd be scared to death to so much as set foot in London, though I'd go there with you if you want."

"Thank you, Meg."

"But what I want to say is that—even if I was this Sarah with all she might have done, I recall none of it, so it isn't the real me now, not Meg Milligrew. If I ever was this Sarah, she's gone, just like she's dead, because I am loyal to you now, Your Grace. I believe that, but can you please believe it too?"

"Truly. And if we do ever learn that you were once someone else, we shall just rely on this Meg to see it through, the Meg my aunt knew and loved and trusted. And I too."

Elizabeth pressed her hands over Meg's fists, which clenched the handkerchief on her knee. Though amazingly she didn't show it, the girl was trembling so hard, her fear vibrated clear up Elizabeth's arms to make them tingle.

NED WAS SLUMPED OVER, writing the play for the princess, when Lord Cornish's man opened the library door without knocking. Ned stayed his scratching quill.

"Visitors at the gate for you, Master Topside."

"For me? No one in these parts knows me."

"A ragtag group of players. One says he's kin to you—Wat Thompson."

Ned banged his fist down so hard that ink slopped and blotting sand flew. "At the *front* gate?" he demanded before recalling there was but one gate in this moated manor.

He knew now he'd made a massive mistake to so grandiosely announce to his uncle that he was going to serve the princess. They'd obviously tracked him through hearing where she lodged. Who knew what mischief they intended? No doubt they were down on their luck and wanted to perform for a hefty fee or expected him to dole out what coin Her Grace had entrusted to him. And after Uncle Wat and Grand Rand—the sodomites—had failed to use his prodigious talents and had treated him instead like . . . like one of the lads.

"I'll walk out to see them straightaway," he said. But he took his time, going to his room far back in the warren of small servants' chambers to wash his face and don a fur-lined cape and his only plumed hat. His feet dragged until he emerged from the inner court. Then he strode directly out toward them, under the arched gate, across the draw-bridge, and over the moat where they waited, all four of them, hats in hands before Wat's horse and the cart and mule, laden with scenery and costumes that looked to be a jumbled mess. No one could ever pack their goods like he could.

He silently cursed not only them for coming, but himself for having to blink back tears that prickled behind his eyeballs but did not fall.

"Uncle, Randall, lads," he greeted them formally with a mere inclination of his head. The breeze blew the plume before his face to tickle his nose and make him want to sneeze. Tossing his head to clear the plume, he stopped a good ten feet from them. "Will you tell me you just happened to be in the neighborhood?" he challenged.

"We only wanted to tell you in person, nephew," Wat said, stepping slightly closer, "that we are very proud indeed of your well-deserved success, are we not?"

The others chimed in. Ned kept his narrowed eyes on his uncle's countenance. They were down on their luck, for certain. And they had not replaced him yet.

"We had just hoped," Wat went on, "for old time's sake, in passing through, we would offer to feature you for the princess, your patron, in a piece. However bright you shine in her royal eyes, my boy, we could make you glitter like a gem set in golden filigree."

"That is kind. But I did the king's speeches in *Triumph at Bosworth* for Her Grace and the entire household the other night. I may be called her fool at times, but I play the best parts now. And I'm writing a play for her at her special, fond bequest."

"Ah, and most excellent it will be too, I warrant," Grand Rand dared to put in. Ned still did not look his way. Their betrayal pierced him again. True, he had sworn to his father on his deathbed he'd give The Queen's Country Players his loyalty, but Uncle Wat had gone back on his word to be a second father to him. He owed them nothing now but his disdain.

"I regret I cannot ask you to stay and play for the household here," he informed them loftily. "The princess is under some constraints by her guardian not to entertain overmuch, not with her sister mayhap on her deathbed."

His voice caught again. His father's wan, wasted face came to him so very real, and his uncle's face so resembled his father's.

"I see," Wat said quietly.

"You have heard of that?" Ned plunged on. "That I soon may serve not an exiled princess but the queen?"

Wat and Rand exchanged lightning-quick glances that said it all. They were willing to lick his boots to curry her favor, and, as usual, they would use and abuse him to get what they wanted.

"Of course," Ned added, "I will ask the Cornishes to send out beer and food to stay you for your continued journey, especially since Ightham is so distant from the other places you might play. And may I suggest a venue," he said as the errant thought hit him. Aye, this would even the match between them, and if they ever ran into each other again someday, he would be kinder to them after they paid their penance.

"Is another noble household nearby?" Wat asked.

"Not quite, but not far. I'll tell you the very way to go. You must inquire at the Queen's Head in the village of Edenbridge, where I've visited myself, the place closest to

Hever where the Princess Elizabeth's own royal mother was reared. Be sure to announce that you call yourselves The Queen's Country Players, Queen Mary's. And, Uncle Wat, remember the way you always used to say you were fresh from London? Emphasize that, too, but leave the lads just out of town till you've set it all up, and then you can enter in fine fettle."

Ned felt only the slightest prick of guilt.

"WHY CAN I NOT FIND anyone I want, when I want?" Elizabeth groused as she left Jenks, Sir Thomas, and their other male companions in the inner courtyard after her short, aborted ride an hour later.

A flustered Lord Cornish met her at the door and sent his man to fetch down either Kat or Meg with a fresh pair of boots. Between rumblings of thunder, something unseen in the forest had spooked Griffin, and he had bolted to skim a hawthorn thicket. Though she was not really hurt, Sir Thomas had insisted they return to the manor house.

Jenks went immediately off to tend Griffin's scratches, but Elizabeth wanted an herbal wash for her own scrapes as well as a replacement for this left boot on which she'd broken a heel shoving away from a tree trunk.

"Can't find your girl Meg," Cornish's man reported, out of breath, as he came down the central staircase. "And hear your Mrs. Ashley's been overseeing the laundresses getting things off the bushes out back afore it rains."

"Then fetch her from out back, man," Elizabeth ordered,

trying to keep her temper leashed. "Or else the Lady Blanche will do or Lady Bea—"

"I'll summon my wife forthwith," Sir Thomas put in as he came clomping over to stare at Elizabeth's snagged skirts. She ignored the offer of his arm to limp on one heelless boot toward the stairs.

"Never mind, I'll tend to things myself," she called back over her shoulder. "I believe it is just not my day."

She knew Penelope Cornish always took a nap in the late afternoons, so she didn't ask for her. Bea had not even appeared at breakfast, but not being able to summon her household women vexed her no end. She hobbled up the steps and past the window at the turn of the staircase. From that vantage she saw Kat and Meg. She had a good nerve to open the casement and screech at them like a Billingsgate fishwife.

Kat was not only overseeing Lady Cornish's laundresses harvesting the linens spread on bushes and hedges but was lugging a big wicker basket herself, so she'd be complaining about sore muscles tonight, when it was her own fault. And Meg stood beyond the moat at the forest edge, though, thank God, she appeared to have neither Ned nor Sam with her. Mayhap she was after mushrooms again, but didn't the dolt realize thunder portended rain?

" 'S blood," Elizabeth hit her fist on the window frame and muttered, "we should be laying plans for Leeds, and we're all at sixes and sevens till Ned gets that damned play done."

Though she knew her staff had never thought she would

be back posthaste after setting out, she banged the door to her chamber open and into the wall. Where was that bootjack, and would it even work since the heel was missing? If she tried to just pull the boot off bare-handed, she'd scrape herself with the protruding nails, which kept tripping her on the floorboards. Could English craftsmen make nothing sound in these modern times? When she got to London next, she'd buy a hundred pairs of boots, all imported ones, Spanish leather or not.

As she plopped down on the hearth bench, she saw the maids had not even straightened her bed today, when it should have had its linens changed. No, rather, it seemed, she realized, someone slept in it.

She stood, bootjack in hand, and limped closer to the bed as thunder rattled like cannonballs outside. Her left heel snagged the carpet; she almost fell. Some sunlight or a lantern would help in this dimming room, but she discerned a mussed coverlet, a nightcap, and the slightest bit—tip—of reddish hair. But Meg was outside, so . . .

In the half shadow of the hanging tester of the bed, she put her hand out and gripped the corner of the counterpane and top sheet. And pulled them back.

Not a drop nor blotch of blood stained the pristine white sheet around the corpse. But wearing her favorite beribboned nightcap, its dark eyes staring wide open, its tongue lolled out, its black-tipped tail curled nicely around its sleek red rump, a dead fox sprawled in her bed. A delicate crucifix dangled from its neck, the very one she had put on poor Will Benton weeks ago in his grave at Wivenhoe.

Chapter The Sixteenth

he real red-haired fox is next.

Elizabeth had reread the beautifully embroidered words until they echoed in her ears
and rang in her brain: *The real red-haired fox is next.*

It was the boast—the threat—of the poisoner on a small,
unframed sampler found under the fox's body, pinned to
the crucifix chain when Ned removed the corpse secretly
from her bed. He had carried the dead animal downstairs in
a laundry basket, and he and Jenks buried it in the forest,
but Elizabeth had kept the crucifix and the menacing message. It was encircled by three-leafed clovers, their long
stems knotted nooselike to match the style of the other
hand-sewn warnings.

As exhausted as she felt, Elizabeth knew she could not
get back in her bed that night, though Kat had scrubbed
and aired the ticking and changed the linens yet again. She
would not rest there or elsewhere, she had vowed, until she
had discovered the identity of the poisoner and rid this
world of her.

She had cross-questioned all her people—except Jenks, who had been out riding with her. Kat, who would ordinarily have been in the room but was out back with the laundresses, claimed she had not seen or heard a thing amiss. Prior to going outside, Meg had been in the kitchen sorting herbs with the cooks. Lady Cornish's pastry baker had upheld her word on that.

"Oh, you still nettled your girl warn't there when you come back in with your boot broke," the portly woman named Moll had dared to respond to Elizabeth's question about Meg's whereabouts. Elizabeth was amazed that petty gossip was the real meat and drink of the downstairs staff and the servants of the bedchamber, in small manors as well as at court.

"I am not nettled if she was helping you," Elizabeth assured Moll through the potent cloud of garlic that enveloped her. "By the way, your saffron crusts are excellent."

"Thankee, ma'am—Princess," Moll blurted while her florid face bloomed brighter. "Aye, Meg was in and out of the kitchens."

"In and out?"

The woman shrugged her rounded shoulders so hard her pigeon breasts bounced. "Tell true, Princess, I figured she was sneakin' out to see Sam in the stables, 'cause he gone sweet on her of a sudden like she slipped him a love potion or somethin'."

"Say nothing of my questions," Elizabeth had warned her. "I do not want Lady Cornish to think I am displeased with any of the efforts all of you make here in the kitchen."

Moll's thin eyebrows had scooted halfway up her high forehead. "Oh, course not, Princess. Wouldn't think nothin' like that."

Elizabeth had also been circumspect in questioning the Cornishes' chief laundress. She did not want the Popes to know any of this—if they didn't already. She worried incessantly that Bea could at least have expedited the fox's arrival in her bed. As for Ned's whereabouts when it was delivered, he claimed he had taken a brief walk outside the moat but spent the rest of the time in Lord Cornish's deserted library, penning the short play *In Praise of Our True Queen.*

"Our true queen—Mary?" Elizabeth had asked him testily, leaning over his shoulder to skim the lines. She had to read by twin rush lights he had lit, for the storm still raging outside had darkened the day.

"Of necessity, as you commanded," he told her defensively, rising and looking rather guilty, she thought. "You said, Your Grace, it was for the ears of Irish Catholics. See, I've copied out the parts for you and Jenks and kept him to a minimum with mostly mimed actions, even a bit of swordplay. We'll rehearse a few days—"

"We haven't the time anymore, not since She has clearly demonstrated she has the most-intimate access to my person and my life. 'S blood, I am safer going after her than waiting here—supposedly guarded—as Cecil would no doubt have me do. We are greatly undermanned with just you, Jenks, and me as players, but we must ride to Leeds tomorrow night. If we but knew these parts, we'd go tonight."

"Tomorrow? But—"

"You and I are apt pupils, and I need something else to do but brood. Give me my part," she insisted and seized the sheet he'd indicated. "And Meg tells me you can do an Irish brogue or Spanish tongue, so you'd best polish them too. Work on your speeches and then, after I go up from supper, come privily to my room and we will go over them. Damn, but I'd give a fortune if we had a few more men along to take our part. Something else is eating at you, I can tell. Out with it."

"I—nothing. I just mayhap need to make a few revisions, write in a few more parts," he said, snatching at her paper.

She pulled it out of his reach. "More parts for whom? It's far too late for that. The three of us will have to do, whatever ill befalls. I will not wait here to be poisoned in my bed by someone who obviously has been watching me for who knows how long. At least, I warrant, since Jenks, my cousin, and I dug up that body at Wivenhoe, for surely neither of them would have told the poisoner that I put a crucifix—one my sister once gave me—around poor, murdered Will Benton's neck."

"Your Grace," he said frowning, as if he were hardly listening, "if I could fetch us a few more players—two men, two boys—ones I know well, ones who—"

"What? But we need them now. Are they hereabouts?"

"If they haven't had their skulls smashed in, as I—I arranged—and hoped for," he said, sighing heavily. At least she was relieved to discover that what made him look so guilty had naught to do with her or Bea Pope. "If you send Jenks on the road to Edenbridge," he rushed on, "he might stop them in time and bring them back privily. They'd need horses, but—"

"Your old friends were here? Your uncle? And you sent them on? I heard some players were turned away but assumed the Pope was the villain. Ned, how could you?"

He flushed; his fine features clenched to make him look the chided boy caught with his hand in the sweetmeats. "They betrayed me," he blurted, "especially my uncle. I didn't tell you aught of what really happened. But vengeance felt so good—so good. I still think they need watching, my uncle and Randall Greene, but I warrant we're desperate, eh?"

She seized his shoulders and stared close into his eyes. "Deadly so. Can we get them back to leave tonight?"

"Tonight? But you just said tomor—"

"But now all of you can do a set play, which will give me time to look around. I'll go in as just another boy, and they won't think a thing of it if I'm not on stage while the rest of you keep their interest. Send Jenks for your players, but keep them in the forest here till we go out tonight. I am sorry for the rain, but they cannot be seen here with us."

She thrust him toward the door. "Tell Jenks to promise them horses to ride, food—some coin. And Ned, I understand about betrayal and vengeance, even in one's family. And may God grant us no more surprises on this day."

BUT THREE MORE CAME CLOSE upon the heels of her words, and she hated things in threes. Death came in threes, Tom

Seymour had told her once, referring to her father being thrice widowed—twice by his own decree and once through the death in childbirth of Tom's sister, Queen Jane. Elizabeth had seen it other times, and everyone believed it, high and low, astrologers and clergy too.

First Cecil's letter reporting information she had requested came much faster than she could ever have hoped. His man left the missive for Jenks in the crotch of the dead chestnut tree as they had arranged, and fortunately, Jenks met him in the damp forest as he was leaving the missive.

"Here it is, delivered safe into your hands, Your Grace," Jenks said, out of breath where he had found her sitting alone in the back of the gardens after the rain passed. "I'll needs double my speed now to get to Ned's people and bring them back. Oh, forgot to tell you, Cecil's man said he come straight from London, not from Stamford."

She looked up, alarmed. "London? Cecil said nothing of going direct to London. But then," she added, "he did need to see his usual sources immediately, and they're all tied to the court. So then, he is near Queen Mary," she added under her breath, "for she bides at St. James's Palace." She closed her eyes to picture the brick palace, lying just outside London in the fields and marshes hard by a park so large it seemed in her mind to swallow the forest outside Ightham. Elizabeth had asked Mary to go riding with her in St. James's Park that day when Mary had ordered her away from London because, she said, Elizabeth was poisoned by her mother's Boleyn blood and by iniquity.

As Jenks bowed and hurried away, she sat staring after him. Surely, Cecil's getting near his sources to help her was the only reason he would hie himself to London without telling her. He had admitted he was ambitious, but only for his success through hers.

Breaking the seal on his letter, she stood and walked farther away from the house, past the sundial, and sat wearily on the stone bench, though it was still damp from the rain. Glancing around to see that she was indeed alone, even scanning the windows at the back of the manor house, she stared at the first of two pages. No matter what words came before her eyes, she kept seeing, hearing, thinking, *The real red-haired fox is next.*

She forced herself to read slowly enough to take it all in should she be forced to destroy it soon. At least it was in Greek instead of Latin this time, so that would stop some prying eyes. First he conveyed something her cousin Harry—so he was suddenly in London, too, when she had told him to stay quiet in the country—had wanted her to know. Harry thought that Waldegrave's mention of St. Anthony's fire could refer to a sort of plague that had swept through France, *feu de Saint-Antoine,* the French called it.

"Smut rye!" she translated aloud as she read on.

"What's that, Your Grace?" Meg asked as she walked up to join her. Kat was somewhere out here too.

"Sit down and listen carefully. Cecil writes that St. Anthony's fire is not an herb but a poison fungus that can taint rye bread. If aught happens to me at Leeds, you must get

word to Jenks's friends at the tavern in Edenbridge that
Kentishmen loyal to me might be in deadly danger from
eating rye bread."

Meg sat and leaned closer, her eyes wide on the letter.
"Oh, no," she said, squinting at it. "Ned's been teaching me
and I still can't read a word of that."

Another time Elizabeth might have laughed, but she said
only, "It's in Greek." She began to translate the explanation
Cecil had included: *"St. Anthony's fire is a black fungus that
infects grain, especially rye. It causes nausea, vomiting, severe
head pain . . ."*

She paused, recalling her own headaches lately, but that
was because of all the strain and because she was heir to
them by nature. She had not eaten rye bread but only fine,
stone-milled white manchet, at least since Wivenhoe, hadn't
she?

"Head pain and . . ." Meg prompted her.

"Also, *violent changes of temperament,*" she read on, with a
shudder. She had that, but hardly caused by poison fungus,
surely not. *"In small doses it has some medicinal use, as you
well might ask your herbalist Meg—"* she translated before
she caught herself.

"Cecil means not to trust me, I know it," Meg cried. "I
can read between his lines at least."

Elizabeth shook her head and went on. *"I have been informed that this fungus is properly used after birth to make the
womb contract to normal size but must be used in small mea-
sure, for the slightest overdose can be fatal."*

She sucked in a breath at the next fact he had written, then read it in a quaking voice. *"Your cousin says he heard that France had an epidemic in which poison rye bread killed thousands of people.* Thousands," she repeated, whispering that last word.

She hit one palm against her forehead. "That's it! Not only does she want the Boleyns out of the way—especially me—but also my loyalists around Leeds, thousands of them, and she's going to murder them with food poisoning. Meg, go fetch Kat and come back to me instantly, but do not run."

Without another word the girl obeyed. It was then that the second surprise of the afternoon interrupted her continued reading of the letter. Ned walked up behind her so quietly, she nearly jumped out of her skin when he spoke.

"Lady Beatrice," he said, "has been summoned to her sister's in Maidstone."

She twisted around to see him. "Oh, Ned. When?"

"Just about the time you found the fox."

"I swear Bea got it in my bed for that poisoner, then fled so she could not be questioned. Or they mean to strike at me here, and she has cleared out. Actually, now I . . . feel more vulnerable here, just waiting . . . for something."

"Maybe She sent the fox to force you to Leeds."

"Then I will outfox her. I've done everything by night before—dug up Will Benton, went to Bushey Cot, then Hever. Our approach in broad daylight at Leeds must take them unawares. You'd best go pack what costumes and scenery you've assembled, in case Jenks does not find your Queen's Players. Nothing must stop us from riding to Leeds this night."

She hardly paid attention to his fading footsteps as she began to read Cecil's second page. He was trying to trace Sarah Scottwood again, but knew it would take time they might not have. And he had given her a *bad bit of advice when he told her that James Butler's bastard daughter had gone back to Ireland when he died eleven years ago at a feast, along with sixteen of his retainers, evidently from food poisoning.*

"God save us," she muttered and gripped the pages so hard against her knees that the stiff velum crinkled in her hand.

Though the Butlers had served the Tudors, she read on, *your royal father never had James Butler's death investigated—a third insult to their family from your royal parents. Butler's daughter and her mother—once Butler's longtime mistress, whom he had cast off—went to Ireland for a time, but that was before Butler was poisoned. The mother died there and the daughter returned alone, even served at court, though in some minor capacity as the Princess Mary's beekeeper.*

Again a shudder racked Elizabeth, but she read on: *Where she is now, I cannot discover; like Sarah Scutea, she has vanished. I have heard, though, that Butler's daughter—I have not learned her Christian name yet either—suffered through an outbreak of the pox at court, and her face was scarred for life, so deeply that in the old days she would have become a nun and taken the veil. . . .*

Elizabeth stopped reading. Food poison. Beekeeper. The

veil. St. Anthony's fire and a poisoned fox wearing a crucifix Queen Mary had once given her. And a buzzing, swarming danger to her very person. . . .

She tried to hold shut the floodgates of memory, even tried to cling to that promise of God from her favorite psalm by whispering, *"They compassed me about like bees; they are quenched as the fire of thorns: for in the name of the Lord I will destroy them."*

But even that could not stop the terror of being destroyed herself. As if in a trance, she stood and walked slowly toward the corner of the frost-blighted garden, closer and closer to Lady Cornish's beehives and to the greatest—and worst—surprise.

ELIZABETH HAD BEEN ELEVEN YEARS OF AGE that day of memory and thrilled to be back at court after numerous, painful childhood exiles from her oft-married sire. His sixth wife, Katherine Parr, was a loving stepmother to all three royal children, playing ambassador of goodwill to their irascible and increasingly ill royal father. Queen Katherine encouraged their educations and treated them with love and warmth.

Mary and Elizabeth's younger brother, Edward, as heir, held sway. Yet Elizabeth's rooms were hard by those of the queen at Whitehall Palace in London, and Mary was allowed her own small household, including a beekeeper who was also an herbalist.

Mary was twenty-eight that summer, still sadly unwed.

Her girl, who provided all the fine honey for the queen's table, was twenty and sometimes made up Mary's nosegays and tuzzy-muzzies too. The beekeeper seemed moody and quiet, but at times she spoke with a gay lilt and sang among her flowers and her hives.

In the warm afternoons Elizabeth often sat and read in the gardens with her new governess, Kat Champernowne—her name before she wed John Ashley. But today Elizabeth had closed her book of Ovid's *Metamorphoses* and now she strolled the gravel garden paths alone, past the old sundial—her father fancied sundials—and the splashing fountain painted Tudor white and green. Beyond the barge landing, the bustling River Thames lay broad and blinking in the summer sun.

In that hot afternoon, shadows slanted sharply as the Princess Mary's beekeeper appeared around the turn of privet hedge with something in her long-gloved hand. A good number of bees buzzed about her.

"Oh," Elizabeth said, "you gave me a start in that veil and draped and gloved, but I know you now." She wondered why the girl did not dip her at least a hint of curtsy. Had Mary given her such largesse? But she was not too shy to speak.

"My father," she replied, with no apology in her voice, "was always teasing to say my face is my fortune, just like my mother's, so I'm always careful of stings, that I am."

"Of course. Is not the Princess Mary about today?"

"Of course," she said, her voice lilting and almost mocking as she echoed her words. She came closer. Elizabeth smiled to see the bees stay with her, like tiny, trained, flying dogs bouncing off her veil and shrouded shoulders.

"The Princess Mary studies the queen," the girl said when Elizabeth had almost lost her train of thought, "because she will be a queen."

"The Princess Mary?" It was most disconcerting to have to talk to someone when she could not see her countenance. "Only, I warrant, if she weds a foreign king. Our brother will rule after our father, and his heirs after him," Elizabeth explained.

She shook her head; her veil swayed. "She must be queen, as her own mother was. My family served hers well—serves the Tudors too. We are the Irish Butlers, Dukes of Ormonde. You have heard of us, of all my father does for the Tudors no matter what affronts are given by upstart elements like your mother's family, have you not?"

Even in her tender years it annoyed the princess to be rudely lectured. This girl dared speak to King Henry's daughter like this—that *her* Irish family was important and had done great things? Elizabeth had heard that this girl had been born on the wrong side of the blanket, so who was she to boast so? And yet Elizabeth's own painful heritage, where she, too, had once been declared illegitimate, made her hold her tongue on that.

"Your mother was the Boleyn," the girl went on, "who took the place of the Princess Mary's mother in the king's affections, even after the king took your dam from betrothal with my father."

Elizabeth backed away now, wary of the girl's approach

with outstretched hand. People at court knew speaking of Elizabeth's Boleyn heritage was forbidden. And though young Bess had been cuffed once or twice years ago, her father's power—and now Queen Katherine's favor—had of late surrounded her with a hedge of protection. But something unfathomable yet fearsome blew from this girl like an ill wind.

Elizabeth darted a look back in the direction of the others. Where was Kat? Why had not someone come to fetch her?

"I've been wanting to show you something, if you think *you* will ever be queen in the Princess Mary's stead," the girl said, extending her gloved hand farther and unflexing her fingers.

Elizabeth saw nothing there at first, then noted a single, large bee staying in one spot, going dizzily in circles. Rather than running as she should—though princesses never ran—she stood mesmerized while the young, veiled beekeeper placed the large bee on Elizabeth's shoulder and lifted her other hand in the air as if to give someone a sign.

"She's the queen," she said. "See what happens if you dare."

The bees that had been bumping lazily into the girl's clothes seemed to multiply and swoop straight for Elizabeth's shoulder. They covered her sleeve, her bodice and hood. Her neck, her face, more of them, swarming with a deafening buzz around her ears while she stood frozen in stark fear.

She waited for stings, for help, for something. Eternity

came and went. Their fuzzy bodies and shifting legs covered her tightly closed eyes, her mouth. She would die here. She wanted to scream, to run, but she was trapped. She held her breath, terrified they would crawl up her nostrils or in her ears. She felt dizzy, nauseous. Her head pounded. Helpless. Caught. Cursed. She shook all over but mostly deep inside.

They writhed and buzzed on her hands, on each long finger people so admired. She dropped her book. But not one stung her as they moved and hummed and swarmed. And then Elizabeth heard salvation—her sister's distant voice.

"Desma! Desma Ormonde. Where are you?"

Her tormentor laughed and touched Elizabeth's shoulder.

"Here, Your Grace. Coming!"

If she left, would the bees go too? If someone came along and screamed or started swatting at them, what would happen? And if Princess Mary saw what her girl had done, would she punish or praise her?

She got her answer then. Though she dared not open her eyes to see, she heard her sister's voice closer—a quick laugh, an "Oh!" as she must have seen Elizabeth standing there beset. Would she go for help? Had she known of this before?

"I shall not have their venom in you now, Boleyn," the girl said, her voice low and menacing and very close. "After all, you are already full of poison, that you are."

Instantly, as she turned away, the bees left, every one of

them, whirling after the queen bee on Desma Ormonde's glove. Elizabeth heard the girl's fading footfalls on the gravel path, on the grass—and another's too. Mary had seen and simply laughed and gone.

Elizabeth stood in the garden, leaning against the prickly hedge, quivering, before her legs gave out and she collapsed to her knees. She covered her face with her trembling hands. Her skin crawled, solid gooseflesh. Had that indeed just happened, something so bizarre and dreadful?

At least the bees had gone away. She wanted it to all go away. And if she never confronted her sister—never told Kat or the queen what that bastard Irish girl had done—she could keep it buried deep, deep down, just like the bitter loss of her mother and her father's hatred when he had called her, more than once, *you Boleyn bastard!*

"YOUR GRACE. YOUR GRACE, what happened? Are you ill?"

It was not Kat's young face bending over her but one with lines, wreathed in silvered hair. And someone else there, her younger self stepped from the mists of memory. No, it was Meg, Meg Milligrew.

Elizabeth saw she was on her knees in the back gardens at Ightham Mote near Lady Cornish's hives, which buzzed, muted now, like her thoughts. Her letter from Cecil lay on the ground. There were no Tudor hedges, no bright green banners, no Whitehall Palace—and no bees coating her like a second skin. She shuddered so hard, her body jerked.

"I—I know who She is," she whispered to them. "The poisoner. And why—partly why—She wants me dead." They helped her rise. Her face felt wet in the crisp air. Surely she had not been crying. But she was dazed enough to swipe at her wet cheeks.

"The letter from Cecil gave her name?" Meg asked, as she retrieved it and the two of them led her back to the bench and sat her down.

"No, but I remember. She wears the veil not only because she used to keep bees and now wants secrecy. Cecil says she's disfigured from the pox. She used to be beautiful, but she's scarred for life."

"And blames you?" Kat asked, looking as puzzled as Meg.

"Not for that, but she hates me. Her name is Desma Ormonde, or Butler, or whatever she calls herself now. Do you recall her, Kat? And," she added, though she nearly choked on the words, "she used to—mayhap yet does—serve my sister."

Chapter The Seventeenth

HAT NIGHT THE SKY WAS SABLE WITH NO moon or stars, as dark as their quest. Yet Elizabeth held to her belief they must go now.

"Where is that girl?" she asked Kat, then turned to stare at Ned. They were to gather in her bedchamber, but no Meg. "I'll have her head if she's got tangled up with Sam."

"Ned might not want to say so," Kat put in, lifting her eyebrows, "but she's probably dawdling wherever he sat or stood last, or mooning over his every word."

"That aside," Ned added hastily, "she fears sleeping in the bed where you found that dead fox."

"I can't fault her for that," Elizabeth admitted, shaking her head. "We're all on edge, but we must set personal thoughts, even fears, aside for now. Surely Meg is just delayed. When she arrives, Kat, put her to bed with her—with my—headache, and keep a watch lest Thomas Pope comes knocking on the door."

Kat nodded stoically and pressed Elizabeth's hands hard in hers. Elizabeth longed to hug her farewell, but her emotions were jagged enough. She tugged away and sent Ned first down the back servants' stairs, then, in her boy's garb, quickly followed. They tiptoed out the side door and rowed across the moat.

Although Jenks was not in sight, The Queen's Country Players waited with the extra horses he had hired from Edenbridge so none would be missing from the stables here. Elizabeth greeted each player when Ned introduced her. The two men swept into graceful, courtly bows they had no doubt done in numberless plays. The boys just gawked until Ned gave them a quick cuff to make them follow suit. Elizabeth had worried about taking the lads into Leeds, but their presence would help to mask hers.

But still no Jenks. "They can't have gone off somewhere together," Elizabeth muttered. She began to pace, mouthing rich oaths she had learned in earshot of her father years ago. Ned smacked his gloves repeatedly across one palm, while the others hovered.

"Your Grace," Ned said finally, "I suppose Jenks could have gone back to have words with the stable man Sam, since they are both—well, fond of Meg. You see, she's been using him—Sam, I mean—to make me jealous, so—"

"You always," his Uncle Wat put in with a snicker, "did draw the ladies like flies to honey."

"Enough." Elizabeth shuddered at the mere mention of honey and rounded on them as if they were to blame. "I want Jenks here now. This is not like him, damn his eyes!"

They heard running feet from the fringe of forest. Ned drew his sword and Elizabeth the dagger from her belt. She was glad to see both Wat and Rand were quick with weapons too. Ned stepped in front of her. When Wat jerked a thumb toward the lads, they darted behind a tree trunk.

Jenks ran into view, his sword drawn too. "She's gone!"

"Shh!" Elizabeth hissed. "Meg? Gone where?"

"Don't know. It's all my fault. I told her, when she got garbed like you, to just come out to say a quick farewell—for good luck, you know. So she said she would afore our dangerous duty, as she put it. Didn't see her, but found her herb basket out there a ways," he said and thrust it at them. "Even playing you, Your Grace, she had that basket."

"That is hers indeed," Elizabeth whispered. "I've used it. And she would not just abandon it."

"I looked everywhere," Jenks went on, his voice breaking. "Even lit a rush taper. Found tracks of horses and one or more woman's footprints. I—I don't want to think it, but she may have been taken."

"Taken by whom?" Wat asked, but everyone ignored him.

Elizabeth bounced her clasped hands against her lips for a moment. "Show us the prints. Is it far?"

"Just back in the forest a bit. I can relight the rush with my flint box."

"The rest of you, wait here," Elizabeth ordered, keeping her dagger out.

It was dark as pitch, but their eyes became accustomed to it as they moved farther away from the wan lights of the manor house. Jenks led her and Ned to the general location, though he had to find the very spot by where he'd discarded the rush light. Elizabeth gritted her teeth for the interminable time it took him to relight it. The three of them bent down to look closer as the wavering flame threw pockmarks and shadows on the muddy forest floor where it was not obscured by wet leaves.

"See," Jenks said, pointing. "At least two horses, that much I can tell. This boot print's mine from when I was here afore. But this one's a man's and not mine, and those two are narrower."

"And different sizes," Ned observed. "Hold that rush closer. Aye, definitely two women. I'd say this one is Meg's. She still walks a bit pigeon-toed, though I've blazed away at her about it."

"I'll wager you have," Jenks muttered. "Like with horseflesh, folks just mistreat others, so why she cares one whit for y—"

"Silence!" Elizabeth commanded. "This other print, long and narrow—it would match those slippers I saw in Bushey Cot. I remember thinking that the poisoner's foot must be even bigger, yet thinner than mine. See?" She straightened, put a hand on Ned's shoulder, and dangled one booted foot over the print.

"Someone's got her, all right," Jenks said, "and we got to get her back. Bet if we looked about more, we'd find signs of"—his voice broke—"a fox poisoned near here."

"But," Ned said, "I see no signs of a struggle here, or even hesitation."

"Nor," Elizabeth added reluctantly as both men stood, "that she might have been drugged—no drag or stagger marks—and therefore forced to go. And yet," she said, looking into their faces lit by flickering flame, "I maintain she is to be trusted. My aunt believed her, and I too."

"But we cannot rule out," Ned persisted as Jenks stomped out the rush light and they started back toward the others, "that she went willingly with the woman who hit me over the head at Bushey Cot. I've been thinking that Meg might have been like Nettie at Wivenhoe, or the one who visited the veiled woman at Bushey Cot, another herb girl in thrall to Desma Ormonde, alias She and the Lady of the White Peacock."

"You and your fancy speeches," Jenks muttered, shoving Ned's shoulder. "More like she's innocent and they mean to poison her!" His fists up, Jenks spun to a half crouch, but Elizabeth slapped his arm and he backed off. When Ned still rounded on Jenks, she yanked Ned's elbow to swing him around to face her. They stared close at each other, nose to nose.

"I will not have us fighting each other. And we cannot rule out," Elizabeth insisted, "that Desma Ormonde mayhap took Meg to spite me. Or, God help her, since she was out here in my clothing, carrying herself like me, mayhap practicing my speech, then—"

"Hell's gates," Ned whispered, "they think they've taken you!"

"Then I would fear for her even more. But we will know when we find her, and find her we must. Now."

Jenks ran ahead and was madly untying horses' reins from tree limbs when she and Ned rejoined the others.

Jenks swung the two lads onto the same horse, then linked his hands to give Elizabeth a boost up.

"You truly care for her," she said quietly, looking down at his upturned face.

"Can't help it," he whispered, his face so solemn. "Lately—forgive me, Your Grace, Meg reminds me of a great lady I always look up to, one I'd die for. But I'm your liege man, no matter what befalls."

"Well said, better than Ned Topside ever spoke," she murmured and reached down to squeeze his shoulder before raising her voice. As the others scrambled for their saddles, she announced, "Jenks will lead the way, but you are all in my charge, and I in your debt."

They picked their way through the forest before bursting out onto the road at a steady clip, plunging even deeper into the dark heart of Kent.

"LOCK HER IN THE ROOM at the top of the Maiden's Tower, but keep her bound and gagged tight too," Desma ordered Colum McKitrick. She smacked their prisoner, sprawled over his broad shoulder, on the rump to show her utter contempt. In protest, the captive grunted and squirmed. Soon it would all be perfectly, completely over, Desma thought smugly—justice accomplished, execution carried out.

She felt flushed and warm, however chill the air. Though it was a good two hours after dawn, the stiff breeze swept across the lake to lift her veil so high she had to hold it down under her chin. She saw Colum try to peer beneath it. She glared at him; he could not see but must have sensed it.

"Aye, your high and mighty Irish majesty," he teased and started away. "I'll truss Elizabeth of England like a pig in the top chamber of the Maiden's Tower, that I will."

"I had no notion we'd return with such booty," she called after him with a delighted laugh to make him stop and turn back around with a tenuous smile. "We'll celebrate tonight, but now I'm exhausted. So I will take care of her later, that I promise you. She has seen my poisons work, haven't you, Boleyn bitch?" she demanded, walking to them to yank at the flowing red hair. "Let her be stewing on what's to come for a while," she concluded with another laugh.

Desma watched Colum grin and cart the woman off as if she were a bail of hay—or her precious rye steeping in its poisons in the bins of the Maiden's Tower, which St. Leger had told her she could use before he'd gone to London. The castle staff obeyed her well enough, better than Colum and his men, whom she had sent for from home.

In her chamber in the main castle, Desma sent her plump, blond herb girl, Nan, downstairs to fetch bread, ale, and her own—her good—honey. Famished after that long ride, that she was, but she didn't want the household servants in her room with all the herbs and fungus stored and mixed here. Nor did she want Nan underfoot any more than she had wanted poor Nettie or the others, but she needed them at times.

She slumped in a chair to rest; she must not get in bed or she would sleep till doomsday when she must be wary of unwanted visitors—pursuers. And her belly was about to cave in, no denying it.

She rose, removed her veil, and washed her hands thoroughly, always wary lest some of the poisons from the pellets would cling and taint her own food. As she rinsed and dried her face, her stomach rumbled in strange harmony with her albino peacock's screech outside. Where was that simpleton Nan with her breakfast? A quarter hour must be gone.

She replaced her veil and stepped into the corridor. Perhaps Colum had joined his men at breakfast, for she heard the distant rumble of deep voices from downstairs. She would box Nan's ears if she found her dawdling about with those ruffians again. But then she heard another sound.

Muffled, but nearby. A man's murmur, that it was. A giggle?

She listened at the door next to her own. With Lord St. Leger's entourage in London, most of these chambers should be empty, including this one.

She banged it open and saw Colum, still mud- and road-stained, and still riding hard. But now he was playing stallion to her girl Nan while her white legs flailed the air.

"I gave you both orders!" Desma shrieked.

Nan squealed to silence and stopped wriggling. Colum, the cur, merely craned his neck and grinned, despite the blatant view he flaunted of his white flanks. Panting, covering neither of them, the wretch dared to smile at her as if they'd merely met in the corridor on the way to chapel.

"And I did what you said," he told Desma. "As for this,

you wouldna let me have the merest glimpse or taste of you, mistress. A man's got to take his ease somewhere."

"You whoreson bawdy bastard. You are loosed from your service here. Go back to Ireland—or to hell!" She went out and slammed the door.

Breathless, shuddering, she leaned against the walnut paneling in the hall. Colum's dragging Nan into a nearby bed did not disgust her but made her recall another man. Her father had been so besotted with her mother that he had coaxed her into empty rooms in broad day and tumbled her in garden bowers, heedless of who spied on them, back when Desma had the same beautiful face, for her da had told her so.

No longer hungry, she went back into her chamber and slammed that door too. She sank onto a cushioned chair, leaned her head against the carved back, and stared up at the festoons of drying herbs and strung mushrooms along the ceiling. After today she would have to take them down, pack them, and move again. Ireland—perhaps she'd flee there as once before, especially if Queen Mary died, with her supposed heir, the Boleyn bastard, dead too. Aye, back to Ireland where her grandmere, Magheen, had taught her the poison herbs, that's where she'd go.

Desma slumped over her knees and wrapped her arms around her thighs, chin on knees, letting her veil fall away so she stared straight down at the floor. She shut her eyes tight and tried to pray to the patron saint of unwed women, Brigid of Kildare, who had received the veil from the holy hands of St. Patrick himself. Desma had taken the veil of revenge and swore on her life the destruction of the Boleyns and those loyal to them. For insulting her father and having him poisoned. For ruining Queen Mary's mother's life—for turning England away from the true church—for everything.

She sat bolt upright at the knock on her door.

"Just leave the food, you whore," she cried. "Don't you be disturbing me or showing your shamed face, don't you dare."

The voice came in roughest Gaelic to make her shudder and her thighs clench. " 'Tisna Nan, mistress, but Colum come a-calling. I'm the one disturbed and wanting to see *you* now, see that face you hide, if you dare."

"You've been dismissed," she answered in Gaelic. "Keep clear of me."

He dared to open the door. "But you see, mistress, I canna keep my thoughts clear of you." His rakish face appeared around the edge. "I've e'en dunked myself in the lake to dare approach Her Irish Majesty." He grinned, stepped in, and swept her an awkward bow. His matted hair still dripped water. His garments molded themselves to each muscle and angle of his big body.

"Besides," he cajoled, "if you'd but be giving me a peek beneath that veil and smile my way, I'd never e'en been touching the likes of the wench Nan."

"You lecherous liar. Will you be trying to turn this fine castle into the worst of stews by tupping my girl?"

He came closer, slowly, his big hands palm out as if to ward off an attack. "I'm done with Nan. And I thrive on a dangerous challenge e'en as you do." His grin was as crooked as his heart, and his flattery as thick as his brows, but she let him come on. "Now, 'twould be a challenge," he said, "putting me hand and the point of me own private sword up the skirts of the Boleyn bastard, but I dinna fancy her like I do you."

"Leave off your stupid sweet talk with me, Colum McKitrick. I'd never take my girl's leavings or someone who tupped the Boleyn, make no mistake. And my face is mine to share or not so—"

"The challenge of serving you—in every way—shivers me as much as it does you. And you canna be trusted either, Mistress Desma." Another grin, sly, seductive. "But I always say, danger stokes desires, that's the truth. I was feeling a thrill to shoot those poison arrows of yours at Lord Carey and his man, but—"

"And missed the mark."

"—but I'd not miss the mark with you. And bedding you, I'd know you were dangerous as death and revel in it."

"You're mad, man."

"Only for you," he crooned, coming yet closer while she glared at him through the fog of her veil. "I'd be getting close enough to adore your body and face, and what a tumble we'd share."

"Never!" she said with a sniff that sucked her veil against her nose before it puffed back out.

She stood and moved closer to the window, leaning one elbow on its deep stone ledge. He fancied himself an Adonis and witty to boot, that he did. Yet his raw intent excited her, even as he said. However rough and crude was Colum McKitrick, he had a true Irish heart and the gift of words, just like her da.

"Good," he said, with a cocksure nod as if she'd vowed to submit to him. "I dinna hear you say no and see no poison pellets nor tankard of hemlock nor rye bread coming my way. So willna you let me touch you, mistress mine, let me . . ."

She held her breath while he extended his big, calloused hands to finger the rolled hem of her veil. Her breath came fast as he slowly lifted it and peered beneath.

He flinched and gasped as if she'd slapped him.

She felt the stab of desertion again, the fury for herself, for her meek-willed mother. Seventeen years a pampered mistress . . . *mistress mine*. Bearing a child, loved and pursued, coddled, flattered. And then cast out for another woman, younger and more comely, just the way the queen's beloved mother had been by that whore Anne Boleyn.

"Your face doesna matter," he whispered, obviously steeling himself from the shock. "Your body—let me touch you—all of you—e'en your heart."

Desma's mother had died of a weak heart, they said, but Desma knew it was a broken one. Her own—it was broken too. Still, she left Ireland to go back to her da's house in London. She was there that night someone poisoned his rye bread with St. Anthony's fire, him and all his false, fawning fools.

Before Colum could step away, she embraced him in an iron grasp. He lowered his hands to clutch at the soft globes of her buttocks right through her riding breeks and ground his hard hips against her softer thighs and belly. No longer did he try to kiss her lips but lowered his head to nip and nibble on her neck.

While he fed on her flesh and his splayed fingers molded and squeezed her, she thrust her hand into the pouch still at her waist and lifted out the small dagger she kept there. It was a mere four-inch blade, anointed with the very honeyed oil Colum and his men had shot at Lord Carey on the road to Wivenhoe.

As if she embraced him, she positioned her hands behind, then neatly stabbed him in the back, near his heart, forcing the blade all the way in. Shocked, he sucked in a huge, wet gasp. When he shoved away from her, she did not let him go. He tried to flee, but she tripped him. She clung. He shouted for his men, but perhaps they still guffawed over their raucous meal down in the great hall.

She held to him while he panted and struggled, but weaker, ever weaker. It often killed within a quarter hour. Only the mushrooms she called death caps worked quicker. She let him go at last, only to watch him crawl toward the door, then topple on his side, slightly curled, mouth open, eyes glazed, like that fox she had sent the Boleyn.

"You will not be leaving me for another," she told him. "You will not cast me out." She shook her head to clear it. This was not her da, but Colum. "And I will be taking care of our prisoner myself, when she has had time to fear death like this—just like this. But first I will torment and torture her."

She went across the chamber to kick once at his big body. He did not budge. She walked away and straightened her veil, leaning unsteadily against the big, carved bedpost. If Nan knew he had come in here, she would simply claim he had left. If his men looked for him, she would say she had paid him what she'd owed and he must have ridden off with the bounty. By the time anyone found him—smelled him—she would have the Boleyn bastard dead and the rye sent to all the local mills in the name of the Princess Elizabeth.

Staggering with exhaustion, she bent to seize Colum's booted feet and dragged him closer to the bed, then rolled him onto his face so she could retrieve her dagger.

He left a trail of mingled blood, moat water from his damp clothes and head, and worse from his insides letting go. She took a bolster off the bed to wipe the smears from the floor and clean the dagger blade before she rubbed more aconite on it and returned it to the pouch.

She kicked the bolster under the bed, then shoved and rolled the body there, finally drawing the hems of the counterpane to the floor. For one moment she heard herself screaming again, just as when she found Da's body, when she cradled it, then tried to hide it so no one would come to take it away. But no, that last scream—her peacock outside again. She collapsed to her knees, hearing it echo, echo in her head.

Chapter The Eighteenth

HAT LAKE PUTS ANY MOAT I SEEN TO SHAME," Jenks said, squinting off into the distance as they rode closer to the castle. "I just pray God we find Meg unharmed there."

"We will," Elizabeth promised, but her voice broke and she had to clear her throat. "We must."

"It's too lovely a setting to house evil," Ned added.

But it did not look lovely to her. They could see from this vantage of a slightly cresting hill that, besides the main castle itself, several separate towers and buildings surrounded a grassy, inner bailey. Then Elizabeth realized why the mere sight of the place chilled her so completely. She almost turned her horse and fled. Despite its lack of tall outer walls, the color, style, and layout reminded her of the sprawling Tower of London hunkered down on the River Thames.

She shuddered, then began to shake, praying her voice did not betray her fear. "Rein in," she called out.

Side by side instead of single file, they halted to survey

the scene through the scrim of naked trees. Sometimes whispering to each other, they studied and discussed the plan of the place a local man had given them.

A stop to talk to him and the ride had taken them longer than she'd expected, especially with one wrong turn, so it was just after midday now. And Elizabeth had made them dismount and walk their horses through the small village of Maidstone before dawn not to wake anyone, especially Beatrice Pope, wherever she slept there—if she did. At times Elizabeth feared they'd find her here, with the master poisoner.

They were dog tired, but they had rested a mile back to eat cold venison pies, cheese, and drink from a stream, so that would lift their strength and spirits—she hoped. At least anticipation and fear would jolt them more alert, for she felt her pulse pounding. The final act of this drama was about to begin, and she could only pray it would be a historic one for her and not a tragedy.

She shook her head at that wretched comparison, but the players had rehearsed their parts much of the way. With a few new lines praising Queen Mary and the "true church," they had hastily adapted an old revenge play called *The Royal Specter* with ghosts, hauntings, and curses—and moved the setting to Dublin. That ought to suit the Irish, she thought. Mainly, the drama suited their needs with its many disguisings, entrances, and exits for the minor parts, one of which she would take.

She had convinced Ned that he must assume the part of an actor born in Ireland and brought early to England and orphaned, so he could claim he recalled little of his beloved homeland. He had gone along but had fairly gloated when she informed his uncle that Ned—Niall McGowan, they were calling him—would speak for the troupe and pretend to be its master.

She finally spoke again to halt their whisperings. "That old farmer told us all else we're likely to know about that place without seeing it inside. Let's ride."

They funneled toward the single, narrow causeway that led to the protective drawbridge, double barbican, and gate tower. The buff stone buildings seemed to sink their darker reflections in the pewter-hued lake. The horses' hollow hoofbeats and the caw of crows were the only sounds. Until they heard the screech.

Shrill and shocking, it echoed out over the lake—and in her heart. They reined in just before the portcullis gate. Elizabeth saw Ned jerk in his saddle before he twisted around to look at her. She could not see his expression clearly, but her stomach cartwheeled at the memory of that night at Bushey Cot.

"She's here," she mouthed to him, and he nodded grimly.

"What in kingdom come is *that?*" Randall asked, missing what had passed between them. "I swear it sounds like some woman in travail or torment."

Jenks's back stiffened, and Elizabeth could only pray he would not spur his mount ahead in search of Meg. Did this Randall have no sense or compassion at all?

"No," Ned said, "it's a white peacock on the grounds."

"White?" Wat said. "Bloody hell, even if it is, you can't

see it from here. Are you sure you haven't been here before, like that trap in Edenbridge you admitted?"

"Keep your voices down, all of you," Elizabeth commanded quietly from the rear. "Water makes sounds carry. And we are not here to bicker or accuse. That cry gives us warning and hope that our quarry is within, for Ned and I have seen her white peacock up close once before, that is all. Ride on, and everyone must play his part."

She was so intent on their task that she had nearly learned to ignore her pounding head pain. It had not lessened one whit since she'd found that fox, and Kat had coiled and pulled her hair up too taut under her boy's cap for this grueling ride. Poor Kat, she thought: Was she managing to cover for Meg's absence too? Thomas Pope had been told Ned and Jenks had been allowed to go to Edenbridge, but Kat was probably at wit's end over Meg gone missing.

When a guard called down at them from the crenelated parapet to halt and send just one on, Ned glibly gave his false identity and spurred his horse ahead. The gaping maw of the portcullis seemed to swallow him whole. Elizabeth ached to hear what was passing between him and the castle guards. Mayhap he'd been taken to Lord St. Leger or Desma Ormonde herself in the long time the rest of them waited.

She drummed her fingers on her saddle and fidgeted. She hated not being in command. She detested subterfuge. When she was queen, surely she would do everything aboveboard, mayhap except for foreign policy. No more domestic plots against her, no murders of someone dear, no more frustrations or fears when she could act from a position of safety and power.

She held her breath while Ned—Niall McGowan—rode jauntily back out to them.

"Lord St. Leger's in London, my lads, but when the steward said I talked just like some of the men who are staying here—Irish guests, he said—he agreed we could give a performance tonight. Says there's a lady guest here might like a wee bit of an Irish play in honor of Her Majesty and old Ireland too."

Elizabeth remembered to breathe. Her hopes had plunged, then soared. At least they would not have to outsmart St. Leger and his retainers. And she had correctly surmised that Desma would be here. She prayed that this time they could outfox her and not be the ones trapped.

They were soon inside. Like the others, she scanned the grounds and buildings, simply pretending to gawk at their archaic grandeur. The old farmer they had questioned about the place had described the main castle and the even older, attached section called the Gloriette on its own tiny island—a last stand if the place were attacked in times of yore.

Across the grassy inner bailey from the castle proper, she noted, stood the separate, four-story, rectangular edifice called the Maiden's Tower. Under this gunmetal-gray sky, its windows stared blankly down on them. Mayhap its lower floor was a makeshift stable or barn these days, for a cow was tethered near the door and sheep cropped the green where a single white peacock strutted, fanning its huge tail. As they passed closer to the Tower, she noted watering and feeding troughs and a pile of ripe manure, from which the stench drifted their way.

"A pox on them," she mouthed. It would be just like Desma Ormonde to deface and desecrate the Maiden's Tower as she had other places once dear to the Boleyns. The old farmer had said Elizabeth's father had built the place as a small pleasure palace in honor of her mother, Queen Anne.

"The tower 'twas built," the rustic had explained, obviously eager for an audience, "years after the rest of Leeds, years after. And by the great King Harry hisself. And ha' been visited by his poor Kentish Queen Anne Boleyn herself too. A local girl, ye ken, and her girl, Elizabeth, ha' nary a foreign drop of blood in her veins, not like that bloody one now. Elizabeth, aye, she'll make us a queen, pure English someday. . . ."

Even now Elizabeth treasured his words. How much she had wanted to thank him for his loyalty, but she had stayed back with the lads while Ned questioned him. Also, she had wanted to warn the old soul not to eat rye bread, but that might start a panic, when there was one already rampaging in her heart to stop Desma Ormonde's mass slaughter of such folk.

Her pure English father, whom she had both feared and adored, had been cunning and wily but evidently not enough to realize his Irish ambassador St. Leger, to whom he gave this place, had played both sides to harbor hatreds.

And now the traitor must have dedicated himself to keeping Desma Ormonde's curse going against the Boleyns. Let him hide out in London. When she was queen—

Elizabeth almost leapt straight out of her saddle when Ned—in an Irish accent—shouted at her.

"I said, lad," he repeated, pointing rudely up at her, "help the others unload our goods while I go ask where we're to stow them. Get a move on those lazy bones now, or I'll take a stick to your backside."

For one moment she glared down at him, not moving. In all this danger, with lives at risk, the blackguard was enjoying this. She noted that his uncle and the others glanced nervously at Ned, then back at her.

She scrambled to obey.

MEG HAD NEVER BEEN MORE TERRIFIED, though Ned would be proud. This woman—She, in the flesh—was so convinced a mere herb girl was Princess of England, she was going to kill her for it.

The woman came closer with a narrow, open leather box containing glass vials and small pewter cups. Meg bucked hard against the ropes, but it only made her limbs go more numb and her breath come harder against this gag. Wide-eyed, she quieted as the woman Her Grace had called Desma Ormonde moved behind her and set her burden down with a clink, then went back to close the door.

Meg had been studying this room in the tower for at least

two hours but saw no hope of escape. She was four floors up, and the single door was heavy wood. She'd heard it bolted outside when that ruffian Colum had put her up here. Two other Irish louts had looked in off and on, one called Brian; and now the master poisoner herself, like some veiled vision from the dead.

Since Meg knew she had no hope of rescue unless her friends found her fast, her dilemma simply was this: Whether she should save her own skin by telling the truth here—though Desma could poison her anyway—or whether she should play it out to protect the princess by her death, or at least earn her a bit more time.

"I'm going to remove that gag now so that we can have a little discussion, Boleyn," the veiled woman said, bending close to where Meg was tied, hands behind her, her legs to the wooden ones of a heavy, carved chair. Desma Ormonde smelled of herbs, but dry, decaying ones, and Meg's nostrils flared.

"I want," the woman went on, speaking deliberately and coldly, "to hear you admit you are a treacherous bitch, spawn of traitors to my family, just like your mother and your aunt."

When the woman fumbled with her gag, Meg could have bitten her fingers off for degrading Mary Boleyn. Now she knew for certain who had poisoned her beloved mistress and left her to take the blame from Lord Henry, whom Desma had tried to kill too.

"Come on now," Desma coaxed as she poked in Meg's

mouth to get a piece of the damp linen. "Before we're finished here, I will hear you confess and beg for your very life."

At first Meg just planned to glare at her silently, disdainfully, down her nose the way Her Grace did. That would buy her more time to decide whether to be Meg or the princess. But when the woman yanked the linen strip from her mouth, Meg thought her whole throat had come out too. She coughed and gagged, wheezed and gasped.

"Here, poor thing," Desma crooned mockingly, "let me give you a little something to drink."

A clanging bell went off in Meg's head. Poison for certain!

Her captor produced a small cup from her box and moved it toward Meg's lips while her eyes streamed tears. Meg shook her head hard and tried to turn away, but the woman grabbed her hair, yanked her head back, forcibly wedged her teeth apart, and poured the liquid between her lips to make her choke again. Meg tried to spit it out, though it tasted enough like water. The woman threw the rest of it in her face and tossed the tankard into a corner.

"I said I just want to talk—at least right now," she said, dragging another chair close and perching upright on the edge of it.

Meg's gaze darted wildly around the small room, desperate for some way to fight back, to run. Not only was she nearly immobile, but the chamber was sparsely furnished, with nothing that could help her, even if she could shove her chair around. The single table was dwarfed by four

stone columns that stood sentinel in the corners. High brass
hooks where tapestries once must have hung encircled the
tall stone walls. Now they bore only a single, faded arras of
a lady with a deer, mayhap the maiden for whom the place
was named. If only she could escape like that maid into that
embroidered meadow and forest.

Reluctantly, Meg's eyes refocused on the poisoner. She
held herself like a real lady, Meg had to give her that. But
her voice was bitter as vile, and it was so strange never to
see a face. Meg imagined it must be ugly as sin, and cruel to
boot.

"A very special drink for you later, Boleyn, I promise,"
she was saying with a hollow laugh.

Meg licked her cracked, dry lips and took a deep breath.
She tried to steady herself by picturing the princess as, even
in her bonds, she sat up straighter and squared her shoulders. She narrowed her eyes and glared down her nose as
she said her first words to this witch.

" 'S blood, how dare a lickspittle like you assault my
royal person!"

"IF WE GET CAUGHT HERE, we'll tell them we are gathering
cobwebs for the play," Elizabeth whispered to Jenks, who
followed her so closely he kept breathing down her neck.
"Ugh!" she cried as she wiped webs from her face. She
recalled Kat's warning that Desma would be sitting at
Leeds like a spider, waiting to ensnare her.

She heard rats skitter away again and wondered how

Wat Thompson and one of the lads were faring in their underground kingdom of vermin, searching whatever cellars and dungeons underlay the old Gloriette. Ned was to be fereting out who slept in which upstairs bedrooms and perhaps taking a peek in them, while Randall and the other lad set up the scenery. She, supposedly with the nervous Jenks to guard her, searched this dungeon of the main castle.

They stopped at the bottom of the uneven steps and squinted into the vast, black cavern toward the labyrinth of halls and cells beyond. The ceiling of this central chamber was vaulted above two iron doors with grills that the outer guards could look through. As Jenks went to peer through the one in the first door, she stood frozen. Her own captivity in the Tower of London, the clank of keys in locks leapt at her, but all was silence here.

"I'm going to call her name aloud," Jenks said, but his mere whisper echoed. Elizabeth saw that her brave man was trembling so hard his candle wavered. Coming down the stairs he had already singed her sleeve with it.

"No need to do more here," she said suddenly, stepping down beside him to grip his arm.

He started, gasped, and jerked around, evidently thinking she'd spotted Meg—or her corpse. But she lowered her candle and pointed to the scabs of rust, years of it, encrusting the sets of locks to both doors.

"No one's been through here for decades, Jenks, praise God."

"But I was praying we'd find her here, just tied or some-

thing," he said as they turned and made a quick retreat up
the narrow, crooked stairs.

WHEN ELIZABETH SAW THE DOOR to the upstairs chamber
Ned had told her of, she almost wished she were back in
the black dungeon. He had not managed to search all the
upstairs rooms but had learned a bit about the Irish lady
who was his lordship's guest. Always veiled, she came and
went at will, one servant had told him, and was somewhere
about the grounds now. But they didn't know where to go
to invite her to the play, since she wasn't in her chamber,
first one on the third floor overlooking the lake. Besides, she
asked for what she wanted and otherwise liked to be left
alone.

Yet, under the pretext of inviting her—and to keep Jenks
from charging upstairs to bang about in every chamber
looking for Meg—Ned had slipped up the back stairs and
peeked into the bedchambers, including that very room.

"Was Meg there?" Jenks had demanded the moment
Ned returned to where they were setting up small bits of
scenery before the play.

"Not Meg nor the Lady of the White Peacock, but it was
quite a room," Ned had announced.

Elizabeth gasped. "Alike to her one at Hever?"

He nodded. "And to Bushey Cot. Strands of stinking
herbs and toadstools."

"Did you make a thorough search?" Elizabeth demanded.

"If Desma Ormonde's not there, neither is Meg," Ned insisted.

"We must be sure. As soon as the play begins and before my first entrance, I am going up there to search that chamber for anything that may help us, even a letter from my sister. If I don't make my entrance, come after me."

"Since the servants say she's not about and they'll all be in the audience, I warrant we can risk that," Ned had said. "But you will not go off alone outside the castle until I make my exit and join you."

Elizabeth just nodded. He had become so pompous she could have stuck him with her dagger to deflate him. "After Act the Second," Ned declared, "Wat and Rand can manage to carry it alone long enough for you, me, and Jenks to search those other buildings for both of them."

"Join me in the kitchen, where I'll keep an eye on the inner bailey in case she heads this way," Elizabeth had said. "Besides, who cares if a lad just steps out to get away for a precious moment from an arrogant, scolding master of the players? No one will recognize me anyway if I—"

"Unless," Ned had interrupted, ignoring her jab, "it turns out Meg is here but not on our side."

"I told you," Jenks had insisted, "that can't be, and Her Gr—this lad did too. After my sword-fight scene I'll be there to guard you, lad."

She had felt pressed between the two of them. "All right," she had said, "that's the way we will play it. But time's of the essence. Both of you join me in the kitchen as soon as you make your exits."

Now she stood, shaking, with her hand on the latch to the chamber Ned had said was definitely Desma's. She knocked lightly and, when there was no answer, darted in. It was nearly dark outside, so the chamber lay in shapes and shadows.

The smell hit her first, stronger than the usual in the woman's other chambers of horror, but she did not hesitate to close the door behind her. Tonight they must capture— mayhap execute—Desma Ormonde. What putrid hatreds and foul vengeance had driven her was not important now, only stopping her.

"Aragh," she whispered at the stench of the garlands. She saw a veil tossed on a tabletop and a sampler with a circlet of some sort of leaves stretched over an embroidery hoop. She ignored all that, even the coffer in the corner—the one, no doubt, that held rotting mushrooms and fungus, mayhap even the St. Anthony's fire rye smut. She went straight. to the bed, praying that under it she would find the long, narrow box she'd seen there in Desma's room at Hever. She had wanted to peer into the box even then. Although she had heard something in it clink together, it could be where she kept privy messages, mayhap royal ones.

Holding her nose and breathing through her mouth, in the dim light she lifted the counterpane high from the floor. Boldly, she thrust her hand under the bed, groping for the leather box.

She touched an arm—a stiff human one. And snatched her hand back out.

She sat, kneeling, bent over with her hands pressed to her

mouth, certain she would be sick. She had been wrong. Meg was here, dead. Her sleeve was damp. With blood? Or had Desma broken with her practice of poisons to drown her?

It was all her fault. Her fault for trying to stop this poison plot, for using the girl like a sacrificial lamb. But the body beneath this bed—was that arm too thick, the corpse itself too long to be Meg?

She blinked back tears. She only wanted to flee, but she had to know. She reached in again, then decided she must have a light.

She fumbled with a flint box she found on the table before the window overlooking the lake. *Hurry. Hurry.* Dusk and mist were swirling outside as if to trap them here all night. The flint struck; she lit the fat tallow candle, then carried it back across the room to the bed.

"If it's you, I'm so sorry, my Meg," she whispered, kneeling as if in prayer for the dead. "So sorry . . ."

She bent to look under. "Oh, thank God. But who are you?"

ELIZABETH EMERGED FROM THE DEPTHS of hell, shrouded in a sheet, waving her arms and weaving across the rush-strewn floor. Playing a lad who was playing a ghost here in the heart of the enemy's castle, her voice quavered, but that was just as well. At least her memorized words kept her from shouting at the audience that they were all foul traitors and harbored and served murderers.

"I bring a curse to all," she half-whispered, then moaned.

"I curse all who would harm our God-given Queen Mary and those of the true and holy church." She could have vomited at those words; her stomach had gone sour anyway.

She banged her shin into the long bench as she climbed on it, for she could barely see through the eyeholes. She adjusted the sheet as she stood rocking and shaking during the supposedly frightened Wat's speech. Now she could scan the entire torchlit audience as she had not been able to from behind the arras before she made her entry.

The likes of stable hands, scullery maids, and laborers stood along the back wall of the great hall, with its long single table on the slightly raised dais still uncleared from the evening meal. The players had been given supper, but Elizabeth had told them to dump it down the public jakes chute, however sure she was their ruse was working.

The house servants with more status sat cheek-by-jowl on long benches, behind the three men they had come to call the Irish guards. That rabble bore watching. They spoke little English to each other, and what there was of it was rank and heavily accented. They had been loud and rude at first—like the groundlings in London, Wat had said importantly—but they had quieted a bit now, either nodding off or else intrigued by ghosts and blood curses.

But they had seen no one who could be Desma Ormonde. No one veiled at all, except Elizabeth and the two lads in their ghostly attire.

Suddenly, as she made her exit by slithering to the floor to return to the bowels of hell, then bending down to hurry out the door, an errant thought pierced her. She realized how Desma must view the world from behind her veil. The woman must feel separate and secret. And very alone. Her poxed face was like a second mask of the woman she had once been. Mayhap all that had made Desma believe she could judge and poison others and hide from what was true and just.

"Are you demented?" Elizabeth muttered to herself. "No softness or sympathy here."

In the corridor they were using for a tiring-room, she whipped off her sheet and threw it on the pile of costumes. From here on out there would be just two ghosts—the lads—while Ned, Wat, and Randall kept the crowd enthralled. Soon Jenks and Ned could slip out to join her, and they would continue to search for Meg, this time in the upstairs rooms of the Gloriette and in the Maiden's Tower.

She went out to the kitchen to wait for her men to join her. Standing in the door someone had left ajar, she looked out toward the now bare gardens and the grassy bailey. Darkness had obliterated dusk's mere shadows, and a thick fog from the lake hovered like a blanket. But for the strutting peacock, this had earlier looked like a benign, deserted village green to her, sheep, cow, and all. That was probably deceptive, just as everything here was—including herself.

And then she heard a woman's sobs, muted on the breeze.

Her stomach cartwheeled. Meg?

Staying close to the wall, she sidled toward the sound, the sort of crying and gasping where one could barely get a breath. Emerging from the gray mist, beyond a clump of frost-blasted hollyhocks, a square stone well appeared. Could Desma have put Meg down the well and she was gasping for air? No, the sobbing came from behind it. Her heart thudding, Elizabeth leaned forward, peered around, and shuffled closer.

Chapter The Nineteenth

VEN THIS CLOSE TO THE WEEPING WOMAN, IN the dark and fog Elizabeth could not tell if it was Meg. She was seated, slumped with her back against the rough stones of the well, her head in her hands.

But no, she was heavier than Meg. Something told her to tiptoe away, yet why should Ned do all the questioning here? Surely, this was not a trap. She knew she'd have to try to sound like the lad she looked.

" 'Scuse me, girl. Need some help?"

The wench looked up through splayed fingers as Elizabeth squatted down, her back against the well. She could see her round face was smooth and slick with tears. The girl shook her head wildly.

"Only if you got the stomach—I don't—to make me take this stuff—to end it all," she said, between gasps and sobs.

The hair on Elizabeth's neck prickled. The girl had gestured to a small pile of mushroom caps at her feet. Could it be another of Desma's herb girls?

"What's happened, then? Can't be anything so bad."

"I'd do it flat—if it warn't for—the babe," she said, wiping her face with her apron. Her voice sounded as if she spoke from inside a barrel.

"You're a new mother and don't want to leave behind—"

She shook her head again. "Gonna be. 'Cause of that cur, Colum McKitrick."

An Irish name, mayhap one of the guards watching the play. "And now that you're with child, he wants no part of you?" Elizabeth prompted. She felt sorry for the poor girl, as stupid as she must be to have trusted a man outside of wedlock—or in. But she either had to get information fast about the veiled woman or get back to wait for Ned and Jenks.

"Kind of," the girl choked out. "It's her, my mistress. He always wanted her, and—he left me and went to her room—and she kept him. And she said he wants no part of me no more, and I'm too scairt of her to cross her."

"Your mistress . . . the veiled lady? She kept him in her room?"

The girl nodded, then frowned, finally surveying Elizabeth suspiciously from head to toe. "You one o' the lads with the players?"

"Oh, aye, and we wanted to invite the fine lady we heard lived here, 'cause our play is set in Ireland, but we couldn't find her. You know where she is?"

She shrugged. "Somewheres on the grounds. Best keep clear. I am 'cause she got other things to do, and now Colum's one of them." She began to wail again, choking on

her words. "He left here—without me, she said—left to
wait—for her."

Elizabeth's hopes crashed as she watched the wench pull
her apron over her head and sob. She knew she could make
her an ally, tell her that Colum was still in Desma's chambers, dead. But the obtuse girl must not be privy to her
mistress's doings, including where she was holding Meg.
Besides, it would mean more hysteria for the girl and time
lost for Elizabeth. She had to get back to the kitchen.

As Elizabeth stood, she deliberately ground the poison
mushroom caps into the grass with her boot toe. Then,
recalling the dead rabbits, she tried to shove the remnants
against the well, where even sheep could not eat them. She
crept away, but stopped in her tracks when she heard a
voice. She would swear it was her own, drifting through the
fog as if from the sky.

" 'S blood, treason it is, treason to touch the next queen
of England!"

"Meg," Elizabeth whispered. "Meg as me."

She tore back to the kitchen. No Jenks, no Ned. Was she
early or late? She raced into the hall, scrabbling in a pile of
props for a stage sword, though she had her dagger drawn.
Peeking past the arras, she saw that Wat and Rand held
sway on stage, with the two lads as ghosts, but no Ned and
Jenks. She had misjudged the timing and they came out,
saw she was gone, and went looking for her. But where? Or
had they heard Meg's ringing tones and had gone to trace
her too?

Just before she let the arras close, she noted that two of

the Irish guards were gone from their bench. She had to warn her men about that, too, but get to Meg first.

She dashed out and across the green toward where she had heard Meg's voice. It must have come from the Maiden's Tower, one of the upper stories. Those guards or Desma had Meg in the tower and thought she was Elizabeth, and Meg, God bless her, was brazening it out.

She smelled the manure pile again before the tall, solid tower loomed from the night and fog. Yes, lighted top windows, four floors up. She bumped into a clump of sheep, which shifted easily out of her way, and then came face to face with the pallid peacock.

Elizabeth slid to a stop, staring at it, waiting for its warning screech. Its tail still folded, it merely pecked at grain on the ground and walked disdainfully away.

A good sign, she told herself. And thank God she looked like a mere lad. If someone stopped her she could say she heard a woman's cries, seized a stage sword, and went to help. She had no real notion of what she would do to rescue Meg, but she had surprise on her side.

As she stepped inside the open doorway, she saw that the single large chamber on the first floor was indeed a makeshift stable and barn. A single hanging lantern illumined the scene. The cow had wandered in to munch hay from a wooden manger. Piled hemp bags of grain cluttered one corner—some yellow kernels had fallen from one. Next to the single staircase going up, a wood-slatted bin looked to be full of threshed grain, too, but these were dark, pointed kernels. Rye!

She shuddered. The bin was narrow but seemed to extend clear up to the second floor. Taking the lantern, keeping clear of the dribbles of grain that had fallen through the slats, Elizabeth edged up the steps.

"'S blood, you think my people won't trace me and punish you?" Meg's voice rang out, strangely echoing both from the windows and down the stairwell. "Even if I'm dead?"

Elizabeth froze as she heard a low laugh—Desma's. She spoke, but her voice was lower pitched and didn't carry, just as at Hever. She gripped her sword hilt and dagger handle so hard—she held the lantern in the same hand as the dagger—that her fingers cramped and she had to flex them. She forced herself upward again.

The second floor appeared to be divided into two chambers with windows, no doubt from which her parents had once surveyed the pretty scene. She went on, foot above foot, keeping her back to the wall, which at the third floor changed from wainscoted wood to raw stone. She tried the four doors exiting the landing lest she needed a hiding place when she and Meg escaped, but they were all locked.

The grain bin continued even up here, built to fit into the side space of the curving stairwell. Recalling her and Ned's entrance to Hever, she considered starting a fire by catching the wood slats with her lantern flame, but that might trap Meg as well as Desma upstairs, and it would bring too many people.

She willed Meg to keep talking, but there was silence above. Her feet felt leaden. She should have taken Cecil's warnings to heart. She should not risk herself, her future, like this, but Desma had to be stopped before there was no future. Surely Ned and Jenks must look here for her soon, unless those Irish guards had followed them out into the kitchen and the grounds.

Come on, my Meg, she sent her command silently upward, *keep talking. In this situation, I would keep talking.*

" 'S blood," Meg cried from above, as if in answer to her wish, "I have informed both my Lord Cecil and my cousin Lord Carey who you are and that you reside at Leeds, Desma Ormonde, so you will not carry this off!"

"Do you think I care if I am caught after I'm finished with you here? Final judgment day for the Boleyns, that's all that matters now, that and Queen Mary ridding herself of her heir so that she can name another before she dies—a Catholic kin, even Mary Stuart, Queen of Scots, would do—that's all that matters."

Elizabeth was so intent on Desma's words and outraged at their import that at first the thud of feet on the stairs below did not register. But someone—at least two heavy-footed men—were coming up fast. Surely Jenks and Ned would not make all that noise, unless they, too, had heard Meg's voice and panicked.

Panic—she felt it now, hot coals and ice in her belly all at once. Gooseflesh peppered her skin, but she broke out in a slick sweat. Her mouth was dry, and she felt she would be sick. She turned down the wick to gut out her lantern and left it on the side of the stairs. Darkness closed her in like a cloak. She knew she should try to make it back to the second floor. She was surely snared here. She could hide—

but where? Nowhere but on up, hoping there were extra unlocked rooms above. Whether it was poison rye or not, she almost wished she could step into this dreadful grain bin, which had small doors at each level.

As the footsteps came closer, she hurried up to the fourth floor, feeling her way around the last turn of stairs. Light seeped around one door, from which Meg's voice boomed again. Elizabeth jiggled the lock on another door. She glimpsed a narrow third one that perhaps led to the roof, but it did not budge either.

The footsteps belonged to two of the Irish guards. One with a lantern turned into view on the staircase below her to shine it in her eyes, while the other knocked her sword from her hand with his own. She thrust her dagger in the back of her belt to hide it as the one without the lantern laid hard hands on her. Then the door behind her swept open and a veiled woman's shadow loomed to block the light.

"SINCE THIS GLORIETTE was the place of final refuge in a siege," Ned told Jenks, "I thought it was our best bet."

"She's not here. That big tower, then the barbicans, that's where we've got to look next. Now!"

They were both out of breath, both distraught. Not only was Meg missing, but Elizabeth had not met them where she'd promised, though Ned had argued that didn't mean she was in danger.

"Just remember," he told Jenks between gasps as they ran

back through the covered corridor that linked the Gloriette with the castle proper, "we've both known that red-haired lad to do what he damn well pleased—no matter what we'd been told. He may just have gone off on his own—and will save Meg and our skins. You know," he said, grabbing his rib cage to fight a stitch in his side, "maybe I'd better go back up to that poisoner's chamber—and look there again."

"I think Meg's somewheres else on the grounds. I swore on this very sword to someone once—my first master, Tom Seymour—that I'd see Her Grace on the throne someday or die trying. But if I can't save her—Meg too—I got nothing to live for—and maybe you don't either," Jenks said. Deftly, he held the blade of his drawn sword neck level before Ned as they ran along together.

"I see your point. Let's stick together, then."

"WHAT IS THIS?" Desma screeched. "I told you to leave me alone, Brian, so I did."

"We canna find Colum," Brian said.

"But we did find this lad from the players sneaking up the stairs," the other guard told her, giving Elizabeth a hard shake.

She was tempted to tell these men where they could find Colum, but that might be useful later. Mayhap Desma would just order her back downstairs where she could get help from Jenks and Ned before returning here. Thankfully, Meg was keeping her mouth shut now.

"What players?" Desma demanded.

"A troupe led by an Irishman, still doing a play in the hall, but we got worried about where Colum went."

"Irish? You dolts!" she spat at them and bent down so low to study Elizabeth, her veil belled out. Elizabeth was tempted to rip it from her.

"Not fools to stop this lad with a drawn sword," the other man, taller and darker-haired than stocky Brian, protested. He showed Desma the weapon.

"Only a sword from the play, milady," Elizabeth said, her head bowed. "Heard someone cry, but guess it could've been that peacock—or that herb girl out looking for someone named Colum too. Said he was last in your cham—"

Desma slapped Elizabeth so hard across the face her head snapped back into the wall. Colors blurred before her eyes, and she tasted blood. If the men had not held her up, she would have toppled down the stairs.

"In *your* chamber?" Brian asked Desma.

"We decided we'd keep it a secret—our passion," she told them. "And now I've sent him on another errand for me, but he'll be back soon."

The words—lies—blurred by, though Elizabeth tried to seize them—to plan her own. Her head spun and the stairs and even the wall behind her seemed to slide and tilt. Should she say more about Colum's demise? She could only stare back at where she thought this woman's eyes must be behind that veil. An icy aura seemed to emanate from her on the scent of smoky herbs, the same dank atmosphere so suffocating at her Bushey Cot poison garden. She shook her head to try to clear it.

"But Colum's horse is still on the grounds, right, Brian?" the man who held Elizabeth said.

"Then no doubt he took another," Desma insisted. "Pluck off that whey-faced lad's cap."

The surprise at that command and the strength of desperation flooded Elizabeth. She went wild. She tried to knee the one called Brian and shove the other down the steps, but they banged her against the wall again. Her ears rang. Desma herself leaned over to snatch off her cap to reveal the coils and twists of red hair.

Still, Elizabeth kicked and flailed. Then, realizing she was trapped, she reached up and ripped off Desma's veil. Desma shrieked. The man called Brian started to laugh, until he glanced up at Desma's face, lit by the lantern he still held.

"Judas Priest!" he cried, then spouted something in Gaelic.

Desma turned away into the room, and for the first time Elizabeth saw that Meg was tied fast to a heavy chair near the window. Meg cried out, too, when she glimpsed Desma's pitted face.

Elizabeth opened her mouth to tell the men where they could find Colum's corpse, but Desma yanked her veil from Elizabeth's grasp and thrust it into her mouth for a gag.

"Bring the girl in here," she ordered the men. Dragging Elizabeth up the last steps, they obeyed. The gag made her feel she couldn't breathe. Panic pounded against her throat and chest. "Loose her hair and tie her with this," Desma was saying as she picked a long linen strip from the floor.

Brian hesitated. "The two of them," he said, "look a bit like sisters. Colum wouldn't say direct who you brought back with you, but—"

"I don't pay any of you to do my thinking," she insisted, advancing on him. "As Colum told you, this is for Ireland, for all of us."

Brian nodded and moved quickly, tying Elizabeth's hands behind her around a narrow stone pillar. The damp linen strip reminded her of the corpse's clothes under Desma's bed. She struggled and tried to talk through her gag, but Desma slapped her again, scratching her cheek. Elizabeth prayed no poison was caught there. She blinked back tears of defeat and stared into the green gaze in the once beautiful face. The specter of the pox had always terrified her. But for some reason her brain threw pictures of Will Benton's corpse at her, all caught in that shroud.

She blinked hard. She had to concentrate on summoning help and on surviving.

"Well," Desma said, rounding on the two men, "since this lad is a girl in disguise, go lock up the other players. God knows what mischief, or worse, they intend. And come back to report to me when all is secured. Don't be standing there. Go on!"

Taking Elizabeth's sword, they left, muttering, banging the door shut. Desma went over to bolt it. Elizabeth could still feel her dagger pressed between the small of her back and the pillar, but it was nowhere near her hands or bonds.

"I heard you had a girl with you at Hatfield and Ightham Mote who greatly resembled you, but when I saw and heard her at first . . ." Desma said, letting her voice trail off. She turned back and leaned against the door with her eyes closed. "You almost tricked me again, my little red-haired fox."

Elizabeth noted she seemed to speak to both of them. Perhaps, even if she had guessed the ruse, she did not know who was who.

"I cannot believe all you have dared," Desma continued and strode over to pull her veil from Elizabeth's mouth. Rather than donning it again, she threw it on the table in the corner beside the long leather box Elizabeth had searched for earlier. "*You* are the Boleyn, I warrant," she said, her eyes narrowed, her voice accusing, as she strode back toward Elizabeth, "because I could not fathom why you—*she,*" she added, pointing at Meg, "would be out in Ightham Forest alone at night."

"And can you fathom," Elizabeth challenged, "I would be brazen enough to be dressed as a lad here?"

"Oh, aye, that I could." She grinned, her smooth teeth so in contrast to her ravaged skin. "I've seen you do it at Wivenhoe and then at Bushey. And I daresay you went out the window at Hever. Besides," she added with a sneer, "your girl here starts nearly all she says with the old oath *'S blood,* and I cannot fathom you would speak that way.

"And I take it," Desma went on, obviously reveling in her power, "that one of the players here today is that handsome rogue you took on to entertain you, Ned Topside. I'll see to him personally—to all of them, as soon as we are finished here."

"And I take it," Elizabeth countered, fighting to keep calm, "that your informant in my household was none other than Beatrice Pope. Cecil knows that as well as everything, so he's in London now to tell the queen—tell her you've failed in everything except that you both used the Popes as spies."

Elizabeth knew it was a gamble to goad this woman, but she had to know about her royal sister's part in this.

"Your half sister, I suppose you are referring to," Desma said, coming closer, hands on her hips in an almost masculine swagger.

"Of course."

"Another Boleyn lie. I, like others, know you share no blood with her. Like your Ned Topside who visits your rooms at night, your sluttish mother kept a pretty bird, a musician, always sprawled across her bed. It was charged at her treason trial that among her other lovers, her red-haired Smeaton—"

"I *am* my royal father's child!" Elizabeth shouted. "Look at me, listen to me—dare to harm me and you will see."

Leaning forward as if she would lunge, she felt her dagger again but had no notion how she could use it to free herself. If she rocked her wrists up and down, would the stone pillar wear a damp linen strip through? She fought to calm her fury.

"This is not only about you, Boleyn bastard, but about

me—about my loyal, loving father your family insulted time and again."

"I know of those things. They are unfortunate and regrettable. But am I to be held accountable for my parents' faults?"

"The sins of the fathers shall be visited upon the children to the third and fourth generation. But since you shall never bear a child, all the poison will stop with you," Desma declared.

"Then are you to be judged for your mother's being a man's mistress or for your father's casting her off?"

"You know—you know of this?" she asked, her voice awed. For once she looked stunned. "Then do you know that when my father was murdered, despite his utmost loyalty to Henry Tudor, the king did naught to have his death investigated and punished?" Her voice rose in volume and pitch as she gestured wildly. "Just ordered them carted off and buried like so much Irish refuse, that he did. I say your family poisoned my father's food and drink!"

Elizabeth jerked as Meg spoke. "Just like you poisoned my mistress, Mary Boleyn. You sent the poisons in with that girl, so you wouldn't have to even see what you did to her."

Desma half-turned toward Meg, then back to Elizabeth. "Oh, I'm going to see you two die very directly. I'm going to watch every writhing moment. I'll warrant Anne Boleyn would have loved to watch Catherine of Aragon die of poisoned food and drink—"

"Poisoned food and drink," Elizabeth interrupted, deciding to risk all on a hunch. "Knowing you now," she cried, leaning forward again to saw at her bonds, "makes me realize that you are the one who poisoned—mayhap in his rye bread—your own father because he cast off your—"

"No!" she screamed and pressed both palms tight to her ears. "No. Her Grace wants you dead, and I will finally do what I should have years ago in the garden with my bees. But I'm innocent of my dear da's death!"

"As innocent as of the death of Colum McKitrick, rotting under your bed?"

Desma began a strange keening sound as she dashed to her table with the vials and began to pour and mix something. Elizabeth sawed openly at her bonds. Something popped loose, but Brian had wound them repeatedly around her wrists.

Her past, her future, dangled before her like that thornbush crown her grandfather had seized for the Tudors. Desma carried a small glass vial toward her with an amber–green liquid within, greener than Cecil's invisible ink. But Elizabeth could kick at her. She bucked forward, only to hear her dagger come free from her belt and clatter to the floor.

Desma leaned down to retrieve it. She dragged Meg's chair closer to Elizabeth, then sat, smiling, calm, in control again.

"Now," she said, "here's my final, only gift to you, Boleyn. I'll let your girl go so she can testify to the queen of your death. I'll have my men get her fast to London."

"I'd never—" Meg began, but Desma pressed the blade of Elizabeth's dagger to her throat to silence the girl.

"But," Desma said, her glittering gaze yet fixed on Eliza-beth, "if you don't drain this vial, Boleyn bitch, I'll cut her throat and force you to drink it anyway."

"My royal sister ordered you to do all this?" Elizabeth demanded.

"Let us say Queen Mary desires it and approves," Desma countered, giving Elizabeth a glimmer of hope Mary had not hated her this much.

"All right then. I see I am beaten. Let Meg go."

"No, Your Grace, I—" Meg began again until Desma slid the blade so close across her throat, she drew a hairline of blood.

Elizabeth leaned closer, planning to stretch out a farewell to Meg to buy more time, but Desma thrust the mouth of the vial at her. Elizabeth pulled back, then lunged. And toppled toward Desma as her bonds gave way.

Her hands still snagged behind her back, she hit Desma hard and took her down with her. Elizabeth rolled away, tugging at her bonds. The vial broke on the floor, and Desma slipped in the stuff, trying to scramble up. Elizabeth yanked her hands apart, numb, but—

Desma made it to the door, fumbled with the latch, got it open. She tried to flee, screaming, "Brian McKitrick! To me!"

Elizabeth pulled her by her skirts, seized her shoulders, and threw her back into the room. Desma's hips hit Meg, who was still tied, and she rolled to the floor again, her hands in the spilled poison. Elizabeth bent to retrieve her dagger, which Desma had dropped.

"Oh, no. Oh, no, it eats through skin!" Desma shouted, then made it to her feet and charged Elizabeth with both sticky hands raised. Elizabeth swung the dagger at her in an arc, managing to dance out of her way. Some advantages to being dressed as a lad, she thought erratically. For a moment they played a mad game of fox and geese, with Desma trying to smear the stuff on her. Elizabeth kicked her away and managed to make a quick slice through Meg's bonds.

And then they heard men's voices—in Gaelic—as at least three of them thundered up the stairs. Desma made another dash for the door, and Elizabeth let her go so she could free Meg.

"Mistress Desma," a voice shouted in heavily accented English, "we got all the players locked up in the castle's wine cellar."

"Up here! I've got two traitors to our cause we must rid ourselves of. Help me!"

On her knees, Elizabeth sawed hard at Meg's leg ties while Meg managed to free her wrists. "They'll be coming up," Meg said, "too many of them. If they got our men, it's just us. What can we do?"

"God knows," Elizabeth muttered. "And if He wants me to rule this kingdom as His realm, it is He who must help us now."

She dragged Meg out of the chair, though she staggered from being tied too long. Desma had run down to meet her men. They stood, swaying against each other at the top of the stairs.

Elizabeth's mind raced. She could shout to Brian—who evidently had the same surname as the corpse in Desma's room—that Desma had murdered Colum and that she could prove it. She could heave the vials of poisons in their faces when they rushed them. But neither tactic would guarantee salvation. Here she stood, everything to lose, with a single dagger to fight them off.

Below in the darkness of the turn of the staircase, they saw jumbled shadows leap upon the walls. Someone had brought a lantern up as they prepared to rush them. Desma and two or three men. The flickering shadows of sword points danced in the air.

Elizabeth thrust the dagger in Meg's hands so she could have both hers free. She went down two steps to reach the iron latch on the door of the slatted bin. If this was Desma's poison rye, even if it was not—

A shout in Gaelic, then Desma's shrill one: "Death to the Boleyns, even the royal one!"

The charge from below began. Elizabeth meant to pull open the door of the bin, but it shoved out of its own accord the minute she shifted the bolted latch. A river of dark grain—and its musty smell—roared out. She ran back up the steps as it bounced and slid downward. The force of it made her wonder if there was more on the roof, for it spilled out until it was knee-high into the onslaught of the men below.

"Down! Back!" Desma shouted. "Don't get it in your mouth! Let it pass us; go back down."

"Get me Desma's veil," Elizabeth ordered Meg, "and

some of those linen bindings. We have to loose the grain on all the other floors."

"What? How? They're down there waiting."

"Go!"

Elizabeth slashed two eyeholes in the veil, and then tied the hems around her neck with the linen. She could not breathe well, but it would keep her from inhaling or swallowing that grain dust Desma had warned her men about. Slipping on the rye, plowing through it and sliding where it had piled up, she started down. She heard them coming up again, but she prayed she'd get to the third-floor landing before they did. She opened that door, too, and steadied herself by hanging on the slats in the dusty torrent.

Shouts below. Scrambling. A scream.

She risked it once again, sliding down to open the latched door on the second floor. No good retreating upstairs and trying to get out a window as she and Ned had at Hever. Nothing to tie together, and it was much too far. Besides, there was no going up in this flood of grain, only down. Her men—she had to free them.

By the time this grain was gone, she heard no footsteps below. Unless it was a ruse, they had probably retreated outside the building to plan another attack. But she could wait no longer.

"Meg," she shouted up the stairs, her voice muffled through the veil, "hold a piece of petticoat to your nose and mouth and get down here. Try not to breathe, though I think you have to eat it to get ill."

She continued down the now darkened stairwell, sliding,

skidding where it had piled up so deep on the lower flights of stairs that she was amazed. Absolute silence reigned below, and someone had lit another lantern. The river of rye had come to rest in a pool of it perhaps four feet deep on the ground floor. A cloud of dust hovered thick in the air.

She heard Meg coming down. Then she noticed a sword point sticking up through the rye.

Someone had dropped it in their hasty scramble. At least it would give them a weapon. Panting through the veil, taking care not to cut herself on the blade, she pulled at it carefully.

It didn't budge. With her foot she shoved grain away and followed it down. A hand held it. A man's big hand.

She cried out just as Meg slid around the last turn. Elizabeth shoved her away from the sword.

Meg kept coughing; for the first time Elizabeth realized her eyes were watering. Or was she crying? And to see the world through this veil, as if she were that ungodly woman . . .

"Why are you shoving me?" Meg protested, then saw the man's hand. "Oh!"

"I think—they may all be under here—somewhere," Elizabeth wheezed. "Feel for his pulse."

For once, without question or argument, Meg obeyed, plunging her arm into the depths. "Nothing. I think he's dead."

"Desma could be here too. We'll try to dig them out, but we've got to free the others first. The wine cellar must be under the kitchen. This may be the only man here."

"But here's a boot with a leg in it," Meg murmured, pointing a distance over. "Can't be the same one."

Elizabeth seized her hand and pulled her away. "We'll be hidden by the fog outside, but be careful."

They ran in the direction of the castle as Elizabeth tore off the veil with her free hand. Meg had the dagger, she the sword. At the kitchen door they heard voices from beyond the deserted room, so they darted into it and toward the cellar door.

"I only hope the key to the wine cellar isn't on one of those dead Irishmen," Meg whispered.

"At Greenwich it's right by the cellar door. One time, years ago," she went on, so nervous and relieved she could not stop talking, "Tom Seymour took me down and stole one of the king's . . ." Her voice faded as they saw that a light burned down here. It could easily be that one of the Irishmen stood guard.

She gripped her sword handle. She was but twenty-five years of age yet felt worn out fighting her own battles. How she longed for an army to command, a navy and—

"Listen," Meg whispered and gripped her arm, "what's that? Can't be singing."

"I will personally bury those bastards in that poison grain if they've gotten drunk in there while . . . while . . ." Elizabeth sputtered.

No one guarded the door, which was a fine oak one with a bunch of grapes carved into it. Elizabeth seized the big key from an iron ring and unlocked it. Meg lifted the lantern.

"A glorious sight, our next queen, crimson hair loosed to the winds of heaven." Wat spoke first and raised a mug in salute to Elizabeth. Both lads and the four men blinked into the brightness of the lantern. Mugs and a leather bottle lay at their feet, and stacked barrels hemmed them in.

"Deliverance, earthly salvation," Rand cried and staggered to stand to sweep her a bow, though he fell over into a pile of heavy firkins, which didn't budge. One had been uncorked and dribbled dark wine across the flagstones.

"They were drinking to your continued health, my lad," Ned put in hastily. "They knew those ruffians were no match for you. Obviously, you have found and stopped the Lady of the White Peacock. Jenks and I, even in the dark, were trying to pick the lock with this iron barrel hoop, should you need our help, right, man?"

At least, she thought, Jenks had the sense to look sober and sheepish. Yet he wiped his eyes and grinned, going down on one knee before Elizabeth with but a quick darted look at Meg. "I told them no one could stop you, Your Grace, and never the two of you together."

"We have no time for chatter," Elizabeth announced. "Wat and Rand, sober up and now, or I'll leave you locked in here. Jenks, fetch our horses and take them to the barbican and be prepared to go up and force the guard to open the gates for us on my signal. Let the lads sneak into the corridor and try to gather what they can of the costumes and props, especially the other weapons. Ned and Meg, follow me."

Back in the Maiden's Tower, the three of them dug in

the grain with their hands, then with the iron hoop Ned still carried. There had been more rye than she had ever imagined in that bin. Now it seemed they shoved great piles of it around as it kept shifting.

"I want to leave, but I have to know she's gone for good," Elizabeth explained, falling to her knees to dig harder, bare-handed.

She knew she had to keep talking and moving or she'd collapse. Her jaw throbbed in rhythm with the head pain she'd borne for days. She was both afraid Desma wouldn't be here and that she would. Despite it all, she could almost pity the woman, a bastard, betrayed by her father and bereft of her mother.

"It would be God's justice," she went on, "that she killed by poison and died by it. I'll have Cecil threaten Lord St. Leger that if this grain isn't all destroyed—Ah!" she gasped and gazed into the face of her nemesis, which her hands had uncovered for the second time today. Ned and Meg waded over and stared down in silence.

Though she had suffocated to death, Desma Ormonde seemed at peace. Like a swarm of bees, dark kernels of rye rested on her eyes, in her gaping mouth, even in her ears and nostrils. Strange, she thought, how Desma's poison decorated her in death. In the wan lantern light, rye smut and dust glittered from each pockmark on her face. Her raven-dark hair, streaming out from her head, seemed adorned with black pearls of grain.

"Let's ride," Elizabeth said, forcing back a sob and standing. "It's all over now. Whether or not she worked for the queen or only because of the queen, it's over."

"Not until you're queen," she heard Ned say, but, tugging Meg's hand, he was hard on her heels out the door.

Ahead of them as they neared the barbican through the fog, Elizabeth saw that Jenks had not waited for her word to open the gates. Everyone was mounted before the raised portcullis and Jenks held her horse. He had somehow recovered his sword, which he held in his right hand. He gave a little cheer when he saw them all safe, then turned immediately to Elizabeth.

"No one was there, so I raised the grate myself, Your Grace."

"I'm so filthy and thirsty, I've a good notion to dive in the lake," she said as he boosted her up.

"If you'll forgive us, Your Grace," Wat slurred amidst hiccups, "we did bring 'long a few firkins o' St. Leger's wine. Din't want him to owe us, as we're off 'fore they pay our fee."

If she had not been so sore and exhausted, she would have laughed. But as she urged her horse toward the gate, she seized the mug from Wat's hands and downed the rest of the wine.

Malmsey, she marveled, her father's favorite. Never had it tasted so sweet and good.

Afterword

17 November, 1558

DESPITE HER TRIUMPH IN SOLVING THE POISON plot against her, Elizabeth had been in a grim mood the week since. Although she and her privy plot council had not been caught returning to Ightham Mote or accused—yet—for the deaths at Leeds, she felt she had lost Cecil's loyalty. And her cousin Harry was with him in London, so Cecil might have swayed him too.

Cecil had been the one to tell the queen that crowds had cheered Elizabeth in Kent. Therefore, he was the cause of the queen, even from her sickbed, writing to Thomas Pope to take Elizabeth back forthwith to Hatfield. Now, she waited here again as she had for years, watched doubly close by him. He was in as beastly a mood as she, for his wife had not gone to her sister's house at all but, rather, had disappeared—he felt that she had deserted him. Still, not even that or a makeshift picnic when Elizabeth just had to get out of the house really cheered anyone today.

"I suppose this long, boring winter," Ned told her, juggling three walnuts, "we could take up the mystery of where Bea Pope has gone and discover whether she deserted the Pope indeed or it is foul play."

"Did you so fancy a real lady doting on you, Ned, even an enemy spy, and now you long to find her?" Elizabeth said, her voice more goading than teasing. She didn't realize she'd hurt Meg's feelings by that remark until she saw her sour face, but she plunged on. "I swear, I'd become Queen of Araby before I'd lift a finger to look for Bea Pope, the traitor. Besides, I warrant, our mystery-solving days are over."

She tossed an apple at his flying hands, sending the walnuts tumbling. Ignoring Jenks's hand extended to help her up, she rose from the Moorish rug they had been sitting on and strode down the lane toward the village. After she and Jenks had outdistanced the Pope again the other day, he had forbidden her to ride. She glanced back over her shoulder to see he kept his distance, but doggedly, he followed on foot, curse him.

Ahead stood the tall, ancient oaks where she had been caught in a storm the day her aunt had sent that secret missive that began her quest for Desma Ormonde. It seemed so long ago and yet but a scattering of weeks. She did not feel half as free as she had thought she would with Desma gone. More than anything, Desma's words that her royal sister might at the last moment name another heir, a Catholic—Mary, Queen of Scots—haunted her.

"I can read your thoughts, Your Grace," Ned's voice interrupted her agonizing as he caught up with her.

She spun to tell him to leave off but watched, chagrined, as he climbed into one of the oaks and dangled upside down by his knees from the lowest limb. "Family trees," he shouted. "Nothing more upsetting or dangerous."

She just waved him away and shook her head. Never had she been less in the mood to tease or laugh. Though she had paid his uncle well and sent them on their way, she could hardly treat her own kin that way.

She heard hoofbeats before she saw the riders. A group of them, all men, galloped headlong toward her down the lane from the main road, their dark cloaks flapping behind them like ravens' wings. As ever—especially now—she instinctively feared the worst. At the last moment, when the queen heard that her plan to poison her Protestant sister had failed or that she had killed Desma Ormonde, had she sent guards to take her back to the Tower—or worse?

Ned came to stand beside her as Jenks ran up and scraped out his sword. Thomas Pope, huffing, hurried toward her. Meg and Kat were halfway to the distant manor house, swinging the empty picnic basket between them, but they dropped it. She saw them lift their petticoats and come running.

"Go into the forest, Your Grace," Jenks cried. "I don't like the look of it."

She shook her head and stood her ground. The one in front in this pell-mell band of men was Cecil, with Harry right behind him. And, broad-shouldered, her old friend Robin Dudley, whom she had not seen since her time in the Tower. Her stomach cartwheeled.

Boldly, she stepped out into a sudden shaft of sun.

Cecil almost vaulted off his horse and went immediately to one knee, with Harry kneeling close behind him and Robin uncovering his head and going down too. The others—several of her father's old advisers, two of her brother's, none of Mary's. She clasped her hands tightly and pressed them to her lips, waiting.

"Your Grace—Your Majesty," Cecil said, out of breath. He extended to her in his square palm the onyx coronation ring that left the monarch's hand only upon death. It glinted in the sun. Elizabeth stared wide-eyed at it, not moving, not daring to believe.

"Your royal sister—I regret," he said, looking up and biting back a smile that lit his eyes, "that she has sadly departed this life, this vale of tears, and left to you the throne and realm of England, Scotland—and Ireland."

Tears blinded her eyes, but she blinked them back and took the ring. Shaking, she thrust it on the fourth finger of her right hand. It was too big, but she would fast get it fitted.

They were all kneeling now, even her own people and a trembling Thomas Pope, staring up at her.

"This," she said in a clarion voice, *"is the Lord's work, and it is marvelous in our eyes."* She breathed in hard, lifted her face to the heavens, and smiled.

"Rise, all of you," she commanded, turning toward the house. "We have much to do. Cecil, I see now why you wanted me back at Hatfield, and I charge that you shall become my principal secretary and counselor."

"Yes, Your Majesty, with pride and—"

"And purposeful ambition," she finished for him with a little laugh. She realized her head pain was gone for the first time in weeks. It made her almost light-headed as she began to stride toward the house.

"Dear cousin Boleyn," she went on to Harry as the men scrambled after her, dragging horses, "I have missed you, missed you all. Robert Dudley—Robin," she added and blushed as the smiling, handsome young man came close and managed to kiss her hand, even as she walked, "I shall need a Master of the Horse, and I have just the man to work for you, Stephen Jenks by name.

"Gentlemen"—she stopped for one moment and they clustered around her—"Hatfield is not a grand place, but I shall hold my first council meeting in the great hall yet today, where my royal parents used to entertain in their happy days."

She glanced back to where Meg stood between a grinning Jenks and wet-eyed Ned, while Kat sobbed into her apron. "All my people," she called to them, gesturing with one raised hand. "I have need of all. Come on then." She waited long enough to see Kat wipe her face and Meg take both Jenks's and Ned's hands to tug them forward.

Elizabeth the Queen began to walk briskly again, but she could have soared.